Condemned
A Julian Mercer Novel

G.K. Parks

Copyright © 2015 G.K. Parks

A Modus Operandi imprint

All rights reserved.

ISBN: 0989195880
ISBN-13: 978-0-9891958-8-1

Thank you, Rosie

ONE

Everything had become interchangeable. The cities, the women, the jobs, none of them were special. They all blurred together in an indecipherable haze.

Julian Mercer stood on the balcony of his hotel room, staring out over the city. If it wasn't for the Ferris wheel, he might not have realized he was in London. He chuckled at the absurdity. Having been born an hour outside the city and spending his youth at the most prestigious preparatory academies, one would have assumed he would recognize home. But he didn't. Not anymore.

The woman he spent the last twenty minutes fucking opened the door and joined him on the balcony. "You got a match?" she asked, holding up an unlit cigarette. She was completely nude, and her breasts were barely concealed underneath her tousled red locks.

"No." He assessed her as if he had never seen her before. She was pretty. Ginger, as his mates would call it. Pale skin, freckles, and auburn red hair. The reason she left the pub with him was a complete mystery, but he didn't complain an hour ago. "Smoking will kill you."

"Bugger." She ran her hands up his pectoral muscles, her fingers tracing the various scars that littered his chest and arms. "How'd that happen?" she asked.

He looked down, trying to be polite, but completely bored now that their romp was concluded. It had been adequate but not something he had any desire to repeat. Hell, he wasn't even sure what her name was. It seemed trivial and unimportant, so he couldn't be bothered to take note of it.

"Thirty-two caliber bullet." His tone was matter-of-fact.

She stepped back, maybe shocked or perhaps turned on. Another detail he couldn't concern himself with. "What'd you say you do?"

"I didn't." He brushed past her and back into the room. He found his shirt on the floor and put it on. Her belongings he carried to the chair closest to the balcony and dropped them off.

"You're an asshole," she snapped, tugging on her shirt and pants. She shoved her underwear and bra into her purse and stomped to the door.

"Thanks for the lovely shag," he retorted as the door slammed, rattling the dresser. "Birds." Fastening his watch, he glanced at the rumpled bed and felt the familiar hollow void. Maybe the reason he neglected to notice he was in London was because the city brought back the pain.

Picking up the untraceable cell phone, he dialed the only number stored in its memory. After the second ring, Bastian Clarke answered. "You've scared off another one?"

"Bas," Mercer was losing his patience, "is

everything set?"

"Yes, sir. We move in tonight to collect the package."

"I'll see you at the rendezvous point at ten. There's something I have to do first." Mercer took out his wallet, opening the tiny sealed compartment and slipping his wedding ring back on, and then he went downstairs, bought a bouquet of yellow roses, and hailed a cab.

Remaining out of sight, Mercer waited for the elderly gentleman to finish uttering a few quiet words. The rain had picked up and sluiced through the frigid air in sheets. Another obvious indication he was home. Sure, other parts of the world got rain, but it always felt different in England. Perhaps he was nostalgic. After the man left, Mercer swallowed, bolstering his nerves.

"Michelle," he put the flowers down, "I've missed you." He played absently with the silver band on his finger, no longer accustomed to wearing it. "And I'm sorry." The grey marble slab stared at him, unyielding and harsh. "Your dad still visits on your birthday, I see." He blinked back the tears that threatened to fall. He was a soldier, a trained killer. He wasn't supposed to be emotional. "This is ridiculous. I'm talking to a bloody piece of granite." The anger hit hard, as it always did, and cursing whatever deity might be listening and mocking his pain, he kissed the top of the gravestone like always and stormed back to the waiting cab. The sooner this job was concluded, the sooner he could leave. Then maybe it wouldn't hurt so much. He could focus on the job and not the excruciating emptiness.

As the taxi meandered through the streets, he stared at his ring, wondering why he kept it and why it felt imperative he put it on before visiting his wife's grave. "Old habits die hard," he mumbled to himself.

The cabbie glanced at him in the rearview mirror but didn't comment.

Each time Mercer returned from a mission for the SAS, he always put his ring back on before walking through the front door. It meant he was home and that he belonged somewhere. To someone. It was his lifeline, a tether to normalcy, but with Michelle's final breath, he had lost his footing.

Over the last two years, his team, particularly Bastian, had tried to act as his moral compass, but often, it seemed it would be easier not to have to worry about such hindrances. When the four of them were employed by Her Majesty, there were no ethical quandaries, just orders. But ever since being forced into an early retirement from the Special Air Service and becoming a personal security specialist, the lines were quickly blurring. If things continued like they were, eventually there would be no more lines.

The cab halted, and Mercer paid the man, exiting without a word. He trudged back up the steps to his hotel room, planning to spend the next few hours reviewing the building's layout and memorizing the plan and at least one contingency. Opening the door, he drew his Sig and pointed it at the intruder. The scent of cigarette smoke tipped him off that he wasn't alone. Constantly on alert, he was trained to decimate anyone who stood in his way or posed a threat.

"I hope you sent Michelle my best," Bastian remarked, snubbing the butt in an ashtray.

"Didn't you quit?" Mercer asked, annoyed by the intrusion, as he tucked the gun in the holster at the small of his back.

"That was yesterday. Depending on how tonight goes, I'll reconsider quitting again tomorrow. But in the event we all bloody well die today, then there's no

reason I should torture myself in these final hours."
He studied Mercer, looking for cracks on his
impassive exterior. "Jules, you can't go on like this.
She's gone. You need to move on."

"I have. Now, are we going to get to work?"

"No." Bastian Clarke had been an intelligence
analyst. He knew his way around a gun and could hold
his own in a firefight, but his real skills came with
reading marks, hacking surveillance, and predicting
enemy movements. He was also Mercer's best friend,
second-in-command, and the only person not afraid
to mouth off. "Hans and Donovan don't want you on-
site. Not today."

"Who's in charge?"

"Today, I am," Bastian said, watching as Mercer
stalked across the room. "Under normal
circumstances, you barely have the rage under
control, and with it being Michelle's birthday, any
problem we encounter will turn into a bloodbath."
Bastian lit another cigarette and exhaled. "Maybe
you're okay with the killing, but we're not
mercenaries. Minimal collateral damage,
understand?"

Mercer grabbed the cigarette from Bastian's mouth
and smushed it into the table. "If I'm going through
hell, then so are you."

"Deal." Bastian flipped open the dossier they
compiled on the kidnapped child, Louisa Hamberson,
and skimmed through the information. Mercer had
spent the entire week negotiating with the kidnappers
on the parents' behalf, and finally, the two parties
agreed on a location for the exchange. Typically, these
matters were civil. But sometimes, the human
element could get greedy or the package was
damaged, and things would turn ugly fast. "It's still
your op, Commander. So why don't we work on the

exit strategy together?" Bastian offered as consolation.

Julian rubbed the bridge of his nose. He needed an outlet to escape. The woman from the pub didn't help, visiting the cemetery only exacerbated the situation, and working on a mission he wouldn't be a part of would just add to his feeling of impotence.

"Figure it out yourself," he barked, storming out of the room and slamming the door.

Since he was stuck in this godforsaken city for another day, he should at least see if any progress was made on finding his wife's killer. It was the only thing that mattered, and despite his best efforts and the efforts of his team and numerous private investigators he hired, no one was ever caught. The police probably still believed he was to blame, and on those sleepless nights when his past haunted him, he wasn't sure that he wasn't.

TWO

"Rubbish," Mercer snarled, exiting the police station.

He was in a worse mood now than when he arrived. He spent hours at the police station, impatiently waiting for the detective inspector assigned to Michelle's case to make time to see him. It was a cold case now, but it was the same man who conducted the initial investigation two years ago. After an eternity, the man summoned Mercer to his desk. Silently staring, he sized up Mercer like he was the prime suspect back to gloat. It was sickening. This detective was a moron, and it was no wonder Michelle's killer was still walking free. If it wasn't for tonight's planned recovery, Mercer would have shown the incompetent bastard exactly where he could put his nightstick. But he couldn't jeopardize the current op or expect any of his teammates to waste their time bailing him out of jail for assaulting a police officer. Instead, he procured copies of the police reports and left without resorting to physical violence.

Returning to his hotel room, he sat at the table and flipped through the pages. It was old news. He read the same information hundreds of times, but he couldn't help himself. Maybe one of these days there would be a new notation or crime scene photo that would lead to the assailant's identity. And until that day came, Mercer was condemned to read and reread the file.

After the fourth perusal, he closed the folder, sick to his stomach and trembling. He wasn't an investigator. His skill set involved precision shooting, tactical response and rescue, and stealth espionage maneuvers. But surely, he must be more competent than the mentally impaired sows that worked for the London police.

"I'll figure this out. I will find that bloody motherfucker," he whispered, pushing away from the table.

To distract himself, he disassembled and cleaned his handgun, reviewed Bastian's plan for the exchange, and phoned the Hambersons to make sure the money was ready to go. Hans and Donovan were performing the retrieval, and Bastian would remain outside to monitor the situation and provide any necessary cover support. It was a good plan. Unfortunately, it didn't involve him.

Hundreds of push-ups and sit-ups later, Bastian phoned. The exchange went off without a hitch. Hans and Donovan had safely negotiated with the kidnappers and exited with Louisa. Her parents were thrilled to have their daughter back alive and unharmed.

"I've made travel arrangements," Bastian stated. "After I collect our fee, we'll head to Heathrow. I don't see any reason for us to stay in this bloody town another night."

"I agree. Where are we going this time?"

"The United States. We fly into O'Hare and should arrive by the morning."

Bastian coordinated their jobs. He had connections to insurance firms and private security agencies, so Mercer didn't bother to ask why. He simply agreed, assuming it was another kidnapping and ransom case.

Disconnecting, Julian showered and packed, disassembling the heavy artillery and placing it inside the checked bag. He hoped that airport security wouldn't confiscate or question the items likely to set the metal detectors abuzz. He couldn't wait for approval or to send them through the mail. It was time to leave London. And he swore he wouldn't return home again until he knew the identity of his wife's killer, and then he would track that man down and leave him bloodied and broken to die slow and painfully.

Bastian received their compensation and arrived at the airport, money in hand. The four men boarded the plane, exchanging few words. But from the worried looks Bastian tossed in Mercer's direction, it was obvious he believed the sooner Julian was away from the EU, the better off he'd be.

The four ex-SAS had been a team for a number of years prior to Julian Mercer's forced retirement. But after his breakdown, Mercer's superiors believed he was a liability. He couldn't control his rage, and he failed to exercise the proper precautions in ensuring his own safety. When he was forced to leave, his team followed suit. Their loyalty wasn't to the Crown; it was to Julian. Even now, as he became increasingly unstable, the three of them were determined to keep him from coming completely unhinged. If work was something he needed to focus on, then they would find more job opportunities.

Situated a few rows away from Bastian and Mercer, Hans and Donovan exchanged a look. They never expected to become kidnap recovery specialists. Mercenary work was something they were better trained for, but it was too slippery a slope. Wet work was costly. And after years of carrying out government-sanctioned hits and black ops missions, maybe it was time to earn back some cosmic brownie points. Balance was important, or so Bastian insisted.

Hans Bauer was a reconnaissance specialist, and Donovan Mayes was an expert at long-distance tactical resolutions. They both favored a more simplistic approach to crisis management, but they were adjusting to civilian life easily enough. They were each a decade younger than Mercer, who recently hit forty, but not remotely as damaged and jaded. They hadn't seen nearly as many devastating attacks and wars, nor did they come home to find their wife choking to death in a pool of her own blood after being stabbed repeatedly. Although it was Julian's pain, it sometimes felt like something they all shared. Grief was a burden no one was free from carrying.

As they hurtled through the sky, Mercer stared out the window into the darkness. At some point he must have fallen asleep because when he opened his eyes, the pilot was announcing they have arrived in Chicago. Stretching in his seat, he realized it was his first dreamless night since arriving in London.

"Morning," Bastian commented, gnawing on a drinking straw. "I've made room reservations at a four-star hotel since these insurance blokes are picking up the tab. We have a meeting scheduled for this afternoon."

"Fine," Mercer replied, the amusement over Bastian's nicotine deprivation very obviously played across his face. "And you were worried about how well

I was keeping it together." He snorted and dug out his passport as the plane made a final approach before landing.

*   *   *

"That was a complete waste of time," Mercer remarked as he and Bastian exited the meeting. The insurance firm wanted to hire specialists to remain behind a desk and crunch numbers before issuing payouts for ransom demands. It was corporate bullshit, and not something any of them were equipped to handle. Hans and Donovan had taken off in pursuit of their own devices, leaving Mercer and Bastian to devise their next course of action. "Now what? I'm sick of being dragged across the globe for frivolous reasons." He squinted against the bright sunlight that filtered into the lobby.

"Fine. Our next move is up to you. It's your call," Bastian said, stopping at a vending machine on the way out of the insurance building. He offered the snack bag to Mercer, who declined, before shoving his hand inside and devouring a fistful of pretzels. "We'll go wherever you want."

"That's the bloody problem." Mercer had taken another stab at the police file before coming to the meeting, and it left him frustrated and irate. "You're constantly on my back. Just give me some room to breathe. I don't need a babysitter following me around. Do you think I'm going to blow my bloody head off? Because I promise if that was my intention, I'd have done it by now."

"You want some space. Here's your space," Bastian yelled, taking a step back. "You know where to find me whenever you're done having a hissy fit."

"And stay away from the nicotine," Mercer called

after him, "because it makes you even more insufferable than usual." Bastian made a rude gesture and then stormed down the street, heading for Chicago's rail system, the L. "Good riddance," Mercer huffed. He finally had the reprieve and privacy he wanted, but now he had to figure out what to do with it.

He moved throughout the city on foot with no destination in mind. It was unfamiliar territory but easy enough to navigate. The sun set almost an hour ago, and the air had a slight chill to it. His stomach growled, and he stepped into an Irish pub for a pint and some sustenance.

To his surprise, the place was crowded with young adults. This part of town didn't seem that trendy, but maybe he was mistaken. He took a seat at the corner of the bar and waited patiently as the world continued spinning around him. After he ate and could no longer tolerate the infernal racket of the pub, he stepped outside. Glancing around, he spotted a sign for the L.

Waiting on the platform was a collection of various people. Subconsciously, he assessed the group, determining who might pose a threat. The three adolescent men, probably in their late teens, appeared particularly interested in the bags an elderly couple was holding. Mercer took a breath, debating if he would intercede if circumstances presented themselves. It wasn't his problem or his business, but the thought of getting to knock some punks around did hold a certain appeal. Continuing to watch out of the corner of his eye, the men lost interest in their prize and moved away from the platform. *Probably for the best*, Mercer thought, leaning against a support pole and waiting for the train.

Fifteen minutes later, the train came, and he boarded, taking a seat in the back corner. As he neared his stop, the brakes squeaked, but there was another unmistakable squeal. It sounded like a woman screaming. Peering through the glass of the subway car, he was positive the sound didn't originate from the train. As the brakes fully engaged and the doors opened, he cautiously stepped outside. No one else reacted as if they heard anything amiss. Maybe Bas was right, and he was losing it. While walking back to the hotel, his eyes darted back and forth, searching for danger, as he strained to hear any other cries for help.

By the time he reached the hotel, he was certain he must have hallucinated the entire event. Had he been thinking of Michelle and not realized it? Entering through the revolving door, Mercer found the lobby empty. He went up to his room, unlocked the door, and stepped inside. He was alone.

Settling into bed, he shut his eyes and forced his mind to go blank. His breathing slowed, only to be kick-started by another blood-curdling scream. It was muffled and must have come from somewhere outside.

Getting up, he peered out the window. But it was too dark, and the alleys were too dimly lit to see from this height. Reacting, he grabbed his gun and opened the door. He exited the hotel and turned down the street. Half a block later, he heard it again and took off at a fast clip, heading straight for the sound. Rounding a corner, he found a woman on the ground, covered in blood and holding a man in her arms. No one else was in sight.

"Miss," Mercer spoke softly, his gun still poised in front of him, "are you okay? Who did this?"

Spotting the gun, she screamed. This time it was nonstop and deafening. Before he could quiet her hysterics or evaluate the condition of the prone man, flashing lights and sirens pulled up behind him. The police ordered him to drop the weapon and surrender. Despite what Bastian might think, he didn't have a death wish and complied. Before he knew it, he was booked and thrown into a jail cell.

"Bollocks," he muttered, knowing his team would never let him live this one down.

*   *   *

It was early morning before the police officer opened the cell door. The woman Mercer attempted to rescue finally managed to give her statement to the officers. And although they were still suspicious of a British citizen running through the streets with a Sig Sauer, Julian had the proper paperwork and documentation, so they couldn't hold him on anything.

After collecting his belongings and being given numerous stern looks by everyone in the squad room, Mercer was free to go. As soon as he stepped outside, he spotted the woman from last night. In the morning sunlight, he realized she couldn't be older than twenty-five.

She gave him a grim smile. "I'm sorry you were arrested," she muttered. "After everything that happened, I saw the gun and thought they came back to finish the job."

Something about the woman piqued his interest. This was new. Different. And obviously dangerous. It could be fun.

"Who?" he asked. She hesitated, watching him pensively, not trusting the man who had so conveniently shown up to help. Mercer dug through his wallet and pulled out his business card, handing it to her. "Maybe I can offer some assistance."

She read the card and then looked up at him. "Personal security specialist?" Considering her options, she walked away without another word.

THREE

"It's about bloody time," Bastian said. "Where've you been all night?"

"Out," Mercer replied. He entered the hotel only to be confronted by Bastian perched in the lobby, waiting to pounce.

"No shit, really? Did you find some unsuspecting American and woo her with your charm and accent? You're not James Bond. He dresses better and has a hell of a lot better attitude than you, mate."

"He's also fictional."

"Details," Bastian muttered, noticing the receipt stuffed in Mercer's shirt pocket. He narrowed his eyes at it. "Was she a whore? Because I'm not entirely certain how else you would have ended up spending the night in jail." He scrutinized his friend's expression. "Is everyone still breathing? Or did someone look at you the wrong way?"

"Frankly, I'm not certain. A man was bleeding, but no one informed me of his condition." Mercer was enjoying pushing Bastian's buttons. "Then again, that happened before I arrived. It was the impetus for the screaming that led to the alley and the woman. Now if you'll excuse me, I'd like to clean up."

After Mercer showered and dressed, he heard a beep, notifying him of a new voicemail message. He listened as a man introduced himself as Carlton Rhoade and requested a call back in regards to a potential job opportunity. The area code indicated Chicago, and having nothing better to do on this wasted trip, he went to Bastian's room and knocked. When Bastian answered, he put the phone on speaker and pushed play.

Without needing further instructions, Bastian opened his laptop and performed a reverse lookup on the number, followed by a people search and background check on Carlton Rhoade. "Looks like he's a newspaper mogul." Bastian frowned at the screen. "My guy at Interpol can check criminal records, but if you want to hear him out, give the gentleman a call. As far as I can tell, he's not a Mafioso kingpin or on any terrorist watchlist, so he's clean enough for our taste."

"Might as well see what he has to say. Someone ought to pay us, just so you have enough revenue to cover your mini-bar expenses." Mercer nodded toward the emptied snack section near the fridge. "Those cashews were twenty dollars a jar."

Dialing, Mercer waited. After three rings, the call was answered by the same voice that left the message. Not wasting time on questions or basic pleasantries, Carlton Rhoade provided an address and time to meet. He did not offer any hint as to what he wanted or how he came about Mercer's number.

"Another kidnapping?" Bastian asked.

"He didn't say. But it might be more interesting than mucking about around here, watching you consume a fortune's worth of chips and nuts."

Preparing for a second meeting in two days, Mercer and Bastian dressed in their professional best and went to the high-class apartment building. The doorman requested their names and called up to Mr. Rhoade's apartment for verification before letting them inside the building. In the lobby, another man waited in the elevator car, which could only be operated by a key, and escorted them to the penthouse.

"Chintzy," Bastian whispered, catching Julian's eye.

As the elevator opened, the two former military men glanced around, uncertain if this was an elaborate hoax. Typically, they weren't invited to spend time in places like this. Sure, their clients tended to be the rich and powerful, but almost all meetings occurred at a place of business.

"Mr. Mercer?" a man asked, entering the foyer. "I'm Carlton Rhoade. I believe you met my daughter, Katia, last night." Rhoade produced the business card, and Mercer nodded slightly. "Come inside. Please make yourselves comfortable."

"Bastian Clarke," Bastian introduced himself, extending his hand, "please forgive Julian, he forgets his manners." He threw a pointed glance at his friend. "Why did you contact us?"

"Personal security specialists," Rhoade continued, leading the three of them into the living room. "Frankly, I wasn't sure what that meant, but Katia said you rushed into that alley with a gun, prepared to defend her. Is that accurate, Mr. Mercer?"

"There were screams. Someone had to do something. The man that was wounded, is he still alive?"

"For now." Rhoade went to the wet bar, having temporarily forgotten the time, but reconsidered and filled a glass with soda water instead. "Can I get you gentlemen anything?"

"No," Mercer interjected, fearing Bastian might ask for the container of mixed nuts sitting atop the bar. "Sir, would you please elaborate on why you asked us here?"

"Forward. I like that." Rhoade took a seat, making a tired sound as he sunk into the plush suede. "My daughter needs a protector. The bodyguards I've hired in the past have been inadequate. They are more concerned with a paycheck and following the rules established by the private security agencies that employ them. From the information I've gathered on you, you do this freelance. Rules and orders shouldn't apply to a man like you."

Mercer shrugged. "I have my own set of rules."

"Which do not limit you to a great extent," Rhoade said, scrutinizing Julian. He cracked a knowing smile. "I've done my research."

"What are you asking?" Bastian interrupted, uneasy with the current exchange. Why didn't Julian mention last night's encounter in more specific detail this morning?

"I need someone who will keep an eye on Katia, chauffeur her around, and make sure nothing happens to her. Is that something you're capable of doing?" Rhoade asked.

Mercer met Bastian's eyes. They didn't need words to communicate. This was a job Mercer wanted, so it was up to Bastian to determine if it was something they could handle. While Bastian launched into an elaborate explanation of their backgrounds and work details, Mercer stalked the small space of the room, studying the various knickknacks. The words were drowned out because, as usual, he couldn't be bothered with such insignificant details. On the table, he spotted a cluster of photographs of Katia Rhoade from the time she was born until her college graduation. One of the more recent photos showed her with the man from the alley.

"Who is he?" Mercer inquired, cutting into the conversation.

"That's Benjamin Styler, Katia's fiancé."

"Julian," Bastian tossed him a warning look, "we'll get the background work out of the way after our meeting."

"So that's a yes?" Rhoade asked, smiling. "You're willing to guard my daughter?"

"Absolutely. Our team is comprised of four men, each with his own unique set of skills. We'll maintain your daughter's safety until the man responsible for shooting her fiancé has been identified and apprehended," Bastian assured. "Do the police have any leads yet?"

"They're working on it. I've been told their best detectives are taking the case," Rhoade replied. "However," he shifted his gaze between the two security specialists, "from what you've said, you might be able to discover his identity faster. Perhaps you could remedy the situation without involving the authorities."

"We don't do that kind of work," Bastian replied, his voice icy. "But identifying potential assailants and subduing imminent threats is necessary to ensure adequate protection."

"Very well." Rhoade stood and shook hands with each man. "Can you start tomorrow?"

Mercer nodded, leading the way out of the apartment. His mind was picking through the parts of the conversation he actually paid attention to. Did Bas just agree to assist in identifying the assailant? Everything up until this point had been asset recovery, protection, or retrieval. They weren't coppers or inspectors. For all intents and purposes, they were hired guns. The American equivalent of cowboys from the Wild West, or at least that's how Mercer liked to fancy himself, having watched one too many spaghetti westerns in his day. Still shocked by Bastian's promises, he followed his friend back to the hotel in a daze. Even though Julian liked to believe he was calling the shots, when it came to the business angle of their ventures, he was in the dark.

* * *

As Bastian worked his magic with the computers, creating full profiles for Katia Rhoade, Benjamin Styler, and Carlton Rhoade, Mercer elected to nap. The time difference and spending the night in lockup had taken their toll. Opening one eye, he watched as the hotel door opened, and Donovan and Hans entered. It appeared they spent the entire night out partying, and he wouldn't have been surprised to learn that was the case. As Bastian briefed the rest of the team, Mercer listened from his spot on the mattress.

Carlton Rhoade owned and operated one of Chicago's top newspapers, courtesy of a vast inheritance left to him by a great uncle. Having spent years in the journalism industry, Rhoade bought the paper after being fired for allegedly running stories without performing the proper fact-checking requirements. By taking over, Rhoade enacted his own form of revenge against his previous boss and anyone that opposed him. Obviously, screwing with Carlton Rhoade wasn't advisable. The paper was revamped, and those he believed to have wronged him were now jobless.

"Superb way to make enemies," Mercer retorted,

sitting up. All eyes turned to him, surprised that he was awake or even paying attention. "But what does this have to do with the girl and her escort?"

Bastian smirked, pleased that Julian was finally showing an interest in something besides target practice. "Perhaps the assailant has an axe to grind with the Rhoade family, especially since Katia is the only remaining relative Carlton has. His wife left him a decade ago, changed her name, and disappeared. From what I've found, she's living in Canada under a different name and with another woman."

"Kinky," Hans grinned, "although, a tad extreme."

"Regardless," Bastian continued, "it would be reasonable to assume if someone wanted to hurt Carlton, Katia would be the way to go." He cautioned a glance at Mercer, not wanting to draw any type of parallel between this situation and Michelle, but Mercer was unfazed.

"What about the other bloke?" Donovan asked, taking a seat at the desk while he studied some aerial maps of the city and focused on Rhoade's apartment building.

"Benjamin Styler has been in trouble before. He was arrested for public intoxication, possession, drunk driving, indecent exposure, and disturbing the peace," Bastian read.

"Sounds like Hans," Donovan replied. "Or me."

"The point is he might have his own set of enemies. Most of the charges were dropped, and from what I gather, he probably ratted on his dealer in order to get away without any felony charges. Based on the Rhoades' wealth, I would have assumed Styler could afford to buy himself out of trouble, but his family isn't nearly as well-off as the nouveau riche Mr. Rhoade. The Stylers keep up appearances with memberships to the country club and Ivy League educations, but they're lacking a few zeroes at the end of their bank accounts."

"When did these legal infringements occur?" Hans asked.

"The most recent was over a year ago, but that doesn't mean Styler's turned over a new leaf. Maybe he's just been more careful."

"What about the woman? Who has she pissed off?" Mercer asked, skimming through the printouts on Carlton and Benjamin.

"No one. She has no record. Nothing disturbing. She's a photographer for a women's magazine. I'd wager her father used his connections to procure the job for her, but aside from that, there's nothing damning in her history." Bastian shifted his gaze around the room. "Any objections to providing this young lady with protection?"

"Drug dealers and distraught employees are nothing we can't handle," Donovan surmised.

"Sounds easier than kidnappers and trained mercenaries," Hans added.

"Let's not forget," Mercer glanced at the copy of Katia's driver's license that Bastian had printed, "she's just an innocent bystander with questionable ties. She can't help it if the man she fell in love with has made some bad decisions in the past." The room remained silent as his words mirrored more than the current matter. "Bas, come up with a strategy so we can finish this quickly."

FOUR

"Miss Rhoade," Mercer greeted. He was leaning against a black sedan with dark tinted windows. As usual, his team pooled their resources and gained access to something bullet resistant. "Care for a ride home?"

"I'm not going home," she looked at him skeptically, "and I'm perfectly capable of taking care of myself."

"Apparently." Mercer judged her appearance, knowing she would eventually give in and get inside the car after making some type of point about having freedom, independence, and being a modern woman. "That doesn't mean you don't want a ride."

"Fine," she huffed, opening the back door and throwing her camera bag and briefcase inside before maneuvering around Mercer to get to the front passenger's side door. "But if you think I'm riding in back and giving you a tip, you've got another thing coming."

He held his snide comment at bay, looking smug as

he went around the car to the driver's side. Some things were predictable. "What destination did you have in mind?" he asked, checking the mirror for signs of trouble or a tail before pulling out while making a mental note not to drive on the left side of the street. Damn Yanks.

"The hospital. I want to see Ben." She took a deep breath and sighed. "Why did my father hire you? We have enough security at home. Am I really expected to have a babysitter for the rest of my life?"

"No," his eyes diligently continued to monitor the traffic patterns and mirrors, "once this situation is sorted out and the threat is removed, my team and I will be on our way."

"Are you investigating?"

"The police ought to be. My job is far more simplistic."

"What is your job?"

"To make sure you remain breathing." He tossed a glance at her.

"My hero." The bitter sarcasm hung in the air. "How convenient that a bodyguard happens to appear at such a perfectly opportune time, right after Ben was shot."

"Is that an apology for leaving me in lockup overnight?" Mercer queried. She had reasons to be suspicious, but he wasn't her enemy. "Is it wrong to assume you took my business card and gave it to your father?" He caught her eye. "You're not fooling anyone, princess. You're scared, and you think I'm a bloody knight in shining armor. Let me make one thing clear. I'm good at what I do, but I'm no one's hero."

The rest of the ride was in silence, and by the time he cut the car's engine, she was twenty feet ahead of him, making her way to the hospital's entrance.

Mercer kept an eye out but didn't fathom anyone would make an attempt on her life in such a populated and public location. He caught up to her at the elevator, and they rode to the appropriate floor without a word.

When the doors opened, she read the signs to locate Ben while Mercer glanced down the corridor, spotting Hans sitting in a chair outside Styler's room. Bastian doled out assignments to ensure the safety of Carlton, Ben, and Katia until they had a firmer grasp on what was going on and who might be targeted. Katia turned and headed for Ben's room, oblivious to the constant presence just feet from her fiancé's door.

"No wonder she needs protection," Hans whispered. "She's bloody clueless."

"Or in denial," Mercer responded. "Any updates on his condition?"

"In and out of consciousness. They think he'll live, but they're monitoring him closely."

"How'd you find this out?" Mercer asked.

"I might have charmed the pants off a nurse." He smiled wickedly. "American women love the accent. Can't we consider permanently relocating to the States?"

"Stay focused," Mercer berated, following Katia into the room.

Inside, Katia took a seat next to Ben. Silent tears fell from her eyes and threatened to streak the mascara she wore. Mercer remained standing near the door, completely out of place. His normal aloof demeanor retired, and he was intrigued by the number of emotions this one woman expressed. Love, fear, hope, anger, pain, and if Ben opened his eyes, a good chance for passion. As a general rule, Julian tried to shut off his feelings, and for the most part, the only one he regularly contended with was anger. So it seemed strange to see such blatant displays in front of him.

"What's your problem?" she asked, sniffling and wiping her eyes. "You just stand there like a goddamn statue, gawking at me. Haven't you ever seen anyone cry before? Are you a fucking sadist? Do you intend to go home and jack off to this?"

"I'm not your enemy." His words were quiet, knowing that anything she said was simply the result of lashing out against the situation and not at him. She stared at him, silently pleading for something only he could promise. "Do you know who did this?" he asked, sensing she knew more about the situation than she had bothered to share.

"What will you do to them?" Her tone became cold and calculating. And in that instant, it was apparent she wanted revenge.

"Whatever you want."

"I want you to kill them. I want them to suffer. To scream." The tears were falling much more rapidly, fueled by her anguish and rage. "I want you to torture them," she trembled and struggled for air, "for the torment they've caused by hurting Ben."

She burst into loud, gasping sobs, and Mercer closed the gap between them and held her in the confines of his arms. He rocked her back and forth as she fought against his grip. Eventually, she gave up struggling and clutched his shoulders, sobbing into his shirt. He picked her up and sat down in the chair with her on his lap as she continued to cry into his chest.

Hours later, the pitiful mewling noises she was making ceased, and he no longer felt the need to continue the swaying motion to try to calm her. Instead, he looked down to find she had fallen asleep. The emotional toll had become too much for her to bear. Getting up, he carried her out of the room and into the hallway.

"Now what did you do?" Hans asked.

"Come on," he jerked his head toward the elevator, not breaking stride, "Bastian's too concerned about playing defense. I'm still your CO, and I make the decisions. The plan's changed."

Without protest, Hans followed Julian down the hallway. Hospital security could keep an eye on Benjamin Styler for the immediate future.

Inside the elevator, the ding roused Katia, and she opened her eyes, embarrassed by her hysterics. "Put me down," she insisted, and Mercer gently released her legs so she could stand next to him. "I'm sorry about your shirt."

"You mean your handkerchief?" he teased, and she looked away, embarrassed. "It needed a good washing anyway."

He caught the perplexed look on Hans' face. The younger man hadn't seen his boss in such a good mood in the last two years. Whatever happened inside that hospital room might be the first step to getting the old Julian back.

"Did you mean what you said?" Katia asked meekly.

"Yes." Mercer judged her expression. "Are you certain that's what you want?" She nodded. "Make sure because there is no going back once it's done."

"I'm positive."

Her conviction was unsettling, and Mercer realized how easily he could relate. He didn't get to exact revenge on his wife's murderer. Not yet. And he spent countless nights wanting nothing more than to watch the man slowly and painfully bleed to death, but instead, the assailant was still walking around free, someplace safe from Mercer's hand.

"Okay. Once we identify the party responsible, the

rest will follow."

"There are things that I haven't told the police," she admitted. "Maybe some of it will be useful."

"Hans, call Bastian and have him meet us at the hotel. We need to work out a new strategy."

FIVE

This was the most talkative and animated Mercer had been in a long while. He paced the room, rubbing his five o'clock shadow and willing the computers to work faster. Katia was seated on the bed, her back against the headboard and her knees pulled up against her chest. Bastian was entering every bit of relevant data he could think of to get the technology to cooperate while Donovan and Hans cleaned and reassembled their weaponry. If Katia was frightened by the two assault rifles, sniper scope, and box of ammunition, she didn't let on.

"Let's go over this one more time," Mercer insisted, turning to face her. He grabbed a chair and sat down. "You said Ben owed money to some people. Were they his drug dealers or his bookies?"

"He's off the drugs," she insisted, chewing on a hangnail. "But he mentioned being indebted to some people for a few grand. I told him I'd lend him the money, but he said it wasn't a big deal."

"How much?" Donovan asked.

"A couple thousand. I don't know the exact dollars and cents," she retorted, glaring in his general direction.

"Why did he owe them money?" Mercer asked.

"I don't know." She shook her head. "He said he made some bad investments and needed some help out of the mess."

"Sounds like a loan shark," Bastian muttered.

Mercer nodded but didn't turn around to face the other man. "When I found you in that alley, you mentioned you thought they came back to finish what they started. How many of them did you see before the shooting started? What did they look like? Did anyone say anything?"

"Two or three guys, maybe. I barely even saw the gun. It happened so fast." She pressed her chin against her knees to hide the telltale quiver before more tears could fall. "We ducked into this little alcove for some privacy. I didn't notice them until after the shooting, and I certainly never expected anyone to do something like this. All at once, someone called Ben's name and said something like 'you had your chance'. I don't remember exactly." She blinked back the tears. "Then BAM." The sudden increase in her volume made Bastian jump. The other three remained unfazed.

"Just one shot?" Mercer inquired.

"How many should they have taken?" she screeched. "He's fighting for his life right now. A second one surely would have killed him."

"Hell of a shot," Hans murmured. "How far away was the shooter?" Katia looked confused, so Hans stood up and pointed his thumb and index finger at her. "Was he closer than this?"

"No." Her brow furrowed. "Maybe twice as far. Perhaps farther." She shook her head and squinted, trying to recall some details. "We were walking back from dinner and stopped in the alley to…" She blushed. "It doesn't matter, but the shooter never came into the alley. He stayed on the street."

"About six to eight meters, assuming they didn't go deeper into the alley after the shooting," Mercer supplied, estimating the distance from the opening to where he found Katia and Ben on the ground.

"Tight quarters," Donovan interjected. "I'd love to run trajectories, especially with the angles from the buildings." His mind was on determining the perfect vantage point. "Did they say or do anything else afterward?"

"No. Ben just crumpled, and they disappeared." A sob escaped her lips, and she swallowed. "He collapsed onto me, and I just kept screaming for help. It felt like hours before anyone showed up." Her eyes focused on Mercer. "You showed up."

"Did you call the authorities?" he asked. They arrived seconds after he did, and assuming the scream he heard while on the train had been her, then she must have been out there for at least a half hour while Ben continued to lose blood.

"No. I couldn't find my phone, and I was too afraid to let go of Ben." She got off the bed and disappeared into the bathroom to get a tissue and wash the ruined makeup off her cheeks. Maybe she just wanted a moment alone, away from the prying eyes of the four men.

"And no one did a damn thing," Bastian said in a hushed tone.

"Surprised?" Julian asked, irate at the entire human race. "People are apathetic. They don't give a shit."

"So we have a group consisting of two or three men. One shooter. One shot fired. No follow-up threats or additional demands," Donovan surmised. "Shall I go to the hospital to ensure Ben isn't visited by any more of these wankers?"

"Go." Julian jerked his head toward the door, and Donovan disappeared before Katia emerged from the bathroom.

"I'll go have a chat with the coppers," Hans offered. "Maybe they can be persuaded to offer up their leads." He exited, and Bastian leaned closer to Mercer.

"There must be surveillance cameras close by. A busy street like this with shops, hotels, and restaurants must have some CCTVs that caught something. I'll work on decrypting the nearby networks and see what I can find. Do you need back-up, or do you think you can handle the young lady on your own?" It was snarky, but Mercer ignored it.

"Here," Julian reached into his pocket and found some dollar bills and change, "for the vending machine down the hallway. You're running low on pen caps, and I know you can't afford to clean out the mini-bar every night."

"Cheeky bastard," Bastian remarked, leaving just as Katia returned to the main room.

As Mercer studied the darkness outside, he detected a few glitches in Katia's behavior. She was afraid, grieving, and angry, but the way she turned cold and vicious in the hospital room spoke volumes. When confronted about the incident and the party responsible, she simply asked what would be done to them. She had to know who was responsible and why her fiancé was barely breathing. If not, there would have been no point in asking that question and deflecting the one he asked.

Her footsteps faltered, and she cleared her throat. But Mercer pretended not to hear, still contemplating his next move. As she stepped closer, the smell of her perfume grew stronger, but he continued to face away. There was something deceitful about this woman, and it was important to make sure she didn't pose a threat to his team.

"Where'd everyone go?" she asked, sounding a little panicked. Perhaps being alone in a hotel room with a strange man wasn't ideal. "You haven't changed your mind, have you?"

"No." Mercer stood in front of the window, watching her reflection in the glass. "My team will determine who's responsible." He glanced back at her. "We don't keep secrets from each other, so I don't understand why you haven't given us the identities of your assailants. You want us to find them, and we will. But why are you making this more difficult than it needs to be?"

"I don't know who they are." She looked away, the lie blatantly obvious.

"Yes. You do." He spun around to face her. "You've been handling this situation better than most. I've seen a lot of grief and the different ways people deal with it. You're calculating. Every word you say is being weighed. I won't go back on my promise. I intend to exact revenge on your behalf, but no one else is here. It's time to come clean. I work for you. I was hired to protect you. Whatever you say won't change that fact."

She looked angry and chewed on her bottom lip. "Fine. I've seen them before. At least the other two. Not the shooter. They were leaving Ben's apartment a week ago. When I asked him who they were, he said they were business associates."

"What kind of business is Mr. Styler in?"

"He's an online day trader."

"Are you sure about that?"

"Of course, I'm fucking sure. Don't you think I know who I'm planning to marry?" She was annoyed.

"You think you're just so goddamn brilliant, trying to rip my story to shreds. Everything I've said has been the truth."

"You knew the men involved in the shooting," Mercer said, pointing out the flaw in her argument.

"I don't know them. I saw them once. It might not even be the same two men. It was dark in that alley, and I was on my knees about to give my fiancé a blowjob. Do you think I gave a damn about some people on the street?"

"Classy."

"Who the hell are you to pass judgment, Mr. Mercer?" Her eyes bore daggers at him. "At least I have someone to love who loves me," her face contorted, "unless he dies." She plopped down on the edge of the bed. "I don't know what I'd do if..." She didn't continue.

"You'll survive. You might not want to, but you will." He watched her as she filtered through the emotions, coming to rest on hatred.

"Why are you doing this to me? Don't you think I've been through enough without being humiliated and accused of lying? Next, you'll probably say I conspired with them and that I want Ben to die."

"Did you?"

"Screw you." She stomped to the door, but before she could get it open, Mercer grabbed her by the shoulders and spun her around to face him.

"You're angry now. You want blood, and you're willing to lash out at anyone and everyone." Admittedly, he had been testing her, pushing her buttons to get this precise reaction. It was important to discover her motivation for concealing the truth. If she was involved, it'd be better to find out forthright. But her emotions were honest. She didn't want Benjamin Styler to die. "You have to learn to be detached. Unemotional. Right now, you're a liability. That's a risk to my team that I won't allow. Get your shit together and file it away in a box. Only clear thinking will get us the results you desire."

"You're psychotic."

He shrugged and released her from his grasp. "Perhaps." She left the room, muttering curses under her breath. He exhaled and dialed Bastian, requesting he meet Katia in the lobby and escort her home.

"What the bloody hell do you keep doing to these women?" Bastian asked, and Mercer hung up.

SIX

Hans received a copy of the police report, but there weren't any leads. Based on Katia's initial statement, the police were working under the assumption it was a mugging gone wrong. Clearly, the woman had a tenuous relationship with the truth, but her statement still enabled the cops to be granted permission to view the video footage from nearby businesses and the city's traffic cams. However, they were unable to identify the shooter. Then again, they didn't know the whole story.

Bastian accessed similar footage through much less legal means and caught the briefest glimpse of the assailants. Three men had leapfrogged the couple from the time they left the restaurant. First, one man followed. Then the men switched off, and another pursued for the next block or so. Finally, the shooter took lead, and as the previous two men joined him, he popped off a single shot. Then the three continued on their way as if nothing happened. They kept their heads down and their faces obscured from the city's surveillance.

"Do we have audio?" Mercer asked, watching the video play again.

"No." Bastian gnawed on a toothpick. "There aren't any better angles either. Whoever these guys are, they know what they're doing." The footage played through on a loop. "I'd say the shooter has a silencer, so he didn't attract any unwanted attention." He glanced up at Mercer. Katia claimed there was a loud bang to accompany the gunshot. Again, her story was falling flat. "Are you sure she isn't responsible for the attempted murder?"

"Yes," Mercer stated, but he was developing doubts.

"Just consider the facts for a moment," Bastian interjected. "Katia suggests they stop in the alleyway for a tryst. She's on her knees, partially obscured by a dumpster. The men following them know where the couple dined and probably where they were headed. The intended killer comes upon the opening with a silencer, takes a single shot, and keeps going. She doesn't call the police. She doesn't run for help. Instead, she does nothing."

"She was petrified," Mercer insisted. "The shooter and his cohorts probably planned to follow until the perfect opportunity presented itself. Maybe they'd been shadowing the couple for some time. Maybe this behavior is not uncommon for Mr. Styler and Ms. Rhoade." He shrugged. "Plus, I heard her screaming for help. If she was responsible, she would have waited for him to bleed out before making a peep. And in an alley, the reverb from the gunshot would have sounded much louder even with a suppressor. I don't believe she's lying about that."

"But she was in the perfect position to keep Styler occupied and ensure she wasn't accidentally shot."

"She isn't involved."

"Jules, stop projecting. Ben isn't Michelle."

"No shit." Mercer gritted his teeth and fought with his temper. "But you didn't see how she was in that hospital room. Her feelings are genuine."

"That doesn't make her innocent. Maybe she made a mistake and regrets it now."

"Fine. You want to waste your time digging through her background, go ahead. But when the time comes, I hope I can count on you."

"You know I'll follow your lead, Commander." Bastian eyed Mercer curiously, wondering what his friend had in mind.

"I'll be back later. If anything new surfaces–"

"I'll ring you," Bastian completed Mercer's sentence, opening several applications on his computer to create a more complete profile on Katia.

Mercer left the hotel, wandering back to the scene of the attack. There was a single piece of shredded police tape hanging from the edge of the brick at the mouth of the alleyway, but it had been three days. No one else considered this a crime scene anymore. It was just another narrow, dark dead end in a city full of dead ends.

Entering the alley, Julian studied the walls, the ground, and the remnants of Ben Styler's blood that hadn't washed out of the asphalt. It was apparent Mercer wasn't a trained investigator, but he had been in plenty of firefights. And this wasn't like any shooting he'd ever seen before.

Spinning around, he noted the obstructed view, the close quarters, and remembered how easily the gunman had taken the single shot and kept walking. The man barely even broke stride. The shooter had to know where Ben would be positioned within the alley. There was no other way it could have happened with such precision.

"Bollocks," Mercer cursed, hating to admit Bastian might be right. He searched the brick for markings of any kind. A stray bullet, a ricochet, or even some spray paint indicating where Ben would have to be standing for the shooting to go off without a hitch, but there was nothing.

Leaving the alley, he walked up and down the street. A couple of hobos watched as he passed by another three times. They called to him, asking for money in exchange for directions. He ignored them. His eyes continued to search. He was determining how he would have carried out the failed execution. The ground provided no clues. The windows reflected across the street, not into the alley. Even the makeshift Plexiglas shelter for the buses didn't provide any viable views. It was dark at the time of the shooting, further complicating the possibility of hitting the intended target.

Mercer stopped on the street corner and considered if a reflection in a passing vehicle or parked car would have provided an ample view for that amazing shot. But that was too circumstantial, unless Katia planned Ben's demise. Was she playing him like a well-worn drum? How deceptive could one young lady be?

Mercer chuckled at that particular thought. Women were always deceptive and manipulative, and they had every reason to be. They possessed a certain power over men, at least heterosexual men. The prettier they were, the more influence they exuded. Maybe it was evolution's way of making up for the physical disparities. Men were stronger, brutish, violent, and likely to force their point while women had other tricks at their disposal. His mind drifted briefly to Michelle, and he cursed that unidentified man for destroying the woman he loved.

From across the street, he leaned against the brick wall of a pub and stared into the alley, but trying to make sense of the location was giving him a headache. It would have been dark and hard to see without the illumination from a streetlight. How was this single event conducted so perfectly? As Mercer mulled over the possibilities, the only thing that made any sense was the shooter must be a professional, either a contract killer or a sharpshooter. Unless he was a sharpshooting contract killer.

"Rubbish," he muttered, turning and heading back to the hotel.

Half a block later, he felt a tail. He didn't spot anyone behind him or acting suspicious, but he was certain he was being followed. Detouring into a clothing boutique, he browsed the racks of shirts, but his focus was on the street just beyond the large display window. Across the way, a man stopped to read a sign for an upcoming music festival.

Exiting, Mercer continued past the hotel with the man still in pursuit. Rounding to the other side of the street, Julian looped around and yanked the man into a small alcove next to a sealed door of an abandoned building. "Who are you? Why are you following me?"

The man shoved himself free and pulled a chain from around his neck, revealing a badge clipped to the end. "Detective Rowlins, CPD." He glared at Julian, considering arresting him for assaulting a police officer. "Mr. Mercer, I'd like to have a chat with you. We can either get a cup of coffee or you can come with me to the precinct."

"Coffee sounds fine."

"Excellent," Rowlins said, leading Julian to the diner two stores down. "Thank you for your cooperation." It sounded more like disappointment than gratitude. The detective called a waitress over and ordered coffee. Mercer declined, and the two sat, sizing each other up. "They always say the guilty return to the scene of the crime. Were you afraid you left some incriminating evidence behind?"

"I'm not the shooter." Mercer's face contorted into a sneer. "The family has asked that I provide protection and assistance in identifying the shooter."

"Convenient," Rowlins responded, taking a sip and reaching for the sugar packets. "Let's pretend for a moment that I believe you. Are you any closer to identifying this alleged mystery shooter than we are?"

"No."

"Would you tell me if you were?"

"No."

Rowlins stirred the sugar into his coffee and took another sip. It was more to his liking now, and he glanced at the counter, eyeing a piece of pumpkin pie. "Since your brief overnight stay with us, we've run your history. Ex-military. Personal tragedy. And now you're claiming to be a security specialist." He raised an eyebrow, looking skeptical. "Why don't you level with me?" He gave Mercer a dead-eye stare. "You're a mercenary, right?"

"No."

"Are you capable of saying anything besides no?"

"What do you want?" Mercer was losing his patience.

"Katia's father is a friend of my lieutenant, so if you say the family hired you, then the family hired you. But I've been doing this job long enough to know when something's fishy, and you showing up in that alley immediately after the shooting smells like yesterday's catch after it sat in the hot sun all day." He narrowed his eyes. "Why did Carlton Rhoade really hire you?"

"I've already told you, even though that is none of

your business."

"With experience like yours, it's hard to believe that you're just here for protection." He glanced around the diner and lowered his voice, leaning forward. "Carlton Rhoade is a man of action. He knows people and can make things happen. I'd prefer not having more bodies to clean up. The homicide unit is busy as it is."

"This wasn't a homicide. Styler's still kicking."

"Is that a confession?"

"No."

"Just the same, I'm keeping tabs on you, buddy." Rowlins' words were meant to be ominous, but Mercer snorted.

"Your time would be better spent learning how to be a tough guy from actual tough guys rather than the cheap facsimiles Hollywood creates in shitty movies." Mercer stood from the table. "Stay out of my way, Detective."

SEVEN

"Bugger," Bastian muttered, rubbing a hand down his face. "What am I supposed to do with this additional bit of information?"

"Figure it out." Mercer was tired of this job, and they'd only been in Carlton Rhoade's employ for two days.

The profiles on Katia, her father, and Benjamin Styler were complete. Even Bastian's contact at Interpol didn't come to any profound conclusions regarding who might have performed the failed hit. The only lead they had was Benjamin Styler's questionable business associates. The police file that Hans obtained didn't point to any real suspects, and now with the appearance of Det. Rowlins, there had to be more to the story. As usual, Mercer wanted answers and expected Bastian to supply them.

"I'll dig through my sources and try to pinpoint the connection between this unnamed police lieutenant and Mr. Rhoade." Bastian bit his lip, wanting a cigarette with every fiber of his being. "You do realize that it's not a crime to have friends. That's how the majority of the world functions."

"It was the way he said it." Mercer's mind replayed the meeting with Rowlins. "Something doesn't coalesce. Either the coppers are dirty, or Rhoade is." He snatched the Carlton Rhoade file off the top of the stack and skimmed through the financial records, phone logs, and work history. "Based on my experiences, I'd wager it's the bloody bobbies."

"Jules, I know you hate the police, but you have no basis for that. They don't have a dog in the fight. What incentive would they have for dragging their heels on this investigation?"

Mercer contemplated the point for a few moments, turned without another word, and left the hotel room. In twenty-five minutes, Katia would be leaving work, and he was on guard duty. Hans was still keeping tabs on Ben, and Donovan was shadowing Carlton. But acting defensively wouldn't locate the party responsible for the shooting, and that's what Katia wanted the ex-SAS team to do.

The only fact that Mercer knew for certain was the shooter was a professional. And since he didn't finish the job, at some point, he'd return to rectify the situation. This led to two options. Continue to bodyguard and hope to intervene before someone ended up dead or determine who the shooter was and have a pleasant chat concerning who hired him. Katia wanted the man tortured and killed, and Mercer agreed. Bastian wouldn't be pleased. Hans and Donovan would probably shrug it off eventually. But would it change the dynamic of their team? Frankly, it didn't matter anymore. More important things were at stake.

Parking in front of a hydrant outside the building,

Mercer waited for Katia to emerge. His eyes roamed the area, searching for potential dangers. Carlton hired the team to protect his daughter. It made sense because she was in close proximity to the shooting. But could there be more to the story? Maybe Rhoade had received some threats but didn't bother to divulge this information. Like the detective said, something smelled fishy.

As Katia stepped into the late afternoon sunlight, Mercer tabled the thought and got out of the car. Going around, he opened the passenger's side door and waited. She snorted, moving past him, and climbed inside the car.

"Is that supposed to be some sort of apology for the shit you were spewing last night?" she asked after he got behind the wheel.

"No."

"So you're pretending to be a gentleman for some other reason?"

He ignored her, pulling into traffic and watching the mirrors for signs of trouble. "I assume you want to go back to the hospital." It wasn't much of a question, and she barely grunted a response before turning away from him and staring out the window as the city whizzed by.

When he parked the car, he grabbed her arm before she could escape. She jerked away, scrutinizing him. "Now what do you want from me?" she asked.

"Were you threatened?"

She pressed her lips into a tight line, narrowing her eyes. "Why would you ask me that? Ben's the one who was shot. He's fighting for his life because of some business deal that went awry. And you want to know if I've been threatened?"

"Answer me."

"Honestly, I don't know." Mercer took a breath,

attempting to be patient while he waited for her elaboration. "The magazine occasionally gets threats from some lunatics. It gets sorted out in the mailroom. But I take pictures, and most of those crazies are either psychotic fans who want access to the celebrities we interview or are pissed by the note from the editor section."

"What about your father?"

"What about him?"

"Don't play coy."

"He has his enemies. It happens when you buy out a newspaper and fire people." She shrugged. "Whatever. That doesn't concern me, and that sure as hell doesn't have anything to do with Ben. You think someone threatened me and that's why my father hired you?"

"Yes."

She shook her head. "He overreacts since I'm all he has. But the reason you're guarding me is because you showed up in that alley, and I passed along your card and suggested he hire you." Her lips curled at the corners. "You offered your assistance, Mr. Mercer. And I want retribution. You seemed pretty capable with that handgun of yours. Afraid you bit off more than you can chew?"

The words processed through his brain. She wasn't pretending to be a clueless waif anymore. She was calling the shots. Or at least she thought she was. Their initial encounter was the impetus that led to his hiring. This wasn't about protection. She wanted blood and believed he would do as she wished.

"You read me that easily?" he asked, releasing his seatbelt and unlocking the doors.

"I screamed for help, and for the longest time, no one came. But then you did. And you had a gun. There was no guesswork. If the men who hurt Ben were still there, you would have killed them."

"Fair enough." The two got out of the car and went inside the hospital. "When your fiancé wakes up, I'd like a few words with him."

"Of course." She offered a weak smile, and they went down the hallway. This time, she recognized Hans and nodded at him before stepping inside Styler's room.

"Looks like you and the bird are getting along, again," Hans commented.

Mercer leaned against the wall outside the door and checked the hallways. Aside from hospital staff, no one was around. He was unfamiliar with police procedures, particularly in the States, but shouldn't some type of protection be provided to shooting victims?

"Do you think you can do some more digging at the police station?" Mercer asked.

"Digging, plowing, pounding," Hans grinned, "maybe some nailing and screwing, too." He caught the irritated look on Julian's face and cut his crude commentary short. "What do you want, sir?"

"Find out why no one's guarding Styler. Then check into Detective Rowlins. And if you have time with all your farm work and carpentry, find out everything you can on Rowlins' supervising lieutenant and any connection that might exist between him and Carlton Rhoade."

"Wouldn't Bas be better suited for this?"

"He's on it, but you might get the answers faster since you already have an in." Mercer tilted his head, his eyes traveling down the hallway. "I'll keep watch on Katia and Ben until you get back."

"Right-o."

"And Hans, keep it in your pants. We don't have time to waste."

Mercer perched on the vacant chair. His thoughts were random. The only one that repeated itself concerned the shooter. He knew some of the best private military contractors in the business. He worked with a few of them, and the others, he'd run up against a time or two when carrying out his black ops missions. As far as he knew, none of them were working in the area. And furthermore, they weren't sloppy enough to leave the target alive. But whoever did it made a hell of a shot. Running through the usual means for hiring a professional hitman, he phoned Donovan and asked him to run recon on the typical haunts once Carlton was secured for the night.

"Mr. Mercer," Katia said, startling him from his musing, "Ben's awake. He's not terribly coherent, but you can talk to him." Her mascara was streaked, and her nose and cheeks were blotchy and red.

"Thank you." He stood. "You need not cry. I believe we are making progress, as is your intended."

EIGHT

Speaking to Benjamin Styler was like having a conversation with a blackout drunk. Instead of getting answers, Mercer was forced to respond to the same question over and over again. The only thing Ben wanted to know was who Mercer was. After Mercer answered, Ben would nod, but a few seconds later, he would just ask the same thing again.

Mercer rubbed his eyes and stepped farther from the bed. "Is he normally like this?" he asked Katia. "Or did he sustain head trauma?"

She laughed. It wasn't because the question was funny, and the sound of her laugh wasn't pleasant. It was pained. "No. They have him on high doses of pain medication and sedatives. At least that's what the doctors said. He's normally very intelligent and charismatic."

"And where are his parents?" It made no sense why this twenty-six-year-old was in the hospital without his family present or some type of police protection.

"They're on a month-long cruise. They won't be back for another two weeks. Thankfully, when Ben proposed, we had legal documentation drawn up so the other would have access to personal information and finances in the event of an emergency." She took Ben's hand, watching as he drifted back into the morphine-induced oblivion.

"How long have you been engaged?"

"Three months." She glanced at Mercer. "We were just starting to plan the wedding." She sniffed and brushed a tear away with the back of her hand.

"You said the two men that accompanied the shooter looked familiar. You saw them leaving Ben's, correct?" Since Styler couldn't provide any answers, hopefully, Katia could.

"That's what I said."

Her focus was on the man lying in the bed, not on answering questions. This wasn't the proper environment for an interrogation or gleaning additional information, so Mercer went to the plastic bag that held Benjamin Styler's personal effects and removed his wallet and cell phone. Why weren't these items considered evidence by the police? Well, if the coppers weren't going to do anything about it, then Mercer would. He slipped them into his pocket and quietly excused himself.

Waiting outside the hospital room, he studied the corridors, checking for cameras and other security measures. Perhaps someone else visited Styler or inquired about his condition. Approaching the nurse's station, Mercer smiled at the woman behind the desk. Unfortunately, she wasn't willing to hand over any patient information, despite his best attempts to charm her. Clearly, there must be some trick or tactic that Hans used to get information. And at the moment, Mercer wished he knew what it was.

Just as Julian returned to the vacant chair outside Styler's room, the detective from earlier emerged at the end of the corridor. Rowlins narrowed his eyes but otherwise refused to acknowledge Mercer. The detective went to the nurse's station, flashed his badge, and asked a few questions. Their voices didn't carry, and Mercer could only make out an occasional word here or there.

"Detective," Mercer called as Rowlins approached, "are you still following me?"

"No, I'm here to speak to the victim." Rowlins made a move for the door, but Mercer stood, blocking the entrance. "Step aside, unless you want to spend another night in holding for interfering in a police investigation."

"Why aren't officers assigned to protect him?"

"Protect him from whom? You got any leads?"

"Someone shot him, but he's not dead. Don't you think whoever is to blame will be back to finish the job?"

The surprise on Rowlins' face was genuine. "The intel says it was a mugging gone wrong. And muggers typically don't return."

"Who said it was a mugging? Is that the official word around the station, or do you simply believe everything a traumatized young lady claims in the middle of the night? And since you believe it was only a mugging, why were you following me this morning and asking questions about my role?" Rowlins actions were contradictory to his words, and it made no sense as far as Julian was concerned.

"Katia Rhoade gave her statement. She told us it was a mugging. But a few officers overheard her speaking to you the next morning outside the precinct. I'd like to get an official statement from the vic before I draw my own conclusions. I also like to investigate my own crime scenes." Rowlins reached into his pocket and pulled out a business card, handing it to Mercer. "I don't like you or your attitude, but that's not reason enough why we can't help each other out. Why don't you share your information with me?"

"Are you planning to return the favor?" Mercer studied him, unsure of what this detective's motivation was. Hans needed to get some real answers before Mercer placed his trust in the CPD detective.

"I'll think about it." The detective stepped closer. "Now let me through, or I will arrest you."

Mercer entered the room ahead of Rowlins. "Ms. Rhoade, let's go. The police have official business." Katia looked ready to protest, but the stern look on Mercer's face made her change her mind. She grabbed her purse, gave the semiconscious Ben a kiss, and went past Rowlins without a single word. Once she was out of earshot, Mercer spoke again to the detective. "Muggers don't leave wallets and jewelry behind. I suggest you learn how to do your job properly. I'm not trained in these matters, but even I know that much."

Rowlins picked up the plastic bag, noting the watch and ring inside. Before he could inquire as to the whereabouts of Styler's wallet, Mercer left the room. In the hallway, Mercer grabbed Katia's arm, dragging her toward the nearest exit. She bucked and protested, but he didn't loosen his grip. Once they were outside, he let go. She rubbed her elbow, glowering at him.

"Why are you lying?" he snarled, the rage boiling to the surface and creeping into his vocal cords.

"I haven't lied to you."

"Bollocks," he spat, grabbing her and forcing her toward the car. He opened the door, pushed her inside, and slammed the door hard enough that the car rocked. He leaned against the vehicle, fighting to keep his anger in check. When he got in on the driver's side, she was curled into a trembling ball in her seat. "You told the police it was a mugging, but that's not what you told me. Until now, that detective was clueless, and no one from the police department has been assigned to protect your fiancé because of it. Your lies could have cost Styler his life."

"I was afraid," she said meekly.

Clenching his jaw, he gripped the steering wheel tightly. "Afraid of what? Who did this? I want a name."

"I don't–"

"Who the bloody hell are they?"

"Jack Pierce." The name flew from her mouth before she could stop it. Reddening, she took a few steadying breaths, calming her rattled nerves. "But I'm not even sure that it was him. And I've told you I don't know who the shooter is, and I don't have a name for the other man that I saw."

"Why the fuck didn't you tell me this two days ago?"

"Because I doubt my own recollection. Jack hasn't been around for quite some time, and those men...the ones near the alley...they looked like the same men from Ben's building." Her lips trembled, but she managed to steady her voice. "And there isn't a chance in hell Jack would have been visiting Ben at home."

"But you're afraid of him?" Mercer turned to face her. "Why are you afraid of this Jack Pierce fellow?" She bit her lip, hesitating. "Answer me."

"Because Ben told me he threatened to kill him." She blinked, swallowing to keep her emotions in check. "And he said that I should avoid Jack at all costs because he has no idea what Jack is capable of."

"You expect me to hunt down the party responsible

for the shooting, but you're too afraid to share that kind of information. When did this happen?"

"Like six months ago." She sighed. "The reason I didn't say anything, Mr. Mercer," her speech came out clipped, "is because I don't even know if Jack is behind this. Ben and Jack had a falling out, and Ben hasn't mentioned Jack in months. Like I told you, I didn't get a good look at the guys, but they looked like the men that were leaving Ben's last week. And I doubt Jack would have been by to see Ben." Her volume increased as if that would make the facts sink into Mercer's thick skull. "It seemed premature to say anything to the police. I thought if Jack wasn't to blame, he might use this opportunity to his advantage and come to the hospital and do something to Ben."

"Then why the hell didn't you tell me?" Julian's anger was under control again, at least for the moment.

"I wasn't sure what you'd do." She met his eyes, no longer afraid. "You might be just like everyone else and take the easy way out. You'd put an end to Jack while the guilty still go free." Letting out an unsteady breath, she squeezed her eyes closed. "I don't want there to be any mistake. When you get the guy, I don't want to have a single doubt that it was the right guy. The thought of someone getting away with this is unbearable."

"Tell me about it," Mercer muttered. He rubbed a heavy hand down his face, forcing calm rationality to take hold. He'd have to use other means of determining who was responsible for the shooting because Katia's information was proving unreliable.

NINE

Bastian rubbed his eyes, exhausted and aggravated. Ever since they began working for the Rhoades, he had done nothing but stare at the computer screen, phone in a few favors, and analyze the nonstop flow of data. He convinced himself that once he cleared their current list of suspects and deconstructed the crime scene, he'd take a break, eat a real meal, and get some sleep. But that was before Julian returned with physical evidence, new names to analyze, and more questions pertaining to a possible police cover-up.

Jack Pierce was now their main focus. As far as Mercer's team was aware, Pierce was the only person who ever made a threat against Benjamin Styler. Although, nothing that came out of Katia's mouth could be believed at this point. She lost all credibility after Mercer confronted her at the hospital about her bogus police statement and failure to fully disclose. But despite these obvious lies, Mercer wasn't willing to walk away. Bastian shook his head at the absurdity. If this was a typical kidnapping and ransom, they would have left at the first whiff of deception. But this was a brutal, vicious attack of a very personal nature, and it was obvious Mercer was projecting. What would happen to Julian's sanity if it turned out Katia was to blame? Bastian cringed at the notion and pushed on, hoping to find a workable angle.

Jack Pierce graduated from the same Ivy League university as Styler. The two men were in the same fraternity, interned at the same high-powered corporations, and from the thousands of photos Bastian discovered across various social networking platforms, the two were practically inseparable until six months ago. After further digging, it seemed apparent the argument was over business. Pierce was recently given a seat on the board of his father's corporation, Pierce Industries. The twenty-six-year-old millionaire was hailed by the business pages as the prodigal son. Despite a rocky start and questionable personal investments, Jack Pierce reclaimed his throne after insisting the company embark on a new product line. This dulled the crushing loss he endured earlier in the year with half a dozen bad investments.

"Never mix money with friendship," Bastian chastised the computer screen.

After a couple more clicks, it was obvious the bad investments were made through Styler. Obviously, Ben wasn't as astute a day trader as he should be. His stock tips were off, and his friend cumulatively lost nearly a million dollars over the course of the previous year. That seemed like an excellent reason to threaten someone and exact some revenge. No wonder the friendship dwindled.

Bastian printed out a few of the news stories, photos of Pierce, his personal information, and everything else Mercer would want to know. Then he closed the computer and rang the commander. As soon as the rest of the team was caught up to speed, Mercer revised their game plan.

"Get some sleep, Bas," Mercer ordered. "With a potential target in sight, I'll need you field ready tomorrow morning."

"Aye," Bastian replied, not needing to be told twice. He picked up the phone and wallet that Mercer swiped from the hospital. "I'll get these analyzed before we head out tomorrow."

Mercer nodded, and Bastian excused himself. With any luck, building security could protect the Rhoades while they were at home, and hospital security would protect Ben. The team needed a night off. After reviewing the newly gained information and dismissing the team, Mercer dropped onto the bed.

Why is Katia lying? Or perhaps the more accurate question would be is Katia lying. No matter how he turned the facts over in his mind, it didn't make any sense. She wanted Styler's attackers caught. Clearly, she loved Ben. But was she afraid of the men responsible for the shooting? Or was there a much darker secret lying just below the surface?

As night turned to day, Mercer drifted in and out of sleep, his mind never stopping for more than a few seconds as he considered her motivation for lying. She wanted the men who did this to die, not be arrested. That would explain why she misled the police and that annoying detective, but it didn't explain why she didn't divulge the truth to him. Didn't he promise he would take care of this in the manner she requested? And what about her father? Was he an overprotective parent, or were these threats originally aimed at him, his daughter, and his soon-to-be son-in-law?

Julian sat up in bed, letting out a frustrated exhale. Carlton Rhoade never said the exact words, but it was apparent he wanted a private military contractor to handle the matter. Furthermore, Carlton had looked into Julian's background and discovered quite a few disconcerting facts. Mercer's former status with the SAS and his personal loss should not be fodder for potential employers.

Grinding his teeth, Mercer hauled himself out of bed and began the endless string of push-ups that signified the start of a new day. As soon as he got the chance, he would confront Carlton and Katia. Being jerked around was not acceptable.

* * *

"Mr. Pierce," Bastian called as the man exited his apartment building, "may we have a word?" Pierce glanced from Bastian to Mercer. "It will only take a few minutes."

"Are you reporters?" Pierce asked.

"No," Mercer responded.

"Lawyers or process servers?"

"No." Mercer was losing his patience. "We need a few moments of your time, I must insist." Without waiting, he stepped closer to Pierce, putting an arm around the man's shoulders and pressing the muzzle of his Sig into the man's ribs.

"Bloody hell," Bastian sighed, scanning the immediate area. At least the building's doorman didn't seem to think this gesture was anything other than outwardly friendly.

"Fine," Pierce said, sounding more annoyed than frightened, "you can have my money, just take it and go."

"This isn't about money, Mr. Pierce," Mercer replied, hauling the man toward the SUV which was illegally parked at a hydrant. "This is about your former acquaintance, Benjamin Styler."

"Now what has Ben gotten me into?" Pierce asked, exasperated. "That jackass cost me millions. Let me guess, he had to borrow in order to pay back some investors, and you're collecting for his loan shark. Mafia, right?" Pierce rolled his eyes. "This is unbelievable. Just tell me what he owes, and I'll pay it. There's no need for violence."

Mercer yanked the rear door open, shoving Pierce inside and climbing in next to him. "This isn't about money."

Bastian got in the front and pulled the car away from the building. Either they'd take Pierce to the abandoned warehouse near the wharf that they had scoped out for privacy, or they'd drop him off at work. It simply depended upon the answers he provided.

"What do you want?" Pierce asked, his anxiety level increasing now that they were on the move. "You can't just kidnap a person. If I don't show up at work in the next ten minutes, they'll know something is wrong. The police will come looking."

"Tell me where you were four nights ago," Mercer instructed, a firm grip on the gun.

"Let's see," Pierce shut his eyes, attempting to recall, "I worked late, went to a bar afterward, had a few drinks." He opened his eyes. "What does any of this have to do with Ben?"

"Were you alone?"

"No," Pierce shifted his focus to the barrel of the weapon, "I was with a couple of co-workers?"

"Names would be useful, Mr. Pierce," Bastian added from the front, his focus split between the interrogation and the road. "Where is this bar?"

"Ethan Hart and Avery Anastaz. We went to Sky Bar. It's inside a hotel."

"When was the last time you spoke to Mr. Styler?" Mercer asked, realizing the bar in question was inside their hotel. Clearly, it put Pierce and his associates within the vicinity at the time of the shooting, and if Katia was right about three men being involved in the shooting, then Pierce looked good for the attempted murder. Although, according to Katia, he wasn't the shooter, which probably meant one of his alleged co-workers was.

"Goddammit," Pierce wiped at the layer of perspiration that erupted on his brow, "can you please stop pointing that thing at me? I'm answering your questions. Please, I'll do whatever you want. I can give you whatever you want, just stop."

"When?" Mercer asked, not wavering.

"I don't know. It's been a while. He screwed me with a bunch of bad stock tips. I was pissed and said I never wanted to see him again, and if he showed his face anywhere near me or my dad's company that I'd kill him. It's been months, seven maybe. I don't know." He took an unsteady breath. "I'll pay for him to get out of whatever trouble he's in, just let me go. Please. I have nothing to do with his deals or the people he's screwed over."

"Julian," Bastian said, stopping the car outside a high-rise office building, "that's enough."

Mercer nodded. The SUV doors unlocked, and he holstered the gun. "We'll be in touch, Mr. Pierce."

TEN

"Is it him?" Mercer asked.

He and Bastian were reviewing the CCTV feeds from the night of the shooting. Three men were visible on the feed, but the quality was far from stellar. Even though they had examined the feed before, Bastian thought it was worth another try now that they could use Jack Pierce as a possible point of comparison.

"I can't be sure. They are of a similar height and hair color," Bastian said, attempting to adjust the image levels in order to determine if the man on the feed and Jack Pierce were one and the same. "But the angles aren't conducive to facial recognition, at least not the version I'm using."

"Make a call and see what our friends can tell us," Mercer suggested, checking the time to make sure he wasn't late to pick up Katia. "What about Styler's phone?"

"After I broke the password, I went through his list of contacts, recent calls, text messages, and even locations pinged on the GPS, but there's nothing sinister."

"Katia said Styler owed someone money, and Pierce was under the same impression. Shouldn't there be a record?"

"It's not on his phone or e-mail. He might have a burner, or he handles deals like that in person. I'll see if I can get his business records. Maybe there's something buried within his online day trading. I'll pull up everything I can. After that, I'll check out Pierce's two co-workers. If all else fails, I'll have a chat with them."

"Bas," he waited for the other man to turn around, "thank you." It wasn't a typical sentiment for Mercer to convey, and Bastian simply nodded.

"You might have to run this information by our copper pal. I've run his background, and I'd say he's one of the good ones. He's not particularly highly ranked in the department, which probably means he doesn't cater to his superior's every whim, but it also means he's probably honest."

"That will be our last resort," Mercer decided. "Any progress on rooting out the connection between Carlton and the homicide lieutenant?"

"Not yet. I only have two hands," Bastian smirked, "and one of them has to hold my nuts." He popped a handful of cashews into his mouth, having raided the newly restocked mini-bar again this morning.

Mercer rolled his eyes and continued out the door. Instead of picking up Katia, he went to the hospital and switched with Hans. He needed access to Styler without the hysterical liar manipulating him with her outpouring of emotion. With any luck, Ben would be awake and alert today. The doctors were decreasing his medication as his condition improved, and it was about time since someone needed to provide Mercer with a few honest answers.

Upon entering Ben's room, the recovering man put

down a spoonful of green gelatin and looked up. He offered a friendly smile, looking better than he had in days.

"Mr. Styler, do you remember me?"

"Julian, right?" He squinted, making sure he recalled the correct name, and Mercer nodded. "Katia hired you." Again, Mercer nodded. "Before you ask, I don't know who's responsible. I didn't see anything."

"What is the last thing you remember?"

"Are you a detective? You sound just like the police officers that were here last night and this morning."

"I'm not a detective. I'm a resolution specialist."

"So you're going to resolve my problems?" Styler snorted. "Good luck with that."

"Answer the question." Mercer's mind turned over Styler's attitude and remark. Bas was right. There was more to the story.

"The last thing I remember is the sound of my zipper and Kat's warm breath then searing pain cutting through my chest." He chuckled. "I thought it was a heart attack. But then I saw red. She screamed, and everything went dark. I guess that's what it's like to get shot.

"Sometimes," Mercer mused. "Do you mind if I ask why you were engaging in oral sex in the middle of a dark alley?"

Styler laughed and then winced, clutching the side of his chest. "Katia recently moved back in with her dad while her apartment underwent some renovations. So we have to sneak a few moments here and there." He rolled his eyes. "Her father treats her like a little girl, not the grown woman that she is."

Mercer nodded, no longer interested in the reason for their public tryst. "I spoke with Jack Pierce this morning." He watched for some telltale sign to emerge on Styler's face, such as fear, anxiety, or unease, but all he saw was guilt.

"Jack didn't do this."

"How can you be so sure? Katia said he threatened to kill you, and you told her to stay away from him."

"Kat has a complicated relationship with the truth. She tends to be overly dramatic at times, but Jack's my best friend. Well, he was. Business got in the way. We had a falling out. He said he'd kill me. Destroy me. Make me lose the thing that I love most since I lost his millions." He snorted. "There are a lot of things Jack might do to get even. He'd probably try to woo Katia. Shit, I wouldn't put it past him to screw her in my own bed, just so he could gloat about it. That's just how we are." He blinked, toying with the gelatin container. "Were. But he would never actually resort to physical violence."

"And you consider this individual your best friend?" Mercer asked, clearly confused.

"Yeah. At least that's how we were in college. Everything was a competition. We liked to make bets and play our games. Things lacked real meaning. I kinda forgot what the real world was like when I invested Jack's money. I thought the tips I gave him were sound, but," he shrugged and sighed, "I was wrong. Jack flipped. We haven't spoken since."

"I see." Mercer picked up the medical file at the end of Styler's bed and skimmed through the pages. There was no indication of previous injuries, so no one had beaten Styler or roughed him up prior to the shooting. The chance of his attack being the result of a loan shark or someone collecting on a debt was dwindling. "Katia believes she saw Mr. Pierce and two of his associates on the street around the time of the shooting."

"Maybe. This is a big city, but we hang around the same neighborhoods. Jack and I used to frequent a few bars on that street back when we were buds. Jack probably still goes to them. He works just around the corner." He exhaled slowly, physical discomfort beginning to reflect on his face. "But I'd say Kat's probably imagining things. She's never even seen Jack up close. Her only knowledge of him has been through old pictures. I doubt she could pick him out of a lineup."

Mercer's brow furrowed. "If you and Jack were practically inseparable, why didn't the three of you ever spend time together? How long had you and Katia been involved?"

"Kat and I have known each other for a while, but we didn't get serious until my falling out with Jack. That put a lot of things in my life into perspective, and three months later, I proposed."

"She mentioned some men leaving your building recently. Was Pierce one of them?" Mercer made a mental note to ask Bastian about the surveillance from Styler's apartment. Hopefully, they'd be able to identify someone suspicious. Perhaps the guilty party stopped by to deliver a threat, or whoever was hired to commit the hit scoped out the area and conducted some surveillance prior to the shooting.

"Jack hasn't been to my place in forever." Styler squinted, trying to figure out who these men were that Mercer was asking about. "The only people who've been to my apartment in the last few months are Kat, her dad, a couple of investors, and a few of my business associates." He pushed himself upright, wincing. "Shit, that hurts."

"I'll need names," Mercer said, waiting expectantly.

"Do you have a pen and some paper?"

"I'll remember."

Ben rattled off a list of six names, not including Katia or Carlton. When he was finished, he took an uneasy breath and hit the button on his morphine drip. "They said the bullet broke two of my ribs and lodged in my lung. A few inches higher and it would have gone through my heart. But still, it hurts like a motherfucker."

"Well, it's either this or death," Mercer said. Ben let out an uneasy laugh and closed his eyes, tired and likely enjoying the effects of the drugs that just entered his system. "Did you give the police officers that questioned you the same information you gave me?"

"I think so. They didn't ask as much as you did. They wanted to know where my wallet and phone were. They think the muggers took them." His speech was becoming thick and slow. "I didn't even realize we were mugged. I'm just glad they didn't hurt Kat, and she still has the ring. It was my grandmother's." Styler sighed, sinking deeper into the pillows. "Nana would be pissed if some thug had her ring. Hoodlums, that's what she called them." He snickered. "Hoodlums in hoods." His eyes remained closed, and he drifted into the abyss.

Stepping out of the room, Mercer took a seat in the hallway and dialed Bastian. After giving him a new list of names to run, he disconnected. Katia's rendition didn't line up with Styler's. Sure, there were some similarities, but it didn't make pinpointing the shooter any easier. Perhaps this was a random act of violence. But what would be the point? The angle and shot were extraordinary. Hell, even Donovan would have had trouble with those angles, and he was the best shooter Mercer knew. The shot was taken before the man was even in front of the mouth of the alley. It was around the corner of the brick wall, and the single bullet ripped through Styler's chest. An inch and a half higher and it would have gone straight through his heart. Styler's back had been against the brick wall, and frankly, it was a decent cover position to block an assault from the street. If it weren't for the surveillance footage, Mercer would have thought the shooter was in the alley and fired straight across. Why not enter the alley, pop off a round or two, and go on?

Only one thought came to mind. The shooter had to remain undetected and unidentifiable or else Katia would pose a problem, and clearly, that was unacceptable. Mercer considered the possibilities. Who wanted Ben Styler dead and Katia Rhoade alive and well?

When Hans escorted Katia down the hospital corridor toward Ben's room, Mercer stood. Her eyes flicked to his face, and she offered a slight smile. But before she could say a word, he spoke.

"Hans, keep a close watch on Styler and a record of who comes and goes."

"Yes, sir."

"Do you think someone will come back to hurt Ben?" she asked, her eyes darting to the room, frantic to see her fiancé. She burst through the door before Mercer could say another word.

Hans looked up. "What the bloody hell is going on now?"

"After speaking to Styler, it seems less likely this is solely a vendetta against him. I believe someone wants to remove him from Ms. Rhoade's life," Mercer said, watching as Katia kissed the unconscious Ben and ran her fingers through his hair. "Until we know for certain, we need to provide him with round-the-clock protection. We'll cease shadowing Mr. Rhoade in order for you and Donovan to maintain eyes on Ben."

"Do you think that's wise?" Hans asked.

"We were never hired to provide protection to

anyone except Katia. Let Carlton's security worry about his protection. He hired us to protect his daughter, so if something were to happen to him, that's not our problem," Mercer replied with a slight shrug.

"The same could be said for Benjamin Styler."

"Perhaps, but I do believe Ms. Rhoade would put a bounty on our heads if any harm were to befall Mr. Styler."

ELEVEN

"What are you thinking?" Bastian asked. He and Mercer were at the hotel bar. Bastian hacked into the security system, but the server didn't store files for more than forty-eight hours. Any record of Jack Pierce and his associates had been erased and written over two days ago. Bas signaled to the bartender, and two more whiskeys were poured. "Thanks," he mumbled.

Mercer took a swig. They already questioned the bartender and passed around a few photos of Pierce and his co-workers. While the faces looked familiar, no one remembered exactly what night it was or what time the gentlemen might have left. The police could get access to the credit card receipts, but Mercer didn't want to ask for help. He didn't trust any cops after his run-ins with the London bobbies.

"Ex-lovers or a possible obsessed stalker," Mercer sighed, swallowing the rest of the contents in one gulp, "that'd be my next guess. Why else worry about Katia's well-being? If you're hired to kill, collateral damage is occasionally unavoidable. There'd be no other reason for such extreme care to be taken in order to remain undetected."

"So you don't think she was a target?" Bastian asked, skimming through some of the data he printed on Pierce's business and associates.

Jack Pierce seemed clean, particularly after their conversation earlier in the day, but that didn't stop Bastian from performing his due diligence. From the bio listed on the company's website, Pierce Industries was family owned and operated. Jack served on the board of his father's company, as did his brother, Daniel. Initially, Jack had been booted out when Styler's investments resulted in a substantial loss for Jack. But after improving his financial portfolio and pitching a new product line to bolster sales for his father's company, Jack returned to a position of power, just in time for his brother to step down and pursue his own ventures. The information on the two co-workers Jack mentioned was still being compiled, but as of yet, Bastian couldn't find any connection between either of them and Benjamin Styler or Katia Rhoade. And the six names that Styler provided turned out to be dead ends.

"No." Mercer shook his head. "It's more likely she's the reason someone wants to eliminate Styler."

"But whoever the shooter is had to know exactly where she'd be and the position she'd be in." Bastian raised an eyebrow pointedly. "Jules, how would they have known what she was planning to do with her beau after dinner? Plus, from what Styler told you, things were just getting underway. And from the angles in that alley, the timing would have to be perfect or else Katia might have still been upright and shot in front of him. Are you sure you aren't reading more into this than what exists? Maybe she was the intended target."

"Bloody hell," Mercer cursed. "Styler said they've been having these romantic meetings ever since Katia moved back in with her father. Whoever fired that shot must have discovered this and waited for the chance to end Styler." He saw the skeptical look in his friend's eyes. "This is rubbish. I don't believe for one goddamn second that Styler was an accidental casualty. He has to be the intended target. He just does." Mercer gulped, pain seeping into his voice.

Julian caught the look on Bastian's face, that worried glance that Mercer was allowing his personal tragedy to blend in with these current events. Julian growled and slammed the glass down. He wasn't accustomed to being this on edge while working a job, but the circumstances were far too similar. And his mind kept drawing needless parallels.

Bastian spoke softly, hoping to provide some solace. "We still aren't sure that Michelle wasn't his intended victim. Jules, you couldn't have known what was going to happen. There's no way of determining whether the man showed up at your house to kill you and found Michelle instead or if he waited for you to leave so he could get her alone."

Mercer's face contorted, and he blinked back his feelings. "Why did you ever agree to investigate for Carlton? We don't investigate. We perform recon, devise a plan, and resolve the situation. We aren't equipped to determine who's responsible or why." He picked up the glass and slammed it back down, barely managing not to throw it across the room. "Since you clearly want to pretend to be part of New Scotland Yard, you figure it out." He stood, signed the receipt with his room number, and went upstairs. Just a few minutes of peace and quiet was what he needed to force the nightmarish thoughts back into the recesses of his mind.

Opening the door to his room, Julian drew his gun and pointed it at the intruder. If this had happened two minutes earlier, he would have pulled the trigger without a moment's hesitation. Maybe he was slightly unhinged. It was no wonder the Special Air Service didn't trust his judgment anymore. The man acknowledged the gun with a level of calm that most people never exhibited.

"Any chance you misplaced your carry permit?" Detective Rowlins asked, nodding at the weapon.

"Shall I report this intrusion to your superiors?" Mercer replied, reluctantly putting the Sig on the dresser and shutting the door. "I'd like to see your warrant."

"And I'd like to see the paperwork explaining why you think you can act like you're the only authority in my city." The two continued the staring contest until finally Rowlins broke eye contact, reaching into his jacket and pulling out his notepad. The police department insignia on the cover added an official air to this otherwise informal and illegal meeting. "What'd you do with Benjamin Styler's belongings?" Mercer remained silent, refusing to answer the question. "Okay, let me ask this another way. Did you discover anything useful?"

"Are you really that pathetic at your job that you expect someone with no experience in the matter to guide your investigation?" Mercer narrowed his eyes. "Get out."

"I've dug through Styler's background. The kid's not exactly a Wall Street tycoon. His stock tips only work out about sixty percent of the time. Most of his investors have lost a significant amount of money. But he's sticking with the business. He works from home, moves money around, and his personal portfolio isn't bad. It's better than a cop's salary but doesn't come close to comparing to what Katia's inheritance will be worth." He continued speaking, ignoring the disgusted look on Mercer's face. "Despite what Ms. Rhoade's statement might reveal about the night in question, I've done my own digging into the kid's enemies and hers. Ballistics has run trajectories, and I've seen security footage from nearby DOT cams. That was a hell of a shot."

"Aren't you bloody brilliant?" Mercer muttered, hoping the detective would take the hint and leave.

"Indeed, I am." Rowlins cracked a smile. "I'm smart enough to know Carlton hired you to eliminate the threat, regardless of what anyone says to the contrary. The only problem you're facing is determining exactly where the threat is coming from. Jack Pierce dropped by the precinct earlier today to file a report. It seems like you're needlessly turning over a lot of stones."

"And you possess the correct morsel of information?"

"Not yet." Rowlins stood. The two men were approximately the same height, but Rowlins was softer, not nearly as regimented and sculpted as Mercer. Then again, Rowlins was an investigator, not a highly trained former military specialist. "But I believe we can help each other. Two heads are better than one."

"And what do you want in return?"

"The opportunity to keep the death toll down."

Mercer snorted. "Who said anything about a body count?"

"This isn't a kidnapping and ransom recovery," Rowlins continued, demonstrating his familiarity with Julian and his team. "Nor is this a black ops mission. There are only two reasons why Carlton Rhoade would hire you. And obviously, if you're spending your nights alone in a hotel room, it isn't because you're the newest addition to his personal security team."

"Strangely enough, we might have been hired to investigate," Mercer offered, hoping to cast doubt on Rowlins' inclination that they were employed to carry out the wet work.

"So share your findings since we're both investigating. I'll apprehend the shooter, and justice will be served."

"That's such a simplistic view of this world." But before Mercer could launch into a tirade about the ineffectualness of the so-called justice system, Bastian barged into the room. "Fuck it," Mercer cursed under his breath.

"Jules, I–" Bastian stopped midsentence, noticing the unfamiliar presence in the room, but he recognized the man from the photos in the CPD's personnel database that he analyzed earlier. "Detective," he nodded and extended his hand, "Bastian Clarke, I don't believe we've had the pleasure." They shook, and Bastian cast an uneasy glance at Julian. At least the handgun was on the dresser and not pointed at the policeman. "Is there something we can help you with, mate?"

"I was hoping we could work together to identify the shooter," Rowlins said, his gaze focused on Mercer. "We can trade leads. I've looked into Jack Pierce, but he alibied out."

"Did you speak to his co-workers? Hart and Anastaz?" Bastian asked.

"I spoke to Ethan Hart and ran through some credit card statements. Hell, Hart even showed me his copy of the receipt."

"That saves us some time," Bastian said, mainly to himself. "We've been considering the possibility the shooter intended to act in a manner that would ensure Ms. Rhoade's safety."

"Bastian, silence," Mercer snapped.

"Pish," Bastian replied. "We're running short on leads. Perhaps Katia has some romantic entanglements in her past that could be to blame," he offered, sharing Mercer's latest insight with the detective. "We aren't aware of all the possibilities. Is there anyone we haven't considered that the police department might be checking out? It's been brought to our attention that Mr. Styler might have owed some crooks an indeterminate amount of money, but we have yet to establish who his debt collectors could be."

Rowlins bit his top lip, briefly resembling a pug with an underbite. "Are we really gonna do this? Because I don't want my balls to end up in a sling if our sharing time turns into a one-sided thing. My lieutenant is tight with Mr. Rhoade, and I'm sure between the two of them, someone will have to pay if things go sideways. And that someone won't be me." He shifted his gaze between the two former SAS. "And you gotta promise that I get the collar. I refuse to stand for any vigilante bullshit on my watch." He narrowed his eyes at Mercer. "But then again, you said you aren't a hired merc, so that won't be a problem, right?"

"Right," Mercer replied, even if his promise to Katia meant walking a fine line.

TWELVE

Det. Rowlins didn't have much to offer beyond what Hans and Bastian already discovered when they pulled the police records, but at least the team knew what leads led straight to dead ends. It was unlikely Jack Pierce and his associates were responsible for the shooting, but someone obviously was.

"Have you accessed building security? Katia mentioned seeing two of Styler's alleged business partners leaving his place a week before the incident. She thought one of them might have been Jack, but clearly, that's been proven false," Bastian said, pondering if it'd be easier to get the information from the police instead of having to procure it in some other manner. "And the general consensus is Styler owes someone money."

"No," Rowlins shook his head, "we had no reason to check the security cams at Ben's apartment since the attack occurred in public. The official story was a mugging gone wrong, even if the muggers never even entered the alley."

"Then why the bloody hell would you buy into such bullshit?" Mercer asked.

"Because that's what Ms. Rhoade insisted," Rowlins spat. "When we brought her to the station to take her statement, she didn't have any I.D. with her. It made her story about the mugging seem believable."

A thought crossed Bastian's mind, and he stopped chewing on the end of his pen. "Were any of her personal effects recovered?"

Rowlins shook his head. "After she reported her wallet and phone missing, we had no basis for questioning her story about the mugging, even though it seemed more likely that she was pick-pocketed. It's possible her phone and wallet were lifted before the couple made it to the alleyway which would explain why Katia couldn't use her phone to call for help. A couple of uniforms canvassed the area, but nothing was recovered. The lieutenant was more concerned with finding the gunman than figuring out what happened to Ms. Rhoade's phone and wallet."

Bastian eyed Mercer, not ready to share his thoughts in front of the policeman, despite the give and take. "Was her father present when she gave her statement?"

"Yeah. He showed up with some lawyer."

"And so your boss took every word she said like it was gospel. But why would she need a solicitor?" Mercer asked. "She was a victim, not a suspect." He thought back to the morning he encountered Katia outside the precinct. Even though she appeared to be alone, he remembered a few men in off-the-rack suits lingering nearby. If they were dressed nicer, he would have assumed they were legal representation. Perhaps they were part of the personal security team that Carlton Rhoade employed. But he didn't recall seeing Carlton nearby. "Tell me everything that happened the night of the attack and the following morning."

"We received an anonymous tip of a woman screaming. Dispatch sent a couple of unis to check it out. They came upon an armed man in a dark alleyway, a single victim with a gunshot wound to the chest, and a hysterical newspaper heiress. You were arrested. Styler was taken by ambulance to the E.R. Katia went with him. The responding officers questioned her. She was in shock, but she explained who she was and why she didn't call for help."

"On account of the alleged mugging," Mercer interrupted, and Rowlins shrugged.

"After the doctors said Styler was in stable condition, we took her to the precinct. Her father and legal counsel were waiting. She filled out an official police report, offered the vaguest description imaginable of the men responsible, and said you must have shown up to help since she didn't recognize you as one of the assailants."

"And there was no evidence to indicate Jules was responsible," Bastian added.

"Right. The bullet was from a different caliber weapon than your handgun." Rowlins' eyes darted to the dresser. "And after you were released and Katia thanked you, you officially fell off our suspect list."

"Except you followed me." Mercer's eyes grew cold. Maybe he no longer distrusted this particular cop, but he still didn't like him.

"In case you haven't caught on, I'm not great at following the official line of bullshit. Corruption happens. Palms get greased, and sometimes evidence disappears. It's been going on for a while. There are people with extensive amounts of money that control aspects of the system."

"So why are you opposed to letting us handle this matter ourselves?" Mercer asked.

"Just because the system is fucked doesn't mean I shouldn't do my job. Not all of us are scumbags," Rowlins said defiantly.

"I've yet to see that proven," Mercer replied, opening the door. "I'll let you know what we find, but I better not regret it."

"Detective," Bastian said before the man could leave, "I'd wager the men who accompanied the shooter and the men who visited Styler a week ago are the same. It's what we've been led to believe. Names or, at the very least, the surveillance feed from Styler's apartment would be beneficial."

"Yeah, I'll get back to you on that." Rowlins went past, offering his hand to Julian. They shook, and an uncomfortable alliance was formed.

After the detective left the hotel room, Mercer locked the door and sat on the bed. His posture remained rigid, and he shut his eyes to sort through his thoughts. When he opened them, he found Bastian analyzing the contents of the mini-bar.

"Take what you want," Mercer offered, "and pass me the bourbon." He took the proffered individual sized bottle, unscrewed the top, and downed the contents in a single swallow. "So what did you come here to say?"

"That you might be right." Bastian shut the fridge without selecting anything. "And now it seems even more likely after speaking to the investigator. I'll scrub some more camera feeds and see if this pick-pocketing theory pans out. If it does..." Bastian waited a moment, letting the implication hang in the air.

"That means the shooter wanted to make sure they had the proper target. Perhaps Katia's belongings were meant to be verification of the kill. Which means either of them could have been the intended victim." Mercer shook his head. "But that was an amazing shot. I don't believe for one second that the shooter missed his target."

Bastian ran a hand through his hair. "I'll get started on the surveillance feed. I'm thinking of a way to chart movements, and I'll map it out on the aerial views I've printed. Assuming Katia and Ben had a similar routine, it might be possible to approximate locations for a strike. Once Donovan reports in on his findings concerning private military contractors in the area, we may end up having some solid ground to stand on."

"All right, get to work. And stop being so friendly with the copper. I don't care for him."

"You don't care for anyone."

Once Mercer was alone in the room, he considered his options. He could conduct his own reconnaissance, attempt to have another chat with Benjamin Styler, or get piss drunk. They were fast approaching the fifth day since the attack, but this wasn't a kidnapping with a limited window for recovery and extraction. Although the longer this went on, the farther away the assailant could run. Dragging his heels on this wasn't the way to go. If he did that, he'd be no better than the London police, and that thought was sickening.

Tucking the Sig into its holster, he left the hotel, unsure of his next destination. It was nearly midnight as he strolled down the block. His eyes swept the street, and he was conscious of the sights and sounds surrounding him. It was a city, like most other cities, and people could be found out and about at all hours of the day and night. Traffic was lighter now, and the streets were lined with parked cars. Halting his procession at the mouth of the alley, he scanned for visual confirmation that would have made that single gunshot possible.

Parked in the space right before the opening was a

large delivery truck. In the dark, with the streetlights serving as the perfect backlight, the windshield acted like a mirror. Mercer rubbed his chin, contemplating the chances of this vehicle being present the night of the shooting. He didn't remember seeing it, but parked cars were something he had paid little attention to. Circling around, he checked for other vantage points, but nothing else showed a reflection of the inside of the alley.

This was planned. It had to be. There were too many moving parts for this to not have been an orchestrated hit. This was premeditated and anything but accidental. Styler was the target, but that meant someone had to force him into this particular spot or else the conditions wouldn't have been perfect. The only name that came to mind was Katia.

Determined to find another possibility, Mercer backtracked to the restaurant the two had left before reversing course and mimicking the path they must have taken. He searched the street, remembering the surveillance footage Bastian had shown him of the three men tailing the couple. There were cross streets, large intersections between the restaurant and here, but this was the first narrow, enclosed alleyway. It was dark, but the area was commercial and not sketchy like the less trafficked areas of the city.

"Still lost?" one of the hobos from a few days ago called.

Mercer ignored him the other day, but now, he was intrigued. "Perhaps," he said, cautiously approaching.

"With that accent, it's no wonder, buddy," the homeless man said. He shook his metal coffee can at Mercer. "Whatcha searching for?"

"Answers." Mercer dug into his pocket and found a twenty. "Were you out here four nights ago?"

"I live here," the man practically spat. "This is my

house, and I suggest you wipe your feet before stepping inside."

"My apologies. Do you remember a woman screaming?"

"Goddamn, that bitch was loud. I thought I was gonna enjoy the show like usual," his eyes flicked across the street, and his hand traveled into his pants, "but then she just starts wailing. I had to pack it in."

"How often does she put on the show?"

"Every four or five days." His eyes lit up, and he adjusted himself. "It's better than Cinemax."

"I thought you lived out here," Mercer replied, losing interest and digesting this new tidbit. He turned, looking straight across the street and directly into the alley, but he knew from the CCTV footage that no one was acting as a spotter that night. Instead, the assailants must have been familiar with Katia and Ben's routine.

"That doesn't mean I don't know about Cinemax. I'm still a man with working parts." The hobo exposed himself, and Mercer walked away, uttering an endless string of expletives.

THIRTEEN

"We need to talk," Mercer announced, barging inside.

"Mr. Mercer, do you have any idea what time it is?" Carlton Rhoade asked, pulling his robe closed. "This better be important."

"Where's Katia?"

"Asleep." Carlton rubbed his eyes and went into the living room. "I'll ask you again. What is this about?"

"Someone's been stalking your daughter." Mercer studied the expression on Carlton's face. "And you don't seem surprised."

"It's been taken care of."

"Are you sure about that?"

"Of course, I'm sure." Carlton glowered, standing up. "And that situation does not concern you."

"Well, it should concern you." Mercer scanned the room, but the place was empty. "After all, she's not my daughter. But it's reasonable to assume the shooter was well-versed on Katia's habits and routine. And based on the few facts I've gathered, I'm assuming her stalker probably hired the assailant to extinguish his competition."

"He said it was taken care of," Carlton mumbled to himself, heading across the room. "But since you've identified a threat, you will protect her. It's that simple." Carlton went to his desk and pulled out his checkbook. "Name your price, Mr. Mercer. I want you to remove the problem and anyone associated with this dangerous man."

"But you just said that issue was resolved." Mercer fought to remain neutral and detached. "And a few seconds after that proclamation, you're trying to hire me to provide a solution. I want names. Who threatened your daughter?"

"I don't have a name." Carlton signed the bottom and tore out the check, leaving the rest blank. "I'm sure you can decide on a fair fee." He tried to hand it to Julian, who scoffed at the notion.

"Explain," Mercer growled.

"Two months ago, I received an envelope with a few photos of my daughter. They were taken of her while she was asleep inside her apartment. The next day, I received a letter asking for twenty thousand dollars. I paid, but I needed assurances that Katia was no longer in any danger. So I asked one of the investigators at my company to look into the matter quietly. He was already checking into a few other personal matters and knew that discretion was of the utmost importance."

"What did he find?"

"Nothing. He said it was a dead end, claiming Katia was safe and that I wouldn't be receiving any more demands, but that answer was far from satisfactory. He left me no choice but to take matters into my own hands. That's why I offered to renovate Katia's apartment as an engagement present, so she'd have to move back here while state-of-the-art security was added in addition to whatever upgrades and cosmetic changes she wanted. I hired additional building security, and there have been no other communications since. Like I said, it was resolved."

"Until Benjamin Styler was nearly killed."

"Are you positive there's a correlation?" Carlton asked. "Styler's a bad seed. I'm sure he has plenty of his own enemies, and thankfully, Katia wasn't harmed, despite her proximity to him at the time of the shooting."

"You are a fool." Mercer sneered, turning and heading for the door. "And I can clearly see the family resemblance." Ignoring the protests of his employer, Mercer slammed the door. On the bright side, he felt certain Katia was not to blame for the failed assassination attempt, nor was she the intended target. At least not yet. Pulling out his cell phone, he dialed Donovan. "I want a progress report regarding the local contractors."

"I'm still looking," Donovan replied, letting out a sigh. "It's been slow going on account of trading off with Hans to guard this bloke, but I've identified a handful of men that have the necessary skills to make the shot. It could be one of them or someone else. Didn't Bas tell you I passed him the list and he has been monitoring their movements and activities?"

"No." Once again, Bastian failed to disclose something important because he was afraid of what Mercer would do with only partial knowledge of the situation. "Has anyone been to see Styler?"

"No one. The police have finally established a permanent presence, and they don't seem to care for the protection we've been providing."

"If you encounter any issues that you can't handle, tell them to contact Detective Rowlins. It appears we are working in tandem with him."

"When did that happen?"

"Ask Bastian, he'd know."

Mercer disconnected and glanced around the street. He'd been on the move throughout the conversation, and now he was contemplating his next destination. Before he could hail a cab, he spotted a light reflecting from one of the parked cars outside Rhoade's apartment building. He smiled; the feeling of progress and impending violence coursed through his veins. It was the calm before the storm, and tonight, all hell would break loose. Unable to wipe the grin off his face, he went to the vehicle, smashed his elbow through the passenger's side window, and opened the car door while simultaneously pointing his Sig at the startled man. The man dropped the camera with the telephoto lens and backed against the door, hands in the air.

"I'd suggest you cooperate," Mercer said, removing the keys from the ignition. "Because if you make a run for it, you'll be dead before you hit the pavement." The man in the car looked ready to soil himself but didn't move a single inch. "Is there a boot release?"

"Huh?" The man raised his hands a little higher in surrender.

"Bloody hell," Mercer muttered. "A trunk release?"

"Ye-yeah."

"Good. Open it and get out slowly."

The man did as he was told, and Julian stepped out of the vehicle with his gun still pointed at whoever this man was. He went around the front of the car, shoved his hostage against the rear door to pat him down, and then ordered him inside the trunk. Once the lid was shut, Mercer holstered his gun, took the pair of black leather gloves out of his pocket, slipped them on, and then climbed into the driver's seat. He put the key in the ignition and headed for the abandoned storefronts his team scoped out near the docks. On the way, he phoned Bastian and asked him to monitor the police frequencies for any word on this possible abduction.

"I really shouldn't let you go anywhere alone," Bastian remarked. "Were you spotted?"

"It's four a.m. The possibility doesn't seem likely but remain on standby," Mercer instructed. "Once he's secured, I'll give you the relevant vehicle information, so you can start building a new profile. We have much to discuss."

"Shall I meet you?"

"No. Stay by the computers in case I need your technological genius, but send Hans."

Mercer drove to the building they were temporarily renting and killed the engine. Getting out of the car, he performed a quick visual sweep of the area and the inside of the dilapidated warehouse. Inside was mostly open space with the exception of a few offices. The windowless one in the corner would serve nicely as a makeshift prison, and after dragging a single chair into the room and collecting the roll of duct tape, Mercer went back to the car to collect his prize.

When the trunk lid opened, Mercer feared he would have to subdue his unwilling guest, but the man looked dazed and frightened. Making quick work of securing his arms behind his back and placing an extra piece of tape over his mouth and eyes to make the man mute and blind, Julian hauled his prisoner out of the car and dragged him into the building. After he was secured to the chair in the center of the room, Mercer removed the tape.

"Shit." The man winced, his skin red from the removed adhesive. "What do you want? Please, don't hurt me."

"Who are you?" Julian asked.

"John Welks. Let me go."

"Who were you photographing?"

"No one. I wasn't."

"Bullshit." Mercer snorted, a smirk emerging on his face, and he slammed the ball of his foot down on the man's ankle in just the right place to snap the bone. The scream ripped through the room, echoing in the small enclosed space. "Want to give that another go?"

"I was hired to keep tabs on Katia Rhoade," Welks choked out. The obvious threat of further violence had loosened his tongue and his resolve.

"By whom?" Mercer asked, but Welks shook his head. Stepping forward, Mercer eyed the other ankle. "How long have you been stalking Ms. Rhoade?"

"I haven't," Welks replied, practically pleading. Julian made a move, but before he could inflict more damage, Welks sputtered, "I'm a private investigator."

Surprised by the words, Mercer took a step back, cocking his head to the side and processing this new bit of information. The man didn't have a wallet on him, or it would have been discovered during the earlier frisking. Slamming the office door and making sure it was locked, Mercer returned to the car and searched the interior. Inside the glove box, he found the vehicle registration, a thirty-two caliber handgun, and a wallet.

"Goddammit," he cursed, dialing Bastian.

FOURTEEN

Hans ran both hands over his face and took a deep breath. "What do you want us to do with him now?" he asked, glancing at the locked door. "We can't just bloody well keep him here indefinitely."

"I know that," Mercer snarled. "But he has answers that we need. It doesn't make a damn bit of difference who he is. Either someone hired him to keep tabs on Katia, or he's the stalker." He let out a huff. "Or he could be our shooter."

"Doesn't seem to me like he has the balls."

"It could be an act." Julian sighed. "I'll give it another go, and then I need you to keep an eye on him. The last thing we need is for him to escape."

"Right-o. Shall I ring Bastian and see if he's come to any conclusions on this new wrinkle?"

Mercer nodded, opening the door and stepping back inside. Welks had managed to tip over the chair and was sideways on the floor. He appeared to be in utter agony. He lifted his head off the ground and looked up at Mercer.

"Let me go," Welks insisted, attempting to sound intimidating despite this submissive position.

"Do you prefer licking dirt off the ground?" Mercer asked, crouching to the man's level and leaning back on his haunches. "Or would you like to be upright? There is no escape, and frankly, I don't care what position you're in because it won't affect what I'm going to do to you." The man remained silent, so Mercer stood and kicked him once in the stomach. The man let out a gasp, but being tied to the chair meant there was no way to protect the softer parts of his body. "Don't jerk me around," Mercer continued. "Why are you tailing Katia Rhoade?"

"I was hired to keep tabs on her."

"By whom?" Mercer circled, but the man remained speechless. "I will find out. And the longer you make me wait, the worse it'll be for you. Do you really want to die for some bloke that paid you to take pictures?"

"He'll kill me."

"And you don't think I will?"

Welks audibly swallowed. "Who are you?"

"Does it matter?"

"You broke my fucking foot. You kidnapped me. You won't get away with this."

Mercer stopped pacing and remained completely still. "Do you hear that?"

"No. What?"

"That's right. There isn't a goddamn person coming for you. And trust me, there won't be enough of you left for the authorities to make a positive identification." Then he went to the door and slammed it shut, leaving the man inside.

"How'd it go?" Hans asked. The entire exchange had taken less than five minutes.

"Bloody fantastic," Mercer retorted. "What'd Bastian say?"

"He's working on phone records and client lists. He thinks he should have a name within the hour. He's also researching Carlton's communiqués in order to determine who sent the photos of Katia."

"Check on the prisoner in twenty minutes and make sure he doesn't try anything stupid. Keep him blind and deaf in terms of our identities and job, but if he decides to talk, you know what to ask."

"How am I allowed to ask?" Hans mused, watching the darkness pass over Mercer's face.

"Any way you'd like. But keep him alive," Mercer went to the exit, "and try not to hobble him any worse than I've already done. In the unlikely event he's nothing more than a pawn, he shouldn't be permanently crippled."

"Yes, sir."

Considering his options, Mercer couldn't afford for Welks to be located before he spilled his guts, so memorizing the man's home address, Mercer took Welks' car and parked it on a nearby neighborhood street. Hopefully, no one would be the wiser. Determined to search through the man's house and belongings for a lead, Mercer took a single step onto the walkway but halted his procession when a woman emerged from the house. She offered a friendly smile.

"Can I help you?" she asked, obviously on her way to work at such an early morning hour.

Caught by surprise, Julian shook his head, but she continued to stare at him. "My apologies."

He stepped off her walkway and continued down the street. The encounter rattled him. The last thing he wanted to do was drag an innocent into this mess, so he'd just have to wait to search Welks' home when no one was around.

Returning to the hotel, Mercer hoped Bastian had a business address for Welks and some idea of who sent the photos to Carlton. They were getting closer. This would end soon enough; he could feel it.

Stopping by Bastian's hotel room, the information was still being tracked and compiled. John Welks was a private investigator at Piper Investigations, a large security firm. It would be difficult to gain access to his office without tipping off building security and the staff, but that didn't mean the files and client information couldn't be accessed from off-site. Bastian was devising a plan. He also phoned Rowlins and informed him of the implied threat to Katia that Carlton had received. The detective hoped to obtain a warrant to review her apartment's security footage for the last few months, so at least that was one less thing Bastian needed to worry about.

"Jules, get some sleep. You've been up all night. And if Katia's life is actually in danger, you have to be sharp."

Grudgingly, Mercer nodded, leaving this mess in the hands of his teammates. Returning to his room, he stripped down and got into bed. Sleep, he willed his mind. Turning off the outside noise was easy. It was a trick he learned from spending too many nights in warzones, but shutting off the internal noise was a bit more difficult. Forcing his mind to go blank, he finally fell into an uneasy sleep, but the nightmare came back.

When he came home that afternoon from the market, he never expected to find his wife on the kitchen floor like that. The grocery bag he was holding crashed to the floor. Glass jars shattered. Cans rolled to the corners of the kitchen, but he paid them no heed as he knelt on the floor, pulling her into his lap and begging for her to live. He would have gladly died in her place. Cradling Michelle in his arms, he held her impossibly close. She couldn't breathe, and she was losing blood too quickly for anything to be done. He called for help, but by the time anyone arrived, she was gone. The paramedics had to pry her out of his arms, and after the police took one look at the apartment and his blood-soaked clothing, they arrested him on the spot.

Awakening with a start, he buried his face in his hands. Tremors coursed through him, and he labored to get his breathing under control. Despite his calloused exterior, his insides were shattered beyond recognition. The encounter with Welks was supposed to alleviate some of the inner turmoil through a justifiable channel for violence, but when he encountered the man's wife leaving her house this morning, Julian knew that he couldn't put an innocent person through this type of anguish. Welks might not be innocent, but his wife certainly was.

After spending another twenty minutes collecting himself, he showered and dressed. When he opened the bathroom door, he raised the Sig but quickly lowered it. Bastian was making himself comfortable in Julian's room.

"I told you we're not in the business of getting our hands dirty," Bastian said, noticing Mercer's clearly rattled visage. "It makes it worse. I know it does."

"We needed answers."

"Did you get them?"

"Not yet." Mercer focused on the open laptop. "What did you find?"

"Fair warning, you're not going to like it. It appears Mr. Welks is on retainer at Rhoade's newspaper. What's even more disturbing is the fact that there is no record of anyone hiring him to surveil Katia. I took a trip to the security firm, spoke to a few people, borrowed a computer or two, but whatever Welks is doing isn't sanctioned." Catching the ire burning through Mercer's eyes, Bastian continued, hoping to put the fire out before something exploded. "That doesn't mean John Welks is the stalker or responsible for this. From what Gladys said, most of the investigators freelance on the side."

"Who the hell is Gladys?"

"The receptionist."

Bastian continued to speak, but Mercer tuned him out. Welks said someone hired him, and whoever that someone was would kill him if he talked. That didn't necessarily mean it was true, but normal people were more afraid of the devil standing in front of them instead of the one waiting in the wings.

"What about private phone records?" Mercer interrupted.

"I'm having trouble accessing them. Our mate at Interpol is working on it, but we don't have them yet. And our copper friend doesn't have enough evidence to get a court order for the records."

"All right." Julian turned and left, wondering if Katia would have any insights to share on these recent developments.

FIFTEEN

Mercer was tired of the norm. It was exhausting. This existence that he never wanted but was condemned to was wearing him down. Katia Rhoade was an heiress that had difficulty with the truth. Her father was equally untrustworthy, and Benjamin Styler's activities and business practices were questionable. Why couldn't anything be black and white? The important things were, or so it seemed. This should be simple, truthful, and the culprit should already have been dealt with. There was no reason for the added complications, but everyone's questionable background and activities made straight answers practically impossible to obtain.

After picking Katia up from work, Mercer took her to the hospital and asked questions about her apartment renovation, the reason for it, her routine with Ben, and how frequently they dined at that particular restaurant before enjoying dessert in that alleyway. She blushed, angry and humiliated, but for once, she actually provided some answers. Her responses mimicked what Carlton and the hobo had told him the previous evening. It was apparent anyone who wanted to make a move against Katia or Ben would have had ample opportunity.

Benjamin Styler wasn't any more adept at varying his routine. He typically worked from home but had a standing lunch meeting with a few of his business buddies to talk stocks and trading tips. The group of four or five men would exchange tips, share investment advice, and strategize on ways to land new clients. Nothing seemed particularly sinister about these meetings of the minds, but it forced Mercer to draw into question the reason why Styler would be indebted to some unsavory chaps.

"Do either of you know John Welks?" Mercer asked, shifting his gaze between Katia and Ben.

"Nope, doesn't ring any bells," Ben offered quickly.

"He works for my father," Katia declared, giving Ben's hand a squeeze. "You met him at the Christmas party. He's that P.I. that they occasionally use for fact-checking."

"Oh, right," Ben said.

"What else does he do?" Mercer asked, hoping someone would say something useful.

"How the hell should we know?" Ben asked, but Mercer just shrugged. "You know something. You must, or you wouldn't be asking these questions. Did he shoot me?"

"Benjamin," Katia scolded, using his full name like a parent would a wayward child, "why would someone my dad employs want to shoot you?"

"Why, indeed." Mercer arched an eyebrow. He wasn't sure how, but he knew he had hit upon something. Now he just had to figure out how to get the information out of Styler.

Julian slipped into the background, letting the two

lovebirds bicker over the implied accusation. When he couldn't take the arguing any longer, he stepped into the hallway. Donovan was outside the room, filling in for Hans who was currently guarding Welks. Donovan shifted his gaze down the hallway, and Mercer spotted the two police officers stationed like sentries. Apparently sharing with Detective Rowlins came with a couple of perks.

"Are they fighting again?" Donovan asked when Katia's voice carried through the door.

"They do this often?"

"A few times that I've noticed. She wants him to tell her about his debts and if that's the reason someone wanted to kill him. He insists his debts have been paid, and that it's old news. Then she cries and begs. He apologizes, and then they snog for a bit." He shook his head, grinning. "Whenever he's released, they're going to have some wicked make-up sex."

"But he won't tell her who he owed. And he won't tell us." Mercer contemplated those facts for a moment, pondering what reason Styler would have for hiding such inconsequential facts. "We've checked his financials but didn't find anything conclusive."

A thought emerged, and after giving Donovan instructions to take Katia home when she was ready to leave, Mercer went down the hallway, nodded curtly to the LEOs, and took the car to the warehouse. He had a few new questions to ask Mr. Welks. Since Welks was Carlton Rhoade's private investigator, he might know plenty about Ben Styler and his business transactions. Luckily, earlier that morning, Mercer had done his research on Welks, but the man had few exploitable weaknesses and no known vices.

Bastian had run a preliminary background on John Welks. He was a private investigator for Piper Investigations, and his main client at the firm was

Carlton Rhoade's newspaper. Welks owned a small townhouse and had been married for eleven years to Teresa Landon Welks, a college professor. Their joint bank account was decent but not particularly extravagant. They had no children and a limited number of extended family members. On paper, Welks was just a working-class stiff.

When Mercer arrived at their makeshift prison, he sent Hans to pick up some first aid supplies, pain relievers, and a few basic necessities. By now, Welks was in agony; his ankle was swollen so badly his shoe would probably have to be cut off. The man was tired, hungry, and in pain. If he was going to talk, now was the time. And if he cooperated, he would be rewarded.

When Julian entered the room, Welks looked up. His eye was swollen and puffy, and his cheek had a gash. But other than that, he didn't look too much worse for wear. Seeing Julian, Welks shrunk as far into the seat as he could, given the restraints. He was afraid, and that fact satisfied Mercer.

"Please," Welks rasped, "I told your partner the same thing I told you. Just let me go. I won't say a word about you. I won't go to the police."

"I don't want to hurt you. I will, but I'd prefer not to. Your wife would like you back in one piece, and I don't want to disappoint her."

"You fucking animal, I swear to god, if you lay a hand on her, I will kill you." It was the proper response, and Julian smiled. "What have you done to Teresa?" Welks asked, horrified.

"Nothing. Yet. Let's get down to business. You're on retainer at Carlton Rhoade's newspaper. You've met his daughter and her fiancé at the company Christmas party. And that's just the bloody tip of the iceberg, isn't it?"

Welks swallowed, hoping to find his voice, but his

mouth was dry. "How could you possibly know that?"

"Tell me everything you know about Benjamin Styler, and I'll consider sending you on your way."

"I...can't."

"Why not?" Julian's question was met with silence, so he continued. "You would rather protect someone who gives you a paycheck than your own wife?" Mercer's face contorted. "What kind of man fails to protect the woman he loves?" He turned the internal guilt and anger outward, focusing the intensity of his feelings on Welks.

The fear reflected in Welks' eyes wasn't faked, and he began spilling his guts, believing Julian would slaughter him if he didn't provide answers to the questions. "Mr. Rhoade asked me to investigate Ben. It was right around Christmas, and they had just announced the engagement. But Mr. Rhoade was afraid Ben was using Katia. The kid had money troubles. He used drugs recreationally, got caught in the midst of a buy, and narced on the dealer to get himself out of trouble. The kid was a mess. Bad business deals, late payments on his bills, questionable morals, no real loyalty to anyone except himself, but he's turned it around recently."

"How recently?"

"Over the past six months or so. And I told that to Mr. Rhoade." Welks pressed his lips together. "Please, whatever you do, don't tell him I said this." Mercer's face contorted in a question. "I know he hired you to guard his daughter. I've seen you bring her home in the evenings and pick her up from work."

"So you admit to spying on Katia."

"I wasn't."

Mercer slapped him across the face as a warning. "I found you outside with the camera. Don't fucking lie to me."

"I'm not," Welks snapped.

"Bollocks," Mercer muttered, circling the room, "then what the hell were you doing with that camera?"

"Making sure no one else showed up." At those words, Mercer stopped pacing. "Since I was already on retainer for Mr. Rhoade, he asked that I investigate the shooting. He wanted to make sure whoever came for Ben didn't come for Katia too." Welks took a deep breath. "I didn't realize Mr. Rhoade also hired you to investigate. I'm assuming that's how you determined when I first met Ben and Katia."

"So since we're both employed by Carlton Rhoade, why the secrecy? Why are you so afraid of Mr. Rhoade? When I questioned you earlier, you said your boss would kill you if you talked. Do you expect me to believe that Carlton Rhoade is a killer?"

Welks shrugged. "He might be. Someone from the newspaper contracted the hit on Benjamin Styler, and I have no way of knowing that it wasn't Carlton himself."

"Rubbish."

The story Welks shared was contradictory. Why hire an investigator to look into a shooting if you were to blame? It made no sense. Shaking his head, Mercer left the room.

"Jules, are you okay?" Hans asked, worry etching his face.

"Dandy," Mercer growled. "Do what you like with him. I need some air. I can't think straight." Without another word, he returned to the car and went to the police station. Someone there must know how to conduct a proper investigation.

SIXTEEN

Police reports were considered public information in most instances, and Mercer requested everything they had on Carlton and Katia Rhoade and Benjamin Styler. When the desk sergeant failed to comply with his request, he asked to speak with Detective Rowlins. Rowlins appeared almost instantaneously and ushered Mercer upstairs to his desk.

Twenty minutes later, Mercer was still reading through the police reports. Things that weren't necessarily public information were also pulled, and Rowlins possessed enough knowledge of Styler's history to grab the records regarding his drug connections too. When Mercer finished, he shut his eyes and exhaled slowly.

"It's not the drug dealer or any of his known associates," Rowlins said, tossing the manila folder on top of the stack. "I've checked. Styler doesn't owe them any money. The last time they were even in contact was over a year ago."

"What do you know about John Welks?"

"The private dick that works for the big security firm?" Rowlins shrugged. "Not much. They're heavy hitters over there at Piper Investigations. They work a lot of corporate security and high profile cases." He chuckled. "You planning on using him as a job reference or something?"

"No. Do you think he has any clue how to conduct an investigation? He's a glorified fact-checker for a newspaper."

"Carlton Rhoade's newspaper." The detective leaned back and sipped his coffee. "You want to share that lead that's circling through your brain like a toy car on a Hot Wheels track?"

"I found him with a telephoto camera lens pointed at Ms. Rhoade's bedroom window," Mercer said, leaving out the rest of the information he had gotten while interrogating Welks.

"Do you know what other photos he's taken? Because I'd love to check out those snapshots."

"That's just it." Mercer gave the pile of intel a dirty look. "The memory card was blank." Bastian was analyzing the camera's data, but initially, he didn't find any incriminating photos of Katia or Ben. So either Welks replaced the card before Mercer got a hold of the camera or the P.I. hadn't gotten a chance to take any candid shots last night.

"Strange. Maybe the guy was only using the lens to zoom in. Perhaps he's a modern day peeping tom. Did you hear about that guy that was photographing ladies underwear using a telephoto lens? I swear, just when we start to get an edge over these sickos, technology jumps light years ahead, and they find other ways to be disgusting."

"Have you made any progress on the information Bastian has shared with you?" Mercer asked, diverting the conversation back to the matter at hand.

"Not yet. The system takes time. We have I's to dot and T's to cross. And just so you know, I like your friend better."

"Good. You can bother him the next time you have pointless questions that need answering, but I do appreciate the intel." Mercer jerked his chin at the stack of files. "Someone will be in touch."

"I'm counting on it," Rowlins replied.

Back on the street, Mercer noted the pedestrians on the sidewalks and the groups congregating near the bus and taxi stands. His eyes darted through the throng. Something was eating away at him. Perhaps it was the situation getting the best of his imagination, but he had spent years honing his instincts. Continuing on a random path, he turned down another street, keeping his pace steady. Crossing the street, he monitored the reflections of the people behind him, but he didn't spot a tail. Seeing a sign for the L, he took the steps up to the elevated platform.

He waited, leaning against a support pillar and appearing lost in his own thoughts. After fifteen minutes, the train came. He entered the nearest door, walked through the car, and exited from a different door just as the chime sounded to indicate that the doors were closing. No one else exited, and none of the people that were waiting on the platform were the same from before the train arrived. Reassured that no one was in pursuit, Julian went down the steps and back to street level.

He only made it a few feet when a car horn blared in the distance. Turning to see what the commotion was about, he barely had time to dive out of the way of a speeding black van that was intent on mowing him down. The van missed, knocking off the back bumper of another car before shooting back into traffic. Screams and expletives echoed through the air. This was no accident.

The van pulled a tight u-turn, launching itself between two parked cars and knocking off both side mirrors. People jumped out of the way as it careened out of control, bouncing like a pinball between the row of parked cars and numerous storefronts while hurtling down the sidewalk, directly toward Mercer.

Julian darted across the street, pulling his Sig from its holster. As soon as the van found a break in the parked cars, it launched off the sidewalk and into the road, another car t-boned it, spinning both vehicles. More horns blared as the pile-up continued to grow. But the van righted itself and kept going. The side door falling off as it jerked through traffic, slamming against other motorists. The delay gave Mercer time to fire into the windshield, emptying his clip before ducking into a building alcove to avoid any possible return fire. Sirens blared, and the driver of the van panicked, crashing into the back of a pick-up truck and forcing the impeding vehicle forward just enough to allow for an illegal turn and escape from the approaching police cars.

After conducting a quick scan of the area for other threats, Mercer breathed a sigh of relief. Holstering his weapon, he continued walking down the street like nothing happened. Everyone's focus was on the numerous accidents, not the man that just opened fire in broad daylight. This was like any other city or any other situation. Acting naturally and uninterested ensured no one paid a bit of attention, and right now, Julian couldn't afford any undue attention. Whoever was behind the wheel had been waiting for him.

Continuing calmly down the street, only the telltale shaking in his hands provided any indication of the adrenaline coursing through his veins. Cautioning a glance across the way, Mercer realized at least three people had been injured by the van. It was possible pedestrians had been killed or maimed, and that didn't include any of the people in the affected vehicles. Ambulances and fire trucks rolled in, adding to the growing chaos. Whoever did this wanted Mercer dead, and they didn't care to destroy any obstacles that got in the way. This needed to end. And it needed to end tonight.

Shutting his eyes, he recalled every detail that he could. The van was black, an older model from the 1990s, with no license plate, and tinted windows. Oh, and it was missing a door and both side mirrors, and it had a dozen or so of his bullets lodged inside of it. Finding his phone, he dialed Bastian.

"Hack into the city's DOT grid. We need eyes on a black van." He gave the current address and told Bastian to turn on the television. A news helicopter was lingering overhead, likely reporting live on the unfolding chaos that just erupted. "The bastard tried to kill me."

"Obviously, he wasn't quite successful," Bastian remarked, the sound of the television filling the background. "Are you okay?"

"I will be once he's dead."

Mercer's trek away from the scene led to less trafficked streets, and he hailed a cab and went straight to the hospital. The police were guarding Styler in Donovan's absence, but obviously, whoever was responsible had big brass ones. And Mercer didn't doubt for a second that the perpetrator would open fire in a hospital. However, the assailant's newly acquired target seemed to be Julian Mercer, and that added a whole new dynamic to this mess.

Mercer returned to Styler's room and barged through the door. His entire focus was on the man in the bed. Ben offered an uncertain smile, confused by the brusqueness and reappearance of the ex-SAS bodyguard.

"I'm sick and tired of playing games," Mercer bellowed, shoving the chair beneath the doorknob to keep everyone outside. "What the bloody hell is going on?" Styler moved to open his mouth with another unhelpful comment or non-answer, so Mercer intervened. "Someone just tried to kill me. So don't you dare speak a word of bullshit. I'm not in the mood."

"What?"

"I'm assuming your attackers want me dead. Just like how they'd prefer you to be. So talk. Who do you owe money to?"

"No one. They were legitimate business expenses, but I paid off my debts. I came into some cash recently, and that was that."

"Katia," Mercer stepped forward and watched Styler's Adam's apple bob uncontrollably, "believes you still owe money to some unsavory chaps. That those people are the ones responsible for the attack. Are you saying she's wrong?"

Ben tapped the hospital call button repeatedly, fearing Mercer might strangle him. "No. I mean yes. She's wrong. I'm in the black. My name's not in anyone's ledger. Honestly. I promise." His eyes grew wide as Mercer continued the approach.

"Where'd you get the money?" Mercer heard hospital staff outside the door.

"I...um...found an untapped revenue source."

"Meaning?" Loud banging erupted from the other side of the door, and Mercer was sure the police would burst through any second. The chair wouldn't hold them off for long.

"I can't," Styler muttered, and Mercer pressed his palm into the bandage on Ben's chest.

Ben screamed, wincing and writhing in pain. But before he could say another word, the two police officers broke through the door and grabbed Mercer, throwing him against the floor and pressing a taser into his back. The electric current ripped through Julian's body, and he remained subdued and twitching on the ground.

As the police hauled Mercer to his feet, Styler met Julian's eyes with remorse. "Thanks for intervening, but that's not really necessary. You don't have to arrest Mr. Mercer. This is all just a big misunderstanding," Styler insisted.

The violent takedown had been more than Styler expected. He had panicked when things had gotten out of hand. Now he regretted his hesitation in answering Julian's questions. After all, Mercer was hired to protect him and Katia, but the policemen ignored his protests, tightening the handcuffs and reading Mercer his rights.

SEVENTEEN

"I'm getting tired of seeing you in lockup," Rowlins said, opening the door. The few other crooks inside the holding cell didn't even bother to glance up at Mercer's release. "Weren't you supposed to be protecting the kid?"

"I'm protecting the girl," Mercer walked haughtily past Rowlins, "but frankly, I might be through with this bloody job."

The detective handed the keys back to the desk sergeant and pulled Mercer aside. "A couple of hours ago, you were reviewing the police files. What changed in such a short amount of time?"

"I believe someone wants me dead." Mercer studied Rowlins, scrutinizing his face for any micro-expressions or signs of guilt. "I was tracked from this precinct through the streets. The results made the news. And I don't take fondly to failed attempts." His gaze turned hard and cold. "There will be lethal repercussions."

"I'd suggest you refrain from making threats inside

a police station and to an officer of the law." Rowlins returned the look. "Are you accusing me of something?"

"You better hope not." Mercer signed the receipt and took the clear plastic bag that held his personal items and continued toward the door. At the front desk, he found Bastian waiting.

"Jules, slow down," Bastian called, tossing a quick nod to Rowlins before chasing after Mercer. "We need to discuss our next course of action."

"I already know what our next course of action is. We're relocating to our secondary location. The hotel is no longer secure. Not that it ever was."

"I've completed the move already," Bastian continued, falling into step with Mercer. "I've also spoken to Styler while you were getting your arse thrown in jail again." He lowered his voice as they exited, both men immediately on alert for potential threats. "I know who sent the photos to Carlton Rhoade." He led Mercer to a new vehicle, having scrapped the last one to make it more difficult for anyone to follow or monitor them while they were mobile. "It seems Styler got creative in paying off his debts."

"How?"

Bastian smirked. "That bloke is one ballsy chap. He took the photos of Katia and sent them to her father."

"Does Rhoade know? Or Katia?"

Bastian shrugged. "I'm still working on that part." He glanced at Mercer, sitting sullenly in the passenger's seat. "Donovan's getting closer to narrowing down the list of local contractors. Not many of them have the skills to make that shot. And a few who could were out of town when the shooting occurred. So the possibilities are dwindling, and once I'm able to identify the two men that accompanied the shooter, that will narrow our potentials even further."

"What's being done with Welks?"

"He's alone, but Hans assured me that he's secure."

"Any idea what happened to the van driver from earlier this afternoon?" Mercer asked, referencing the man that tried to run him down, but Bas just shrugged. "All I can say for certain is it's unlikely he's the same hitman from the alley. The shooting was precise and calculated, and today's attempt was messy and opportunistic. Maybe the kamikaze driver was one of the shooter's two associates."

"Could be, unless it was someone else entirely," Bastian offered. "After all, you do have trouble making friends." Even without turning, he could feel Mercer's icy stare. They rode in silence until the oppressiveness became unbearable. "Since Ben sent the threatening photos and demand letter to Carlton, do you think Carlton suspected his future son-in-law of extortion?"

"If what Welks said is true, then Rhoade might be aware of precisely who Benjamin Styler is and what he's done, or Carlton could still be in the dark."

"Rhoade doesn't strike me as clueless." There was more to the story than what Bastian was saying, but they needed to regroup and strategize before acting brashly, especially now that there might be a bounty on their heads.

* * *

Inside the pre-furnished flat the former SAS were using as their new headquarters, Mercer stood alone, analyzing the maps and intel that covered the walls like mismatched wallpaper. Having spent so much time guarding Katia and getting jerked around by the powers that be, he somehow missed just how much time and effort his men had put into this assignment.

It was easy to forget everyone else's role, but he appreciated their dedication, even if he would never tell them that in so many words.

Donovan's list of capable contract killers had dwindled to less than a handful, and Bastian was analyzing each potential hitman's financial records and calling in favors from every government agency from both sides of the pond to figure this out. After the attempt on Mercer's life and his arrest for assaulting Benjamin Styler, none of the former SAS were guarding the Rhoades' apartment. Carlton's personal security could do a fine job on their own.

"Knock, knock," Bastian called, crunching on some potato chips. "Was there anything specific you wanted me to get out of Welks?"

"Answers." Mercer didn't bother to turn around. He was benched for the evening by Bastian's request. Since someone wanted Julian dead, he couldn't risk leading that party to Welks or one of the other intended targets. And after his violent outburst with Styler earlier in the afternoon, it was apparent that Julian wasn't the calmest person when it came to asking questions.

"Bloody fantastic," Bastian replied sarcastically. "I would have never been able to figure that out on my own." Instead of waiting for Mercer's cheeky response, Bastian left to conduct another interrogation with John Welks. Now that they knew the source of the blackmail photos, Welks' position working for Carlton Rhoade contained a brand new dynamic and one the team could exploit.

The door slammed, and Mercer took a breath, dropping some of his stoicism and returning to the living room. Easing into the flat's pre-furnished recliner, he unclipped the holster from his belt and put it on the coffee table. Closing his eyes, he listened to the sound of his own breathing and focused on his heartbeat. When the tension abated, he opened his eyes and went into the kitchen for sustenance.

It was obvious he'd been letting his rage dictate his actions. There had been no reason to resort to physical violence so quickly, and it was due to his actions with Welks and Styler that Bastian requested he take the night off. The team didn't want Julian to become a liability, and with a killer on his heels, he'd be even more likely to lash out if he didn't find a proper outlet to expel his inner turmoil.

As he removed the wrapper from a frozen dinner and popped it into the microwave, his brain felt clear. It had been a long time, probably since before London, when he managed to focus without the fog of grief and rage clouding his every thought and impulse. And in the quiet safety of the empty flat, he relaxed. His instincts and thoughts were sharper than they had been, and after removing the cardboard tray from the micro, he set to work, compiling a list of facts from the intelligence they had gathered.

This mission wasn't that different from some of the jobs the military had sent him on, nor was it dissimilar from the kidnappings they worked for the last two years. It was rather simple once he got down to the bones of the matter. It was about locations, timing, concluding who had reason and opportunity, and foremost, determining what goal would be achieved by eliminating the mark. Once these questions were answered, the list of potentials would dwindle. Then the remaining names would be dealt with accordingly. He could handle this. His team could handle this. And when he finished analyzing the information, a single wayward thought crossed his mind. Why couldn't they use the same tried and true method to identify and locate Michelle's killer?

Tabling that last thought far away for later consideration before it could turn into an obvious distraction, Julian reviewed the names on the list. Someone with deep pockets paid for the hit. And there was only one name that came to mind. But was Carlton Rhoade so heartless and sinister that he would destroy his daughter's happiness and risk her wrath by hiring professionals to murder her fiancé? Shouldn't a father love his daughter and want nothing but her happiness? And why would Rhoade hire a team to investigate and provide protection if he was responsible for ordering the hit?

Mercer picked through the financials that Bastian obtained through every illegal method possible, and he noted quite a few cash transfers out of Carlton's personal account. But once the money was liquid, it was difficult to trace. The phone records didn't indicate contact with any of the wet work experts that Donovan had uncovered, but as soon as the shooter was identified, the contract killer would lead the team back to his client. Mercer wouldn't give him any other choice. The only catch was they would have to capture him without killing him. That could be tricky, especially when dealing with a professional. Luckily, Mercer's team was their own brand of quasi-mercenary. The skills they possessed should be enough. They had to be because from Mercer's estimation there was no other way to positively identify the party responsible.

Speaking to Welks could only aid their investigation, as would whatever leads Detective Rowlins might discover when checking out building surveillance. But the incident on the street had left a bad taste in Mercer's mouth. He was tracked from the precinct. Someone knew he was there, followed him when he left, waited, watched, and attempted to strike. Even though the attempt on his life failed, Julian wasn't certain the pain in the arse detective wasn't to blame. Cops were dirty, especially in this city, and Mercer didn't want to trust him despite Bastian's insistence.

Tapping his fingers on the table, he ran through his encounters with Rowlins. The detective said Rhoade had friends highly placed in the police department. The questionable police lieutenant could have been responsible for the botched attempt at vehicular homicide, or it may have been another officer of the law. Did Carlton hire a hit squad to take out Mercer before he could uncover the truth? That made no sense. Then again, Carlton's behavior made little sense if John Welks was to be taken at his word. Trust no one. It was the safest course of action, and the only logical one when fact continued to meet fiction.

"Bollocks," Mercer grunted, pushing away from the table.

He was certain he was missing something, and John Welks was the only person who could provide insight and answers. It was up to Bastian to convince their hostage to open up. It was the only way, and Mercer knew that if anyone on his team could appear nonthreatening and apologetic, it was Bas.

EIGHTEEN

"How'd it go?" Julian asked, barely opening one eye. He had fallen asleep in the chair a few hours earlier, and his convoluted dreams had led to one theory that he just couldn't shake – Carlton Rhoade must be involved.

"We've made progress. Welks said he was anonymously contacted via the newspaper's internal e-mail system for information on Styler and Katia. This unknown contact wanted to know everything about Ben's background and daily activities."

"Which explains how the hit was so easily orchestrated," Julian mused. "Does Welks have any idea who contacted him or who was privy to his investigation of Benjamin Styler?"

"The P.I. offered up a few possibilities, mostly former newspaper employees, but nothing conclusive has surfaced."

"Do you think he's on to something?"

"No. The person responsible has access to the internal e-mail system at the paper, so it must be a current employee." Bas scribbled a note and tacked it to the wall. "Welks seems like a decent fellow that just happened to make a mistake. So I'm easing him into trusting me. Once he does, I'm sure he'll be more forthcoming and provide us with additional intel. In the meantime, I'll see if our anonymous e-mailer has left a digital footprint that we can trace."

"Haven't you already poked around the newspaper's server?"

"That doesn't mean I can't look again." Bas sighed and sat down on the couch. "I told Welks we'd cut him loose as soon as we can, and I brought him some ice and a wrap for his ankle and let him speak to his wife in a show of good faith."

"You what?" Mercer sat up straight, fully awake.

"We were knocking on the twenty-four hour window. In another day, she would have reported him missing, and the coppers would have been breathing down our necks."

"He could have tipped her off. They could trace the call. They–"

"You are paranoid." Bastian's gaze turned hard and impenetrable. "There was no need for further violence. He's cooperating. He probably would have cooperated without being abducted and threatened. But I understand why you acted the way you did since he was outside the apartment with a camera. And just so you know, he said he was there to ensure Katia and Carlton were safe."

Mercer scoffed and rolled his shoulders to work the tension out of them. "He was far from cooperative when I asked him questions. Perhaps you should take over all the interrogations since you're so bloody friendly." The words were acidic, but Bastian ignored them. "Let me guess, you believe whoever planned to kill me this afternoon was seeking revenge due to my less than personable attitude."

"No," Bastian drummed his fingers subconsciously, "but in the last twelve hours, a lot has changed. We need to review the updated intel and devise a new plan of action. Donovan and Hans will be here shortly." He found the anger in Mercer's eyes inappropriately placed. "Would you rather turn tail and run?"

"I don't run. I am not a coward."

"So what then?"

"They have made us fools. We are nothing more than pawns in some sick, rich bastard's game. Benjamin Styler extorted Carlton Rhoade by threatening Katia. Rhoade paid the demands to his future son-in-law but probably hired a hitman to kill the kid. Katia is," Mercer's face contorted into a sea of disdain and confusion, "misinformed, dishonest, and quite a handful."

"Face it, you like that in a woman." Bastian's comment was met with hatred. "And your assumptions on the way things are seem sorely misplaced. Rhoade wouldn't risk any harm ever befalling his own flesh and blood."

"C'mon, Bas, you were there when Carlton hired us to identify the party responsible for the attack on Styler. He wanted us to extinguish the threat without asking any other questions. That sounds like someone who fears the truth might come out, and what we've uncovered indicates that Carlton has the means and motive for contracting the hit." He slammed his palm against the wall. "And now I'd wager Mr. Rhoade has hired someone else to remove us from the equation as well. Maybe he realized Welks has been abducted and thinks we're getting too close to discovering his involvement."

"You do realize none of what you just said makes

bloody sense."

"Welks and Styler practically admitted as much. Shall we go knock on Carlton's door and have a friendly chat?" Mercer asked, disgusted. "Rhoade wanted wet work. You sat in his living room and listened to him ask if we were mercenaries."

"Let's say your cockamamie theory is true. Would you have said yes?" Bastian raised a challenging brow, cocking his head to the side. "Regardless of how unemotional and heartless you want to play, I know you, Commander. And you would have refused his request. The last thing you'd ever do is kill an innocent."

"Styler's not innocent. He's a blackmailer."

"Bullshit. The kid basically borrowed some family money to get back in the black. He never directly threatened Katia. And from what I've heard and seen, he wouldn't. He's crazy about her and also a bit crazy, but he isn't a bad guy. Definitely stupid but not evil. You wouldn't have hurt him."

Mercer glanced around the room. "You're a fool for holding my morality in such high regard." He scoffed at the insanity that was quickly overtaking the flat. "You're forced to act like my goddamn conscience ninety-nine percent of the time. What the hell would make you think that I would deem Benjamin Styler innocent and beyond the vengeance I could exact?"

"It's rather simple. If you wanted to kill Styler, you would have done it earlier today in his hospital room." Bastian returned the glare. "You pretend to live on the edge, but you don't. There are a hundred more painful and effective things you could have done to gain Styler's compliance, but you didn't. Instead, you gave him a little jab in the bandage and maybe tore a stitch or two. Big fucking deal." He returned Mercer's stare. "You didn't do any permanent damage to Welks either. And even after reaching some pretty insane conclusions concerning Carlton Rhoade's role in all of this, you have yet to bang down his door, shove your Sig in his face, and pull the bloody trigger. So don't play this game with me, Jules. Because I know you." Bastian let out a resounding, exasperated breath, and stormed into the kitchen, searching for something. "I need a bloody cigarette." Instead, he found a bag of pretzel sticks and a bottle of Irish whiskey.

"I promised Katia I would kill the person responsible for hurting Ben," Mercer admitted once Bastian downed the drink. "At the time, I didn't realize that person may be her father."

"You thought you needed this as much as she did. Maybe you both do, but we don't know for certain it's her father," Bastian replied, slightly calmer now. "From the information I've convinced the private eye to share, I believe that he is still holding back some vital information that will lead us to the actual guilty party. Yes, Carlton hired him to determine who was responsible for the extortion and to keep tabs on Katia and Benjamin, but something else is missing. Based on the facts, the most likely assumption is that the shooter is also receiving information from Welks, and that is the man that has threatened Welks' life and made an attempt on yours."

"How certain are you that a third party is involved?" Mercer asked, wondering if his tirade was completely pointless.

"I'd say it's a strong possibility. The only thing we know for certain is that the party responsible has access to the internal e-mail system at Rhoade's newspaper. It's how he contacted Welks for additional information on Styler. Until we know for certain who that person is, don't jump to any more conclusions. It makes you sound insane." He winked. "More so than usual, mate."

"My theory was based on your notes and intel."

"Which are still incomplete." Bastian rolled his eyes, seeing no point in continuing this argument. He knew Mercer was impatient and had a tendency to run into situations half-cocked when he thought time was of the essence. "Donovan is setting up a few meetings with our possible hitmen. Once we determine who took the shot, we'll find out who wanted the trigger pulled. It should clear this up efficiently and with minimal fallout." He assessed Mercer. "Are you able to hold it together if we have to talk to these contractors in a public setting? Or will that be a problem?"

"I can handle it."

"Even if one of them turns out to be the shooter or the kamikaze van driver?"

"Our mission is intelligence gathering." Mercer met his eyes, agreeing with Bastian's suggestion to wait for further information before acting. "I might not like it, but the contract killer has to lead us to the puppet master. But once we know for certain..." His voice trailed off.

"I know. With any luck, that detective friend of yours will provide a clean-up crew." Bastian headed toward the bedroom. "Like I said, stop pretending to toe the line because it's clear you aren't." And he shut the door.

NINETEEN

It was late, but the pounding in Mercer's skull wouldn't let him sleep. Tension headaches were never fun. And he had numerous reasons to be tense. As soon as Donovan returned with the list of potential shooters, additional meetings could be arranged with the most likely candidates, and if the shooter wasn't willing to divulge his client list, Mercer would force the point. He snorted. Maybe Bas was right, and he didn't have to resort to violence so swiftly. But they were running out of time. Someone tried to murder Mercer in the middle of one of the busiest streets in Chicago. That meant they were getting close, and someone was growing tired of the game.

Without making a conscious effort, Mercer left the flat and found himself outside Rhoade's apartment. He studied the building's security. Several surveillance cameras were posted on the building and in surrounding areas. The doorman was a basic deterrent, as were the armed rent-a-cops that were behind a desk in the lobby. That didn't include the man inside the elevator or the personal bodyguards that were probably permanent fixtures inside the penthouse apartment. That was a whole hell of a lot of security for a single threatening letter that was sent by someone with no intention of doing actual harm.

Perhaps Rhoade had other enemies. Surely, someone must have posed a danger at some point for this level of protection. Pulling away from the curb, Mercer drove back to the hotel they checked out of earlier in the day. Despite some reticence, he left the car with the valet and strolled down the street. There was nothing else to gain from the crime scene. He knew where the shooter had been and how he knew to wait for Katia and Ben. Too bad the man didn't leave his name and number at the mouth of the alley.

The same homeless man was in his usual spot. And Mercer approached, pulling a twenty from his pocket. The man smiled a filthy grin, eyeing the money. He held out his coffee can for Mercer to drop the cash inside, but Mercer shook his head.

"I'm sorry your entertainment hasn't been around lately," Mercer said, nodding across the street.

"I can find something else to keep my interest," the man replied, shaking the can. "How's about you help a guy out?"

"I need some information first." He studied the man, glad that the hobo's pants were fastened and secured around his waist. "Does a delivery truck usually park across the street near the alley?" Mercer pointed, indicated the place where a truck was currently parked.

"Yeah, it's there five nights a week. I've had to move before to get a better view of the show. It's a real pain in my ass. It's not like my house is on wheels, y'know."

"Do you remember seeing anyone else regularly watching the show? Maybe you recall someone following the couple to the alley."

The man thought about it, squinting through the darkness as he recollected. "I didn't see nothing." He shook the can vehemently, and Mercer grabbed it out of his hand. "Hey. That's mine. You can't just take my stuff."

"I don't believe you." Mercer pulled the can away before the man could grab it.

The homeless man clawed ineffectually at the air, wiggling his fingers in the direction of the coffee can. "Fine. There might have been a guy lingering for the last couple of weeks. His eyes were ice cold, and he freaked me out. He would watch from over there," he pointed to a nearby lamppost, "but didn't seem that interested." The hobo lunged for the can again, but Mercer stepped back. "Give me back my money."

Looking inside to see how much change was causing that infernal rattling, Mercer spotted a bullet casing among the rusty coins and other trinkets. Removing it, despite the loud protests, he dropped the twenty inside and shoved the can back at the man. "Thanks for the help."

"Fuck off, thief."

Mercer snorted and returned to the hotel. The police already identified the caliber and weapon, but for some reason, this insignificant metal object seemed to hold importance. Something was odd about it, but Mercer couldn't quite put his finger on it.

Handing the parking slip to the valet, he waited for his car to be brought around and climbed into the driver's seat. He pulled onto the main thoroughfare and immediately realized something was off.

"Do not turn around. Just drive," a deep, raspy voice commanded from the backseat before reaching around and removing the Sig from Mercer's hip. "This doesn't have to be unpleasant like your earlier encounter this afternoon. I just wanted the chance to talk to you in private."

"Did you bribe the valet?" Mercer asked, running through a risk assessment and his options.

"No. He didn't notice me. It's wonderful what can be accomplished using fold-down backseats." Cold, blue eyes stared at Mercer through the rearview mirror. "It's my turn to ask a question. Are you working for Carlton Rhoade?"

"Who?"

Traffic was light on account of the late hour, but Mercer drove at a snail's pace, wanting to find the perfect spot to dislodge the man, preferably through the windshield. He tightened his seatbelt and continued driving aimlessly.

"I'm not playing with you. Rhoade is a powerful man. He hires only the best, and from the rumblings I've heard, that might be you. But I don't want things to become more complicated than they already are. You've made a mess by allowing the police to become involved, and they're getting antsy. They are looking to make arrests. They are investigating. Neither of those things is acceptable."

"I concur," Mercer retorted, but the gun pressed into the back of his seat.

"Don't try anything. And don't expect me to believe that you aren't assisting the cops after you spent the day at the police station." Whoever this man was, he had been tracking Mercer's movements, monitoring the exchanges with Detective Rowlins, and might also be responsible for the attempted vehicular homicide earlier in the day.

"The bobbies arrested me. That's not my doing."

"Stop lying." The metal clicked as the gun was cocked. "Collect your fee and leave town. Or just leave town. I don't care. Your presence is no longer necessary. Do I make myself clear?"

"You seem to know precisely who I am, so why don't you tell me who you are?" Mercer's eyes barely shifted as he considered driving straight into one of the support pillars for the elevated railway tracks.

"I'm simply someone who has a job to do. A job not unlike yours, Julian Mercer."

"You were hired to execute the hit on Benjamin Styler." Mercer's eyes darted to the mirror, hoping to discover some identifying feature that wasn't obscured by the ski mask, but only the killer's eyes were visible. "Are you sure the same man didn't hire me to complete the job that you couldn't?" It was a lie, but only Bastian could read Mercer well enough to determine things like that. The man in the backseat snorted but otherwise remained silent. He wasn't gullible enough to believe that Julian had been contracted to complete the failed hit on Styler. "In that case, I assume you realize that puts us at odds with one another." Mercer shifted, turning just enough so if the man fired, the bullet would be less likely to rip through any vital organs. "If you tell me who hired you, I'll spare your life."

The contract killer laughed. "In case you haven't noticed, I'm the one holding you at gunpoint, so I'll take my chances." The man's eyes darted to Julian's and then back to the road, scanning for signs of danger or a trap. It was clear he suspected Mercer would try something.

Mercer produced a mirthless smile. "Suit yourself, but be aware that since you tried to kill Styler, I'm supposed to kill you." He chuckled. "And who's to say that someone else wasn't hired to eliminate me."

"That might be." The man shrugged, not taking the bait and confessing to being the van driver or knowing who was. "What exactly do you plan to do? I have no issue with you. As long as you stay out of my way and leave town, then there's no reason for us to face off."

"A friendly word of advice, don't make another move against Styler, or I'll be forced to act."

The man blinked, a slight grin tugging at the corners of his eyes. "It's a pity you refused to take my warning seriously. I hoped this would be a civil encounter."

Before the man could fire, Mercer accelerated. The increased speed knocked the gunman backward into the seat cushions, buying Julian a few precious seconds. Julian forced his taut muscles to relax as he drove straight into the center column. The crash reverberated in the small space. The airbag deployed, slamming into Mercer and knocking the wind from his lungs. The plastic burned against his skin, and talc irritated his eyes. The windshield shattered into glass pebbles, and the dashboard practically dropped out, exposing wires and jagged pieces of metal and plastic. The rear tires left the ground momentarily before crashing back onto the pavement with a jarring thud.

Squeezing his eyes shut a few times to clear his vision, Mercer shook his head, released the seatbelt, and turned to see the man crumpled in a heap between the armrest and the passenger's seat. Pain radiated up Mercer's left side and across his collarbone as he struggled to get the door open. Once he was free, he opened the back door, searching for his Sig. He could end this now.

The unidentified man was semiconscious in the front seat. Unfortunately, the crash didn't kill him, but a bullet in the back of the head surely would. The only hitch in that plan was Mercer still didn't know who wanted Styler dead, and eliminating one contract killer would do nothing more than buy some time while a second hit was ordered. The ex-SAS needed answers and a name, not a dead man that could tell no tales.

Clawing through the fragments of the shattered windshield, Julian located his weapon underneath one of the seats and pulled it free. He aimed, but the man remained motionless, sprawled between the front and back seats of the car. And in his current state, he didn't pose a danger, but he would in the future. As Mercer fought with his conscience, deciding what to do with the disabled vehicle and the semiconscious man, flashing lights approached from the distance.

Coming to a decision to avoid another run-in with the local police force, Mercer decided to let the cops handle the situation. "Good luck," Mercer spat, slamming the door and disappearing into the night. If everything worked out like it should, the man would be arrested, and the police would convince him to give up his employer. This might all be over by the morning.

Mercer headed for the closest subway platform. While he waited for the next train, he stowed his gun and caught sight of his reflection in the window. His face was severely bruised, and a cut ran horizontally from his brow past his temple. There was also a good chance his arm was broken or dislocated based on the pain and the way it hung from his side.

Compartmentalizing his injuries, he boarded the train, avoiding the looks from the few people who were on their way home from working a late shift or leaving the bars and clubs. Thankfully, no one approached. Finally, he had some peace and quiet.

When he returned to the flat, he let himself in. Donovan was back from his outing, spreading a stack of glossies across the kitchen table. He was scribbling each contract killer's information on sticky notes and attaching them to the photos. At the sound of Mercer's footsteps, he looked up.

"Should I ask?"

"No," Mercer winced and slumped into the chair, "but I wouldn't object to a first aid kit."

While Donovan retrieved the supplies, Mercer skimmed through the photos, narrowing down the list based on the few features his unwelcome passenger exhibited. Three possibilities remained on the table. After Donovan returned, Mercer slipped out of his shirt and assessed his arm.

"It looks to be dislocated," Donovan said. "Shall I?" Mercer nodded and bit back his scream when Donovan pulled and twisted, popping the shoulder joint back into place. At least it was better than a break. "How'd it happen?"

"I thought you weren't asking." Mercer tapped the photo nearest to him. "Tell me about this one," he commanded, getting up to wash his face and hands in the sink before applying the antiseptic and bandages.

"What happened to the rest of them?"

"I've encountered our competition. Based on build and eye color, it's one of these three bastards." He grabbed the whiskey, downing a few mouthfuls to dull the throbbing in his head and arm. "Now tell me about him."

"Edward Duchamp, discharged U.S. Marine Corps sniper, worked for a few private military black ops groups, suspected of arms dealing and drug smuggling. When he became too questionable for even the paramilitary chaps to deal with, he became a gun for hire. His weapon of choice is still a long-range sniper rifle, but he's tested proficient on handguns and assault rifles."

"Is he connected to Rhoade's newspaper? How does he collect payment and find his clients?" Mercer used the stainless steel toaster as a mirror, plucking the glass fragments from his brow and temple with a pair of sterilized tweezers.

"I haven't found anything to link him to Rhoade. Duchamp's known for doing some contract work for the mafia. He finds his clients through referrals and meets with them at a small downtown bar. Payment is in cash and deals are brokered face-to-face."

"Next," Mercer said, pointing to the second man in the group.

"Jesus Reyes, Spanish bloke, relocated to the States within the past five years."

Mercer held up his hand. "Does he have an accent?"

"Of course, he has an accent, Tex," Donovan replied, attempting a pathetic American accent of his own. "All those Europeans do."

"It's not him. I would have remembered a Spaniard with ice blue eyes. The shooter has a general American accent." He dropped a few glass shards on top of the discarded candidate's photo. "Who's left?"

"Isaac Armann. Classified background. Bastian's still digging up some clues to piece together his past."

"And how does he get hired?"

"Asking around in the right neighborhood results in a phone number. Place a call, arrange a wire transfer, no questions asked." Donovan studied Julian. "From what I can tell, he has an office in the back room of some dive. He's also the only man that refused to take a meeting with me. Shall I inquire further?"

"No." Mercer removed the final piece of glass from his cheek and put the bloodied tweezers down. "It's him."

"How can you be sure?"

"Call it a hunch, but the man in the back of my car wasn't regular military. He was a spook. And that eliminates Duchamp." Mercer flicked the edge of Armann's photo. "And he has a classified background." He met Donovan's gaze. "Phone the precinct and find out what you can about the accident involving our sedan that took place about an hour ago. Find out if anyone was arrested or brought to the hospital." Rummaging through his pocket, he removed the bullet casing and put it on the table. "I'm guessing that belongs to Armann. He might have taken a few practice shots before he fired on Styler."

"Silver, dented," Donovan lifted it, twirling it in his fingers and studying the etchings and marks, "looks like he made it himself, based on the impression from a vise grip. He probably manufactures his own ammunition to keep off the radar." At Donovan's words, Mercer smiled, realizing that was the oddity he couldn't place, and continued toward the door, grabbing a set of keys for one of the other vehicles. "Where are you going?" Donovan asked.

"To protect Styler. If Armann's out of the picture, someone else will eventually try to make a move, especially since three men were following the couple the night of the shooting." Mercer chuckled. "The game is afoot."

"Oh, bloody hell," Bastian growled, emerging from the hallway, "as if James Bond wasn't bad enough, now you think you're Sherlock Holmes."

Condemned

TWENTY

Mercer was sitting in the chair next to Benjamin Styler's bed when morning came. Styler opened his eyes, squinting against the bright glare from the sunlight, and let out a surprised gasp. Mercer nodded but remained silent; he had been dozing for the last few hours, not quite asleep but not fully awake either.

"What happened to you?" Styler asked, still wary of Mercer. "Did the police do that? I've read tons of stories on brutality, but I've never witnessed it firsthand until yesterday."

"The man who plans to kill you did this." There was no reason to sugarcoat.

"What happened to him? Do you know who he is? Where he went? What he wants? Have you notified the authorities? Is that why you're here? Why did they let you in my room? You attacked me."

"Silence." Mercer's arm was throbbing, and the last thing he wanted was to deal with some panicked rich kid. Or faux rich kid. Whatever Styler was. "It is being resolved, and I will make sure that a second attempt also fails."

"Second attempt?" Styler paled. "Why can't you stop this before there is a second attempt?" He launched into more rapid-fire questioning, and Mercer clapped a hand over Styler's mouth.

"Silence." He searched Styler's eyes for acquiescence and saw fear. The kid was scared. Too bad he wasn't more afraid of the man trying to kill him and less afraid of Mercer. "Remain quiet and only speak when I ask a question. Do you understand?" Styler nodded, and Mercer removed his hand. "Did you send the photos of Katia to her father?"

"Yes." Styler looked ready to launch into some excuse but clamped his mouth shut.

"Carlton knows. He does not enjoy being threatened. It appears he hired a private investigator to get to the bottom of it, and someone is using the information gained by said investigator to tail your movements and eliminate you. Do you think that Carlton Rhoade is capable of such action?" Mercer still didn't know who hired Armann, and despite the unlikelihood, it never hurt to ask.

"No. Mr. Rhoade wouldn't do something like that. Yes, I sent the photos, but I needed the cash to pay off my investors. Kat wanted to give it to me, but I didn't want her to think I was just some mooch."

"So you stole from her father instead?"

"No. I..." He looked away. "It's not that simple."

"Does Katia know?"

"No."

"You should tell her," Mercer said resolutely, easing back into the chair. "You should also ring for the nurse and ask for something to relieve your headache."

"But I don't have a headache."

Mercer rolled his eyes. "You're giving me one."

Talking to Styler proved to be too much effort and far too frustrating for Mercer to handle at the present, so instead, he remained in the chair, letting the acetaminophen he confiscated dull some of the achiness. He would have preferred a fifth of scotch, but he was working and needed to be alert.

Donovan had yet to phone with the information on the accident, and Mercer contemplated calling Rowlins directly. However, if whoever hired Armann had clout with the local bobbies, then Mercer didn't want to tip them off on his progress. Frankly, after the attempt on his life yesterday afternoon, he suspected members of the police department might be working with Armann and his crew. And he didn't want to take any additional risks with Ben's safety or his own.

"What a fucking mess," Mercer mumbled to himself, cautioning a glance at Styler who was playing some game on a tablet that Katia brought him. Luckily, the other man was too preoccupied smashing candy or launching birds at things to notice anything was wrong. Mercer shut his eyes, hoping to sneak in a few moments of sleep.

"How dare you?" Katia's voice rang out as she threw open the hospital door.

"Babe," Styler began, but her anger was focused on Julian.

"You could have done some serious damage yesterday, and then you have the nerve to show up here today and sit in that chair like nothing happened. What the hell is the matter with you?"

Mercer gave her a bored look, spotting Bastian behind her. Bastian shut the door and leaned against it, hoping her outburst didn't attract the attention of the hospital's security personnel. She paced, steam practically billowing out of her ears. The longer Mercer remained silent, the angrier she became.

"Jules," Bastian said, drawing the attention of everyone inside the room, "I believe it's time we discuss our findings with the aggrieved."

"Very well." Mercer tossed a quick look to Styler, but Ben didn't say a word. "Ms. Rhoade, your fiancé sent threatening photographs to your father, who in turn hired an investigator to get to the root of the problem. Said investigator is currently in fear of his life, and as of yet, we have not identified who else has hired him to investigate Mr. Styler. While unlikely, we have not entirely ruled out the possibility that the shooting was orchestrated by your father, so please, prepare yourself for that possibility."

"What?" She slumped onto the edge of the bed. "But why?" She turned to face Styler, and Mercer crossed the room to take up a spot next to Bastian. "He's lying, right? Ben, say he's lying."

"Honey, I'm so sorry. I didn't threaten you. Not really. I sent your dad a photo of you when you were asleep. That was it." She remained motionless. "I needed the money."

"I would have given it to you," she snarled. "I offered. You're such a jackass." Styler reached for her, but she batted his hand away. "Don't you fucking touch me."

"But, sweetheart," Styler begged, "I didn't want us to start our lives together with something like money hanging over our heads."

"Oh, so you thought it'd be better to blackmail my father?" She slapped him across the face. "Screw you, Ben." She spun, prepared to flee, only to find Bastian and Mercer blocking her path. "Get out of my way."

"No." Mercer studied her. "I'm not finished yet. Do you know Isaac Armann?"

"No, now move."

"Someone hired him to kill Ben. And apparently,

since my mates and I were getting a bit too close, Armann was instructed to remove us from the situation as well." Mercer looked to Bastian for reinforcement on this theory, and Bastian nodded, having uncovered enough of Armann's history to positively identify him as the contract killer. "So now that my head is also on the chopping block, we need to discuss what shall be done to remedy this situation."

"Get out of my way. I don't care what happens to you or Ben," Katia hissed, hurt and angry.

"You don't mean that," Bastian said, interjecting before Styler or Mercer could say something that would piss the poor woman off more than she already was. "You love him," he jerked his chin toward Styler, "even if he made a mistake. And I'm sure you love your father too. This seems like a family situation that has gotten out of control. Wouldn't you agree, love?" he asked in that calming, soft lilt that tended to gain compliance from his listener.

She let out a harsh breath. "So what do you propose we do?"

"First, I think you should have a talk with your father, so we can completely rule him out as contracting the hit," Bastian said. "And if he did, then he needs to call it off." He shifted his focus to Mercer. "We were unable to locate Armann after last night's accident. When the police arrived, he wasn't in the vehicle or seen fleeing the scene."

"Accident?" Katia asked, noticing the condition Mercer was in for the first time. "Are you okay?"

"Just ducky," Mercer snapped.

"Why would you think my father hired a hitman? Let alone, where would he even find one?" Katia asked. "I'm sorry, but I don't buy it." She swiveled to face Styler. "And oh my god, how the hell could you have sent photos to my father? I'm surprised you didn't tape us having sex and sell that on the internet while you were at it." She seemed more interested in berating her idiotic fiancé than finding the person responsible for nearly killing him.

Mercer couldn't stand the prima donna attitude anymore. "Ms. Rhoade, shut up. I'm tired of the drama, the whining, and the bitching. You are an adult, so start acting like it." His tone immediately silenced Katia. "We're going to have a grown-up discussion, and when we are finished, we shall devise an exit strategy. Then you will call your father. Is that clear?"

"Yes," she said, finally acknowledging that she needed to get her priorities straight.

"Brilliant," Bastian sighed, "shall I begin?"

TWENTY-ONE

Isaac Armann had fled the scene of the accident. Mercer wasn't sure how the semiconscious man managed to crawl out of the rubble of the totaled car, but according to the police accounts, no one was present at the scene. The only signs that anyone had even been inside the vehicle were the blood smears that covered the deployed airbag and a few droplets on the passenger's side floor mat.

Armann was a pro and a local. He knew the ins and outs of the city better than the ex-SAS. He probably had connections or contacts that could assist in his disappearance, maybe even some of his friends were men who possessed badges and guns.

Despite Bastian's insistence that Detective Rowlins was not in on some grand conspiracy, Mercer was still having issues accepting this fact as the truth. He was certain someone at the precinct was assisting Armann or the kamikaze van driver, who were likely working together if the two were not, in fact, one and the same. The events from the last two days were too well-timed to be purely coincidental.

The more important question worthy of contemplation was who was in a position to come across someone of Armann's specific skill set and possessed the means to hire him and his two unnamed associates to eliminate Benjamin Styler. Mercer was willing to blame every rich son of a bitch they encountered in Chicago as the culprit. That left Jack Pierce and Carlton Rhoade at the top of the short list, while Bastian continued to delve into Katia's background for jilted lovers or potential stalkers.

Fortunately, Katia provided some useful assistance concerning her father's potential involvement. Finally dropping the entitled air that she had exuded since their first encounter, she spoke of an article her father had researched early in his career on organized crime and contract killers. By this point, the article was somewhat dated, but it named a few undisclosed sources and served as an exposé enumerating the benefits and detriments of an underground criminal element functioning within the established system of law and order. It sounded like rubbish, but it might have been a glimpse into Carlton's questionable connections.

Bastian had spent an entire evening analyzing Carlton's spending habits and routine, hoping to find a blip in the normal pattern. The only thing that came close to pinging as suspicious was the purchase of a cappuccino from a coffee cart across town from Carlton's typical haunts. It wasn't en route to any of the other locations that he normally frequented, and from what Bastian determined, there was no reason for Rhoade to venture into that sketchy part of town.

"I tried to check through nearby footage to figure out how Armann disappeared, but the city's DOT camera grid hasn't been cooperating with my latest infiltration attempts," Bastian muttered. Despite the fact he had hacked into the servers before, security had been upgraded, and it was a safe bet to assume it was because of his earlier breach. "We might have to share this information with Rowlins."

"He won't be able to do anything. We don't exactly have evidence. It's not like Armann is in custody," Mercer spat, still on the fence over not putting a bullet into the man when he had the chance. Now Armann was in the wind, and he knew Julian would pose a problem. The matter just became exponentially more dangerous, and for once, this didn't seem like a good thing. "We'll have to find another way to determine who wants Styler dead since our previous plan to obtain this information from the hired gun has gone awry."

"I can just ask my dad," Katia said. She met Mercer's eyes. "You can't really believe he's to blame for this. Why wouldn't he just tell me what Ben did instead of hiring someone to kill him?"

"We don't believe your father's responsible," Bastian interjected. "The issue isn't necessarily with your father. It's with determining who else would have known he hired a private investigator to look into the matter. John Welks is the P.I. your father hired. Do you have any idea who might have been aware of this?"

"Maybe his friends at the paper," Katia suggested. "Dad tends to relegate a lot of the workload. I'm sure his assistants must have scheduled meetings or made phone calls on his behalf. They might have even taken a message or cut a check for Mr. Welks' invoice."

"It's still the paper," Mercer mumbled, recalling Welks' insistence that the anonymous e-mail had been sent internally.

"I don't understand what's going on. What does

Ben's asinine behavior have to do with what happened the other night in the alley?" Katia asked.

"Based upon everything we know, it stands to reason that whoever wants Mr. Styler dead is well-off and powerful, and given the planning and trajectory that were necessary to make that shot, we are also working under the assumption that the party responsible stipulated that your safety must never be jeopardized." Bastian pressed his lips together, unsure how much more he should say. "And lastly, the person responsible used the internal e-mail system at your father's paper to request this information from Mr. Welks anonymously."

Mercer let out an exhale and closed his eyes. This was the first time he'd heard the facts laid out so clearly. Either he'd been too preoccupied to notice before, or his team had pieced together a lot of the puzzle while he was crashing cars and babysitting Styler.

"Jules?" Bastian asked, his voice cutting through the monotony. "Are you all right?"

That was the real question, wasn't it? Mercer opened his eyes and stared at his friend. Truthfully, he wasn't, and he hadn't been for a long time. Somehow, working kidnappings didn't take this toll. It let whatever malady that was eating away at his soul continue to fester unnoticed, but this was different. This was a contracted killing. Or maybe two since Julian had agreed to exact revenge on Katia's behalf. The questions spun through his mind, unraveling bits of his sanity and unleashing a hell that he couldn't even begin to control. His vision began to blur, and everything started to dim.

"Jules?" Bastian asked again as Mercer's legs turned to gelatin. "Shit."

Consciousness seemed to escape Mercer's grasp

momentarily as he slumped to the floor in the midst of the discussion. At least a hospital seemed like the appropriate place to have this type of reaction. Bastian knelt next to him, automatically checking his pulse.

"Love, get a doctor," Bastian instructed, turning to Katia.

"I'm fine," Mercer hissed, shaking away the pain and darkness. "I just got a little lightheaded. It's nothing." Bastian continued to give him that annoying, worried look. "Wipe that bloody expression off your face, Clarke, and help me up." It was rare that Mercer referred to his second-in-command by his last name, and Bastian knew better than to argue. He hoisted Mercer to his feet but looked pointedly at the vacant chair which Julian ignored. "Let's have a discussion with that private eye before we bring any of this to Mr. Rhoade's attention." There was too much for Julian to wrap his mind around, and with Armann on the loose, the next threat could be imminent. His focus shifted to Katia and Ben. "The two of you should hash things out. Donovan or Hans will monitor the situation, but I'd suggest you don't leave this room. Do you understand?" It wasn't a suggestion, and Katia silently agreed.

"But I'm supposed to be discharged today," Ben replied. Mercer gave him a hard stare, and Ben shrunk back, correcting his earlier declaration by adding, "Maybe they need to run some more tests. I'm really not feeling very well."

"That makes two of us," Mercer muttered.

"Stay put," Bastian urged, following Mercer from the room. Once the door was shut, he passed the orders on to Hans who was stationed outside in his usual spot and then rushed to catch up to Julian who was already halfway out the door. "Would you stop for one moment?"

"Staying still is what led to that episode. So we're on the move since I don't have time for this."

"Staying still has nothing to do with it," Bastian shot back. "You were in a car accident. And that episode was probably the result of a concussion. At least that's what happens to normal human beings, the ones without such hard heads." He snatched the car keys from Mercer's grip. "And just so we're clear, there isn't a chance in hell I'm letting you drive."

"It wasn't an accident."

"I know it wasn't an accident, but–"

"Bollocks." Mercer's mind was somewhere else. "Running into Welks outside of Rhoade's flat wasn't an accident. He was waiting, just like Armann was waiting inside the vehicle last night." He turned to Bastian. "We're being played, and I'm not positive who's pulling the strings. We need to start over from the beginning." Mercer's mind drifted to Welks, then the attempt made on his life outside the police station, and lastly to the unfortunate meeting with Armann. "This is too simple. One thing inevitably led to another. First, we get Welks, who tells us Ben was blackmailing Carlton, and then Armann shows up to warn us off. It's too easy. Someone else is calling the shots and playing us for fools, hoping we'll blame Carlton Rhoade for this predicament." He glanced at Bastian. "Which, admittedly, I almost did."

"You're daft." Bastian climbed behind the wheel and turned in his seat, checking the back for any unwanted guests. "Everything isn't some grand conspiracy."

"Actually, I'm certain this time it is."

"You're always certain it is. You've been certain it is since..." Bastian faltered.

"Michelle," Mercer swallowed, completing the

sentence. "I'm not wrong. Stop treating me like an imbecile or a loon. I'm neither."

"So now you just happen to have some bloody brilliant skills of deduction?"

"Bas, you're the best intelligence analyst I've ever known. Look at this objectively, like you would a mission. Do you believe the intel is sound?"

"What we've determined on our own is sound."

"And what about everything else?"

Bastian ran a hand down his face then switched lanes and altered course. Originally, he planned to take Mercer back to the flat for a rest, but logic dictated that they reevaluate the intricacies of these new developments with a wary eye. "Unfortunately, I believe you might be correct."

"Unfortunately?" Mercer asked.

"Yes. Which means the poor bloke we have tied up will probably remain in that chair for the next few days, despite the promised early release I hoped to grant him."

"Pity."

"And for the record, I never thought Rhoade was responsible. You're the one accusing him of wanting to murder his future son-in-law."

"Well, that I believe is still true. The only aspect up for debate is whether or not he would actually follow through fulfilling that desire."

Bastian rolled his eyes, and Mercer settled further into the seat, hoping for a few minutes of shut-eye before conducting the interrogation.

TWENTY-TWO

Mercer found another chair and dragged it into the room they were using as a makeshift prison. He sat, afraid that another dizzy spell would show weakness in front of their captive. Welks was only in slightly better shape than he had been the last time Mercer saw him. Crossing his arms in front of his chest, Julian waited, hoping Welks would voluntarily spill his guts in order to avoid more violence.

"I don't know who would want to frame Carlton Rhoade or how anyone could know who you are or where you would be. I told you everything I know," Welks insisted.

"You haven't, and you probably won't. Frankly, I could use some peace and quiet, so if you aren't going to say anything useful, don't speak."

This was a different approach from what Welks had already been subjected to, and he seemed uneasy with this new caveat. He remained silent for a little over a minute, studying Mercer. The office door was open, but Bastian remained out of sight.

"Where are we?" Welks asked, leaning as far to the side as the duct tape would allow so he could peer out the door.

"Shh." Mercer flicked his gaze to Welks and then closed his eyes again. Humans were a social species, and lack of communication would loosen his captive's tongue.

The silence lasted for another couple of minutes before Welks' chair squeaked. "Come on, man, let me go. It's just the two of us. I won't say a word."

"Tell me who hired you."

"I work for Piper Investigations, and they assigned me to assist Carlton Rhoade at the paper."

"And who told you to wait outside Rhoade's apartment building with your camera?"

Welks gulped but didn't speak. The silence returned, and this time, it was deafening. Welks fidgeted, shifting in his seat and contemplating his chances of escape or maybe survival. With freedom less than ten feet away, his resolve to stave off answering Mercer's questions was fading quickly. Freedom was the one thing Welks wanted, and leaving the door open had whet his appetite.

"If I say any more, I could be next. He'll have me killed."

"Who is he?" Mercer asked, intrigue playing across his face. Welks considered his options, but he was doing it too slowly for his interrogator's liking. "Are you afraid of Carlton Rhoade? Because I find it improbable that Mr. Rhoade would hire anyone to photograph his daughter. After all, didn't this start with a few questionable photos?" Something passed across Welks' face that could only be described as 'oh shit', and Mercer smiled. "So this started before the photographs. Something else happened that forced Rhoade to hire an investigator. What was it? When did it happen?"

"Carlton Rhoade is a powerful businessman. I'm sure plenty of things happen that would require a trained investigator. And like I've mentioned, I work for Rhoade's newspaper. I've been on his payroll for years. There's nothing sinister about that. I'm not involved in any of this. I don't know anything. Please, just let me go."

Mercer smiled. Even though Welks never said anything specific, one could make certain assumptions based upon the information. Perhaps it wasn't the most reasonable interrogation technique, but it might just reap some rewards.

"So someone must have approached you because of your connection to Rhoade's newspaper," Mercer mused and rubbed his chin, watching as Welks' eyes grew wide. "Who wanted information on Carlton Rhoade and his personal life and business?"

Desperate to be set free, Welks said the first thing that came to mind. "It was...um...Styler who asked me to keep tabs on Rhoade. That's all I know, so let me go."

Mercer laughed. "You're a terrible liar. I wasn't born yesterday. There isn't a chance in hell you'd be afraid of Benjamin Styler." He narrowed his eyes. "But Styler has enemies. He owed debts until that blackmail scheme got him back in the black." Mercer chuckled at the play on words. "And whoever's paying you under the table has deep pockets. He's untouchable. Am I right?"

"Please, let me go. I don't know who he is. The only thing I know is he's dangerous. I was contacted and paid anonymously. Your partner said I could go as soon as this was cleared up. I've told you all I can."

"What happens when your benefactor goes looking for you and doesn't find you? Do you care about nothing more than your own meaningless life? What about your wife? If this man is as dangerous as you claim, he will stop at nothing to find you and silence you. But if you're forthcoming with me, my friends will make arrangements to keep you safe."

Welks laughed. "Now who's a pitiful liar?" He rolled his eyes. "You'll either let me go or you'll kill me. There's no fucking way someone like you would help me. I'll take my chances."

"That's not all I can do." Mercer stood, towering over Welks. "Look at me." The other man resisted, and Mercer grabbed his hair and yanked, jerking his chin up. "I've already encountered Isaac Armann, so your usefulness is dwindling by the second. When time is up, we'll clear out. We don't have to release you. It takes days for a man to starve. But the dehydration will set in first, causing muscle cramps, delusions, and insanity. It's a horrible way to go. But maybe if you're lucky, the stink from your decomposing corpse will lead the police here before the rats and maggots completely dismantle your flesh. Think about it." He dragged the empty chair out of the room, slamming the door.

"Rats and maggots, really?" Bastian asked, cocking an eyebrow. "Was he quaking in fear or fits of giggles?"

"He wants to leave, but he refuses to help himself. You suggested I don't resort to violence, so what was I supposed to say?"

"I'll give it a go." Bastian picked up a file and went to the door. "I have some information on his personal life, his spending habits, and a few tidbits on his wife. Maybe he isn't as cowardly as you believe."

"I doubt it."

"Honey attracts more flies, Jules."

Bastian opened the door and went inside the room.

His voice was calm, almost friendly, as he began discussing every aspect of the man's work and personal life that they had uncovered as if he were reading a child's fairytale. Once it was obvious they had gotten John Welks' full and undivided attention, Bas approached the subject of Isaac Armann. This was a different angle than asking who hired Welks, and with any luck, the P.I. wouldn't have an issue discussing the key facts he knew about Armann. Hopefully, they'd discover who hired Armann and the identities of the two men that accompanied him into the alley. This was their best bet, and if this failed, they'd have no choice but to question Carlton Rhoade again since they were running out of suspects fast.

"Is it true?" Welks asked. Armann was the final name mentioned before Julian left their captive to contemplate his uncertain future. And now that Bastian was breaching the same subject, Welks was becoming increasingly uneasy. "Is Armann here?"

"Why? Does that worry you?" Bastian asked.

"It should worry everyone. Do you have any idea who Isaac Armann is or what he's capable of doing?"

"Why don't you enlighten me?"

"He's a cleaner. He makes problems disappear, and they never come back. There was an article about men like him a few years ago in one of the papers."

"Rhoade's paper?" Bastian asked, playing dumb.

"It was before Rhoade had a paper. But Isaac Armann was an unidentified source for the article. At least that was the rumor floating around the precinct. He was the only one with cojones big enough to confess to his crimes and career without fear of repercussions. He's one sinister badass, and he isn't afraid of anyone squealing on him."

"I take it his reputation precedes him," Bastian said, and Welks nodded. "And you discovered that he was hired to conduct the hit on Benjamin Styler. Which means whoever wants Styler dead wants it done right and with no fallout. Do you have any evidence that might point us to the man who hired Armann?"

"No."

"But the same person who hired Armann needed you for something. What was it?"

"Just some basic information concerning Carlton's interest in Styler. Nothing heinous. At least, that's what I thought at the time," Welks admitted.

"Who asked you for this information?"

"I can't tell you." Welks looked grim. "I'm not saying this is the case, but if this alleged client of mine can afford to hire the best mercenary in town, do you honestly believe he would even bother to blink before extinguishing me if he thought I posed a danger to him?"

"You really don't know who he is, do you?" Bastian asked.

"It was in my best interest not to find out." Welks bit his lip and stared at the floor. The only thing the P.I. knew for certain was that he should fear this unknown man.

"Aww, bloody hell. We're gonna have to do this the hard way."

TWENTY-THREE

"It would have been faster to beat the answers out of him," Mercer muttered as he tore through John Welks' home office.

"Bugger," Bastian hissed, still attempting to access Welks' computer. Each individual file was password protected, and John Welks had different passwords for everything. "He must have a list written down somewhere."

"Like I said, we should persuade him to give us the information instead." Mercer's head was still throbbing, and he rubbed his face, wincing when his hand came into contact with his battered temple and cheek.

"Shut your mouth." Bastian was frustrated as well. "I'd like to believe you wouldn't actually beat a man into a bloody pulp for no good reason. And I'm assuming what John said is true. He's being paid, but more than likely, it's been anonymous. As soon as I can get into these bloody files, I might be able to trace the source of the communications back to the puppet master."

"Just because Welks doesn't know his client's identity, that doesn't mean there will be an electronic trail for you to trace. Don't you think that this twisted genius would be smarter than that?" Mercer asked. They'd been arguing ever since the break-in. "Welks is a bloody P.I., so whoever contacted him would have been careful enough to avoid detection."

"There's only one way to know for certain. And once we finish here, we'll have to devise a method of getting into his office at the investigation firm." Bastian glanced at the clock, aware that Teresa Welks would be at work until six, so they didn't have much time. "Check for hiding places, removable walls, false bottoms, that sort of thing."

"Bastian, I know what I'm doing."

"Well, after that hit to your head, I wasn't sure your brain was still capable of functioning." It was obvious from Mercer's earlier wooziness that he had a slight concussion, not enough to stop him, but a traumatic brain injury, even slight, was still a traumatic brain injury. Or at least that's how medical professionals regarded all concussions. "Now stop distracting me," Bastian snapped.

Mercer left the office and went into the bedroom, searched the closets, and then dumped the contents of the dresser into the floor. He searched through the scattered clothing, the few satchels that contained jewelry and other expensive possessions, and ran his hands along the bottoms of the drawers and the frame of the furniture. Either John Welks was brilliant at hiding things, or there was nothing to be found.

Repeating the process in the living room, he tore through the furniture, finally coming across an envelope taped underneath the sofa. Inside was nothing more than a bank account number and transaction sheet. That was a strange place to file financial information, and Mercer tucked the envelope into his back pocket and continued searching for something damning.

Going from room to room, Mercer ripped the entire house apart. There would be no way of concealing the intrusion. They didn't have the time to be methodical and neat, so instead, he wanted it to look like a home invasion. And by the time he was finished, not a single drawer or closet was left intact. Inside the linen closet, Mercer discovered a camera bag containing a few rolls of film and multiple memory cards. After a final perusal of the remaining rooms, he went back to the office to see how much progress Bastian had made.

"I've copied the files. Nothing was seriously encrypted, and after I found the password list, it didn't take long. From what I can tell, not much is relevant to the Rhoades or Benjamin Styler, but I copied everything just in case. Should we clean up?" Bastian inquired, but instead of responding, Mercer simply grabbed the computer monitor and slammed it into the floor. "I'll take that as a no."

"We need to get out of here and check his office at Piper Investigations before Teresa arrives home and reports the intrusion to the police." Mercer glanced at his watch. "We're on a time crunch."

"Well, it's a good thing I found this." Bastian held up John Welks' I.D. card. "It has an access strip, so with a little snip and some paste, I should be able to get in and out without anyone questioning me."

"Let's get to it," Mercer ordered, leading the way to the door. "Worst case, you could ask Gladys for a favor."

Bastian diverted to an office supply store, removed one of his numerous falsified identities, and while Julian kept watch, his second-in-command found an

X-Acto knife, cut out Welks' photo, pasted his own on top, and laminated the entire item at one of the self-serve kiosks. Back in the vehicle, the pair continued to Piper Investigations.

"I'll just be a minute," Bastian said, stopping Julian before he could make it out the door. "With the way you look, mate, I don't think it'd be wise for both of us to go in together. They are investigators, and your appearance might ping something in their clue savvy brains."

Mercer let out a growl but remained in the vehicle, watching as Bastian went to the trunk, pulled out a suit jacket and a pair of glasses, ran a hand through his hair, and darted inside. It wasn't much of a disguise, but if Bas wanted to perfect geek chic, he was doing a damn fine job. Beginning a countdown, if Bas wasn't out in the next ten minutes, Mercer would go in.

Bastian went through the front door and headed for the elevators at the back of the lobby. The receptionist paid no attention to him, and he cautioned a quick glance at the directory on the wall while he waited for the elevator. *Welks, John – Office #502*, he read. Taking the elevator up to level five, he ducked his head down, keeping his face obscured from the security camera. When the doors opened on the proper level, he stepped out and almost collided with a man who was getting on the elevator.

"Pardon," Bastian muttered, sidestepping.

"Sorry," the man responded automatically. At least he didn't seem very interested in Bastian.

Turning right, Bastian went halfway down the hall before he realized he was moving in the wrong direction. Turning, he headed back the way he came, hoping that the people inside the two offices he passed wouldn't take notice. He should have performed a more thorough exam of the building's layout before attempting this feat, but he had only examined the security measures and weaknesses, not the arrangement of the office numbers.

Despite his best efforts, he had been unable to break into the majority of the server data from off-site because his attempt to plant a trojan on his earlier trip failed due to Gladys, the overly friendly receptionist, returning to her station far too quickly for his liking. So now Bastian would have to break into Welks' office and personal computer the old-fashioned way. Hopefully, that password list he found printed and taped to the bottom of the locked desk drawer would serve a purpose here as well.

Swiping the card through the reader, he stepped into the small office, flipped the blinds closed, and set to work behind the computer. As he waited for the ancient, decade old contraption to boot-up, he opened the desk drawers, rifled through the contents, and set to work picking the locks on the nearby filing cabinet. After the resounding startup ding, he logged into the network using Welks' password and plugged in his flash drive in order for the brilliant computer worm he created to infiltrate the network. As it began copying and downloading the relevant files and metadata, Bastian returned to the filing cabinet, removing numerous folders that pertained to Carlton Rhoade. He didn't locate anything labeled Katia or Ben, but he was having trouble believing that Welks had clients named John and Jane Doe. Grabbing everything that was suspicious, he dropped them on the desk and flipped through the files.

Skimming the pages led to unrelated cases and clients. He replaced a stack of useless files and narrowed the remaining pile down to information that dealt with Carlton Rhoade and the newspaper.

Returning to the computer, he checked the progress. Forty-two percent and counting. Bastian searched the rest of the office, but there was nothing else to find. Taking a seat behind the computer, he gave the screen another glance. Fifty-seven percent.

"C'mon, love, hurry up," he purred. Just then, he heard voices in the hallway and approaching footsteps. "Bugger." It was stupid to assume they were coming to check Welks' office, but just in case, Bastian considered his options. He could either duck under the desk and hope they didn't notice or he could remain working and insist he was tech support.

The footsteps stopped, and he waited. The office door was locked, and unless they were from building security or maintenance, then no one should be able to get in, right? Shutting his eyes, he took a breath and recalled the data on the security system. The codes were different for each office, so he should be safe.

The conversation continued just feet away, and Bastian could hear muffled words about Welks' disappearance. Did his absence prompt some curious co-workers to check for a clue as to Welks' whereabouts inside the office? Shit.

Bas tapped his fingers lightly against the desk, willing the computer to work faster. As soon as it hit the hundred percent mark, he removed the drive and powered down the computer. He had what he came for, but there was a new chink in the plan. He had no way out. Collecting the folders and placing the drive in his pocket, he took a deep breath and silently approached the only exit.

Bastian cracked the door open a smidge and peered into the hallway. One woman and two men stood about ten feet from the doorway, directly between the office and the elevator. There would be no slipping past undetected. Just as he was about to send a text to

Mercer to provide a distraction, the commander emerged from the stairwell at the far end of the corridor.

"Where the bloody hell is he?" Mercer yelled, storming down the hallway and rattling the first office door he spotted. "I want answers. And I want them now."

The raucous caused the group assembled to abandon their position in the hallway, and Bastian waited a few beats before he exited Welks' office, pulling the door shut behind him. Mercer spotted Bastian and gave an almost imperceptible nod.

"What's the matter, sir?" one of the men asked while the woman phoned for security or perhaps the police.

"I hired you jerks to find out who's been screwing my wife, and you still don't have a name. I want to know who he is. Did he pay you to protect him?"

"Sir, I'm sure we can get this straightened out. Please, calm down. What's your name? Who was working on your case?"

Apparently, situations like this arise often enough, and as soon as the elevator car arrived, Bastian stepped to the side, allowing the security personnel to get off the lift. They were heading for Mercer, and Bas wasn't sure how this would play out. He stepped inside the elevator, pressed the lobby button, and then put his arm against the door just as it was about to close.

Leaning into the hallway, Bas took a breath. "False alarm. Sorry for the inconvenience. There's no need for security. I have the paperwork on your case right here, Mr. Jones," Bas said, doing his best American accent. "Why don't we go downstairs and discuss this like civilized human beings?"

"Sorry for the commotion." Mercer nodded curtly

to the gathering group and headed toward the lift. As soon as he was close, Bastian pulled his arm away from the door, letting Mercer slip inside moments before the doors shut. The baffled security personnel and investigators tried to follow, but they were too slow. "They'll probably be waiting for us in the lobby since I had to disable one of the security guards who didn't want to let me through."

"I'm guessing the gang from the fifth floor will be taking the stairs down to meet us," Bastian muttered, keeping his head down and away from the camera. Mercer had already been spotted, so he yanked the cable out, disconnecting it. "We'll have to make our own exit."

"Plan B it is," Mercer agreed, pressing the number two to redirect the lift to another floor.

TWENTY-FOUR

When the lift stopped on the second floor, Mercer exited, tossing a quick glance down the hallway. No one was waiting for them, so he led the way down the corridor and across a large reception area, passing a conference room and continuing toward the restrooms. Opening the door marked ladies, he checked the room and each of the stalls, making sure they were empty. Bastian locked the door behind him and went to the handicapped stall at the end of the row.

"Let's not tell Hans or Donovan about this," Bastian muttered, balancing on the rim of the toilet seat as he maneuvered a grate away from an exhaust fan.

"Agreed," Mercer replied, taking the grate and placing it on the floor.

While Bastian tugged and fought with the fan to remove it from its lodged position directly above the commode, Mercer cautioned a glance out the small window near the sinks. Thankfully, no police cruisers were waiting outside. The coast was clear for the time being.

"Jules, a little help," Bastian said, finally pulling the blades free and nearly losing his balance in the process. Mercer grabbed the removed fan and waited for Bastian to climb onto the lid of the toilet tank and hoist himself through the newly created three foot opening. "It's a tight squeeze." A few moments of clanging ensued, and then the metal cover leading outside popped open, falling to the ground and landing in the shrubbery surrounding the building. "Pipe's on the right," Bas said before pulling himself out the opening and grabbing onto the drainage pipe that ran along the length of the building, using it to slide down.

Mercer followed suit, barely managing to fit inside their makeshift exit. The drainage pipe was weak. And after Bastian's descent, it wasn't likely to hold, so Mercer gripped the ledge, lowering himself as far as possible. His injured shoulder threatened to unhinge from the joint, and he sucked in a breath to steel himself against the pain.

Glancing back, he aimed for the closest and thickest bush he could find and let go. Branches broke, but at least Julian's leg did not. Getting up, he brushed the leaves and twigs from his clothes and climbed out of the decimated shrub. He would definitely feel that later, but right now, they had to move.

"There should have been an easier way to go about this," Mercer said as the two sprinted to the parked vehicle and took off into traffic. "Did you get everything?"

"Yes. Now we have to sort through it."

"First, we need to dump the car. Head to the business district. Hans left a back-up waiting in a parking garage there."

"I don't think that's necessary." But Bastian's words fell on deaf ears. So he did what Mercer instructed. When they arrived, they wiped the car, walked through the garage, entered an adjacent one, and acquired the third vehicle Mercer had used since agreeing to take this job. Then they returned to the flat. "I'll start the analysis, but this ought to lead to a clear picture of what's going on."

"I hope so." Mercer went into the bedroom, only to return a second later and hand his second-in-command the bank information, film, and memory cards he found inside Welks' house. "Ring Hans and make sure everything is still secure at the hospital. Wake me if they need assistance."

"Absolutely." Bastian was already accessing the information the memory cards held. "Are you sure you're feeling okay?"

"Lovely," Mercer replied.

Shutting himself into one of the bedrooms, he stripped off his shirt and assessed his injuries. After making a couple of trips to the kitchen and bathroom for bandages, antiseptic, ice, and acetaminophen, he settled onto the bed, hoping for a few hours of dreamless sleep.

While Mercer slept, Bastian gnawed on a drinking straw, his fingers dancing across the keyboard as he sifted through the tons of irrelevant information he had copied from Piper Investigations. Once the proper parameters were entered into the computer, he flipped on a second laptop and skimmed through the memory cards Mercer procured from Welks' house. The files contained numerous surveillance photos from different locations. Businesses, apartments, and public meeting places, such as parks and bus stops, had been photographed. Bas didn't recognize any of the subjects in the snapshots, and the majority were location-based. Clicking through the information, he finally stumbled upon two men meeting at a bus stop outside one of the sketchier bars that Donovan had scouted. Isaac Armann was making a deal.

Quickly printing a few photos, Bastian tacked them to the wall. He sat back, assessing the hard work they'd already put in. Then he opened another computer program, cropped the image to focus on Armann's unidentified companion, and cranked up the facial recognition software. If it didn't get a ping, he'd source it out to his contacts at Interpol or MI-6. As the computer ran through the databases to find statistically similar facial proportions and features, he sorted through the banking information that Mercer discovered under the couch.

The routing number led to an offshore account in John Welks' name. The bank itself was located on a tropical island with closed banking policies; however, the account was drained. It was obvious after scanning through the transaction history that the money was transferred into this account from a currently unknown source before being moved into Piper Investigations' business account.

"Odd." Bastian checked the progress the computer was making on Piper Investigations' data and added a financial parameter. It'd be easier to access account information this way instead of requesting help from law enforcement or a few accounting experts who may or may not support themselves through questionable means.

While the computers continued to process, he picked up the only remaining piece of evidence they collected – the film. It might be outdated in the current digital age, but it was also the only way to ensure the information it possessed could not be stolen through digital means.

Rummaging through the flat for the items needed to develop the film, Bastian locked himself inside the bathroom and set to work. When he emerged, Mercer was standing in their makeshift command center, studying the updates posted to the walls. Hans and Donovan were still at the hospital, and given the radio silence, he was assured that Katia and Ben were safe.

"Anything solid?" Mercer asked, watching Bas tape the developed photos to the wall. "I take it we're paying Jack Pierce another visit." He jerked his chin at the close-up of Pierce exiting his office building. "Are those snapshots from the film we discovered at Welks' place?"

"Yes, but," Bastian exhaled and taped a second photo to the wall, "Pierce wasn't the only one photographed."

"Shit."

As Bastian continued to place photographs on the wall, it was obvious Benjamin Styler was under surveillance. The majority were of Ben either alone or with other people. A few additional close-up photos had been taken of Katia Rhoade, Jack Pierce, a few unidentified men, Isaac Armann, and Mercer's team.

"Maybe Welks is a very astute investigator," Bastian suggested. "But more than likely, this is what he uncovered after the extortion led him to Benjamin Styler. However, since the film wasn't developed, he hasn't shown these to anyone."

"What about Armann, Pierce, and those chaps?" Mercer asked, pointing to a few photos of different individuals. There were five unidentified men, but they wouldn't remain unidentified for long. "See what you can dig up and then maybe you should ask Welks about it," Mercer insisted, not wanting to deal with the private eye again unless it was to permanently resolve the issue.

Bastian remained silent, mulling over the implications. "These two gentlemen are leaving Styler's apartment. Perhaps these are the business associates that Katia spotted." Untaping another photo from the wall which was a still from the street cams near the alley at the time of the shooting, Bas held the two next to each other for a comparison. "They appear to be the same blokes that accompanied Armann during the botched assassination attempt."

"What about these two? Are they the same men in the pictures you're holding?" Mercer asked, flicking another snapshot with his index finger. The photo was a wide shot of Jack Pierce with two other men.

"Hang on." Bastian grabbed a magnifying glass from the drawer and compared the men in that photo to the surveillance footage he printed from the street cams near the alley from the time of the shooting. "I can't be certain yet, but they resemble the men with Armann. However, their features seem to differ slightly. This one looks too tall."

"You think Armann found two lookalikes to help cover his tracks?"

"Stranger things have happened." Bastian pointed out the man in the photo with Isaac Armann that was currently being run through facial recognition. "I'm guessing this is the man responsible for the attempt on Styler's life, but it'll take some time to identify him. His face is almost completely obscured by that damn cap."

"Okay." Mercer looked at the computers which were still processing the data. "Let me know what else is uncovered and if that detective ever got building surveillance from Styler's apartment. The faster we can rule out some of these people, the better. I'll go to the hospital to keep watch while Hans and Donovan perform some reconnaissance on Pierce and track down Armann." Without another word, Mercer turned on his heel, grabbed the keys, and left. A bit of sleep dulled his headache and sharpened his senses. The time for battle was growing near.

TWENTY-FIVE

"So you know who wants me dead?" Ben asked. He was dressed and sitting up in bed, waiting to be discharged. The attempts to delay quickly faded, even after his insistence that he was experiencing excruciating chest pain. The hospital staff ran a few more tests which came out negative, so the ruse to stay inside the hospital failed. And the nurse said as soon as the attending physician signed the forms, Styler would be free to go. That meant Ben only had another hour or two to enjoy the security afforded to him by the confines of the hospital. "Why haven't you stopped this guy or turned him in to the police?"

Katia's eyes flicked to Mercer, but she didn't speak. Taking an uneasy breath, she crossed her arms over her chest and waited for an explanation.

"Like I said, we know the shooter's identity, but we have yet to identify the man who contracted the hit on your life. Isaac Armann is only a hired gun with no personal stake in your demise. But I don't doubt that he will try again. Failure is unacceptable, and as long as your heart continues to beat, he won't stop."

"Great. I end up with a contract killer who has a strong work ethic," Ben said sardonically.

"Have you spoken to your father?" Mercer asked Katia.

"Briefly." Katia's focus had remained on Mercer since his appearance. It was obvious the princess was angry with her betrothed. "He wants me to return home immediately and sever all ties to Benjamin." Ben opened his mouth to say something but decided against it after the frigid look she gave him.

"What do you want to do?" Mercer asked. He agreed to protect her, and if she wanted to leave Styler to face Armann's crosshairs alone, then so be it. Mercer and his team would find another way to proceed.

"I'm not leaving. For all I know, my dad could be a part of this." She shook her head, disgusted. "When I accused him of being involved, all he said was 'we'll talk about this later'." She cleared her throat, solidifying her resolve. "He drove my mother away. And he has done nothing but lie since the engagement. How could he have Ben investigated and fail to tell me about it?" She continued to shake her head. "I'm not going back there."

"Kat, listen, I don't want to come between you and your dad," Ben said, and Mercer felt his headache returning.

"No? You sent him photos. What did you think would happen?" She took a deep breath and composed herself, turning back to Mercer. Noting the annoyed look on his face, she tossed him an apologetic smile. "I'm sorry. I will try to keep our personal drama to a minimum." A nurse came into the room and checked Styler's stats, recording them on a sheet. As soon as she left, Katia cleared her throat and paced the room. "Now what do we do? They're ready to kick us out."

"I'll have a word with the police officers outside. Maybe they can delay the hospital staff from sending you home so soon." Mercer returned to the hallway, but the two officers that had been stationed outside were gone. "The cafeteria must have made fresh donuts," he griped, glancing around and spotting the nurse from earlier. "Excuse me, miss," she turned, and he offered the friendliest smile he was capable of producing, "my friend's life may still be in danger. Is there any way to delay his release?"

"I can assure you that he is perfectly fine. Gunshot wounds can be particularly traumatic, but unfortunately, we deal with them almost every day. There's no need to worry. Like I told him and his fiancée, he should feel right as rain in a few weeks."

"That's not what I meant." Mercer shifted his gaze around the empty hallway, not remembering it ever being this desolate. "Is something going on?"

"No, everything's fine."

He could tell she was lying. "What happened to the protection detail?"

"There was an incident downstairs in the ER, but like I said, everything is fine."

"What kind of incident? How long ago?" Mercer's tone was urgent, but she just stared blankly at him. "I suggest you call security and the authorities." She stood there, dumbfounded, unable to form a question. "Now," he barked.

"Sir," her tone became sharp, "please do not address me in such a manner."

"Bollocks." He reached across the desk and yanked the phone from its cradle. Dialing 911 while she voiced a protest, he waited for the operator to come on the line. "I'd like to report a shooting in progress."

She practically leapt across to grab the phone from him, but he swatted her away. Scanning the area, he shifted and opened his jacket. As soon as the gun came into view, she screamed and ran down the hallway. At least that should get security here quickly. As the operator continued to ask inane questions about his identity, location, and reason for the call, Katia opened the door.

"Get back," Mercer ordered, dropping the phone on the desk. "Close the door and stay low."

"What? Why?"

"Do it." He took a step toward her, and a shot rang out inches from his head. Had he not moved, it would have pierced through his brain. He shoved her backward into the room. "Armann."

"Mercer," Isaac smiled, enjoying the game, "it's a shame you moved. I would have made it quick." He fired again, and Mercer ducked into a doorway, pulling his Sig and returning fire. "Stand down, and we won't have a problem."

"Fuck you," Mercer hissed, breaking cover and firing three times, but Armann crouched behind a medicine cart. The bullets lodged ineffectually into the metal. "How'd you get out of the bloody car before the police arrived?"

"Details." Armann scurried from position to position. "You should have killed me when you had the chance. And here I thought you were a worthy adversary." He let out a chortle. "Had I realized you were just another simpering pussy, I wouldn't have bothered to extend such a courtesy to you." He laughed again, firing as Mercer vaulted over the nurse's station and behind the circular desk. "Then again, if you had the balls, you would have killed me after that pathetic stunt with the car."

"Rubbish." Mercer stood, firing repeatedly in

Armann's direction and forcing the man to retreat back behind the medicine cart. Keeping count of the bullets, Mercer fired twice more and hesitated, hoping Armann would fall for the trap.

"Just tell me what room Styler's in. One between the eyes, and I'll be on my way." Armann didn't move from his spot. Julian had one bullet remaining before he had to reload, and he palmed the extra clip, prepared to fire, eject, and reload in one fluid motion. The only problem was Armann wasn't moving. "I studied your gun, and I can count just as well as you can. How stupid do you think I am?"

"A hair above plankton," Mercer growled as heavy footsteps sounded in the distance. "But I'm guessing that might be giving you too much credit."

"Good. I hoped you would underestimate me. It'll make this easier." Armann pushed the cart forward, remaining behind it, and Mercer fired once and reloaded. The new magazine was locked into place before the old one even hit the ground, but in that time, Armann bashed into the first room he came across. It wasn't Styler's, and from the lack of sound, it was either empty or belonged to a comatose patient. "Oh where, oh where, can he be?" Armann sang out, returning to his position behind the cart and scooting it forward in order to repeat the process with the next room in the hallway.

Left with no other choice, Julian cleared the desk and ran full force into the cart. Armann was knocked back by the sudden impact but came up firing. Mercer narrowly avoided the bullet whizzing past and slammed into the cart again, but Armann was prepared this time and turned his hip to absorb the impact as he continued to fire, grazing Mercer's shoulder and forcing the ex-SAS to duck into one of the patient rooms. Mercer pressed his back against the open door and used the reflection from a nearby window to glance around the corner.

"CPD, drop your weapons," a voice called.

Julian spotted a few cops and hospital security approaching from one end of the hallway, and the reflection in the glass showed another few men coming up behind Armann, boxing him in. They moved in groups of two and three, slowly taking up cover positions. Guns were drawn, and it seemed plausible they planned to shoot first and ask questions later. Not that Mercer had any particular issue with the use of extreme prejudice in this situation, but he didn't necessarily want to get hit by friendly fire either.

"Looks like we have ourselves a standoff." Armann smiled, ducking into the adjacent room to where Julian was taking cover. The two men made eye contact through the reflection in the metallic medicine cart, and Armann's icy blue eyes held nothing but psychotic amusement. "Damn, this is turning out to be a lot more fun than I bargained for. Do you think I can collect overtime pay?"

"Who hired you?" Julian aimed, but at this angle, he didn't have a bead on Armann. Hopefully, the police did.

"Get on the ground," a police officer commanded, and Armann stepped into the hallway, closer to the cart.

"Don't shoot," Armann called, slowly raising his arms. In less than a millisecond, he changed stances, gripping the gun in both hands and firing two shots, sending a single bullet through the skulls of two of the responding officers. "At least not until I have a chance to even the score."

Mercer dove out of the room, tackling Armann to the ground. The officers from the other end of the hallway moved closer, and bullets flew past, lodging into the ground near the embattled men. It wasn't surprising. One of the combatants just killed two of their brothers-in-arms, so if they accidentally shot Mercer, he would be seen as collateral damage whose death could be blamed on the crazed shooter. Then again, the bloody bobbies probably didn't have any idea if he was working with Armann or not.

Mercer squeezed off two shots, and at close range, he knew he didn't miss. Armann gasped, clutching his side with one hand and fending off Mercer with the other. Despite the lead in his gut, Armann wasn't ready to throw in the towel.

"Are you going to finish it this time?" Armann asked, but before Mercer could respond, he was pulled away by one of the police officers.

The officer placed the muzzle of his Glock against Mercer's head. "Just give me a reason," the cop bellowed.

Dropping his Sig, Mercer didn't resist being handcuffed. He watched another three officers move in to subdue Armann, first kicking his gun away and then kicking him repeatedly in the process. Before Mercer could even utter a word, Armann grabbed the first cop by the ankle and removed his back-up piece while simultaneously performing a sweeping leg kick and knocking the other one off balance and into the third officer.

"Until next time," Armann warned, grabbing the off balance cop and holding his gun against the man's temple.

The bullet wound was oozing, but it didn't slow down the killer. He stumbled backward, taking his hostage with him. The cop that subdued Mercer aimed his weapon and radioed for back-up, but they weren't close enough to be of any use. The macabre procession continued to the nearest exit, and when they reached the doorway, Armann pulled the trigger, spraying the officer's brains across the wall and fleeing from the building, leaving an obvious blood trail in his wake.

Mercer clenched his jaw and shut his eyes. He might not like or trust the police, but three men just gave their lives in the line of duty. And there wasn't a chance in hell Mercer would let the party responsible get away with it. Isaac Armann was a dead man.

TWENTY-SIX

In the aftermath of the firefight, three men were dead, and a trail of blood led from the center of the hallway to the exit Isaac Armann took. The hallway was roped off, and hospital personnel moved the nearby patients to other rooms, attempting to avoid disturbing the crime scene any more than necessary. Katia and Ben were still in the same room, being questioned by the police. Since Ben was no longer a patient, he was a material witness. Mercer caught a glimpse of the two. Ben had his arm wrapped around Katia's quaking shoulders as she tried to explain what happened and why.

"Call Bastian," Mercer mouthed, hoping one of them would notice. Blood was running down his arm, but until the police decided he wasn't responsible, they were willing to let him suffer. He was seated in a chair with his hands handcuffed behind his back. The irony that he was in a very similar position to John Welks was not lost on him, and despite the gravity of the situation, he snorted.

"Is something funny?" one of the officers asked. "You think it's funny to kill a few cops?" The gravel in the man's voice was full of vengeance. "What can you tell me about your partner?"

"He's not my partner. His name is Isaac Armann, and someone hired him to murder Benjamin Styler."

"Yeah, and according to the reports I read, you assaulted Styler in this very hospital room not too long ago."

Mercer sighed. "I need to speak to Detective Rowlins."

"You need a lot of things. Too bad I don't give a shit." The cop shoved Mercer sideways, knocking him against the wall and forcing him to land on top of his still bleeding arm. "Maybe you need to stop being so clutzy." He yanked Mercer back to an upright position. "If you cooperate, maybe I'll even get a doctor to come look at that arm."

"Check the security footage. I was trying to stop him, not aid in his escape." Mercer let out an aggravated breath.

"Oh, so you want me to just leave you here unattended so you can escape? I don't think so." Before the cop could do anything else, Katia and Ben were escorted from Styler's room.

"Oh my god, you saved us, again," Katia exclaimed, kneeling next to Mercer. Her fingertips traced the skin near the gunshot wound, and Mercer bit back a hiss, looking away. "I'm sorry." She practically spun in a circle, searching for someone who could patch him up. Not finding a single paramedic or nurse, she turned to the officer. "He protected us." She stepped between Mercer and the man interrogating him. "Can't you see he needs help? Why aren't you helping him?"

"Miss," one of the cops said, trying to pull her away, "we need to take you down to the station to answer more questions."

"Go with them. But call Bastian and have him meet you there. He'll protect you," Mercer said before the officers led Ben and Katia away.

"Who's Bastian? Is that the shooter?" the same officer from before asked.

"Listen to me very carefully," Mercer growled, "Isaac Armann was hired to perform the hit on Benjamin Styler. Detective Rowlins is investigating. My team and I are assisting."

"Your team?" He glared. "How many of you are there? I need names."

"Good luck with that because I'm not saying another goddamn word without counsel." Mercer clenched his jaw and gave the officer a dead-eye stare.

"We'll see if you don't change your tune." The man put his hand on Mercer's shoulder, the same one that had recently been dislocated and grazed by a bullet, and gave it a hard squeeze. "It's just a matter of time."

Mercer hid the flinch masterfully, and the man stepped away, taking a seat at the nurse's station. He continued to stare at Mercer, but the two remained locked in a battle of wits. Julian had experienced far worse than this, and he wouldn't crack. Hell, he was more likely to pass out from blood loss than he was to utter another word to a stubborn policeman who was seemingly doing little to track down the man responsible for murdering three of his brothers in blue.

Just as Mercer was starting to get a little woozy, Rowlins appeared at the end of the hallway, accompanied by a few members of the police brass. Although no one spoke to him, Julian could hear some muttered words about the security cam footage taken during the time of the shooting. Reluctantly, the officer from earlier came around the desk to unlock the handcuffs.

"Looks like you're clear for now," the officer said, but his words sounded like a threat.

"We need to ask you some questions," another man with captain bars said, "but first, let's get you stitched up."

"Fine." Mercer looked down, noting that a small pool of blood had collected below the chair from his injury. "Isaac Armann's been shot. He'll need medical supplies or assistance. You need to monitor area doctors, hospitals, vets, and pharmacy supply centers."

"It's already being done. We've issued an APB, and his description was broadcast over the wire. It'll be fine," Rowlins said, motioning some medical personnel around the crime scene tape. They pushed a gurney with them. "It seems you and I may have some things to discuss in private," he whispered.

Mercer waved the gurney away and stood. "I'm capable of walking down the bloody hallway."

Rowlins shrugged. "It's your funeral, buddy." He turned to address the three other people standing nearby. "Captain, I'll take him to the ER, and we'll meet you back at the station after they stitch him up." One of the men nodded, and Rowlins led Julian down the hallway, away from the mess and the other officers.

"Are Katia and Ben safe?" Mercer asked once they were out of earshot.

"Of course, they're safe. They're at the precinct. Plus, your pal, the friendly one, is with them. He was concerned about how well you were holding up. Care to tell me what happened?"

"Someone hired Armann to orchestrate a hit on Styler. He missed the first time, so he came back to try again."

"And how does this relate to the car crash I heard a little something about?"

"Unimportant details."

"Somehow, I doubt that."

"It is none of your concern. Why did the protection detail leave? Why didn't the responding officers take down Armann after he killed three of your own?" Rage boiled to the surface, skyrocketing Mercer's blood pressure and causing him to teeter. Rowlins ducked underneath Julian's good arm to steady him as they continued toward the ER. "Right now, I'm having a hell of a time trusting any of you."

"I'm not your enemy. You're not under arrest. We're just doing our jobs to piece this mess together. And for the record," Rowlins passed Julian off to a nurse who helped him onto a waiting bed, "I wouldn't have let that motherfucker get away." The nurse went to find a doctor. "I'm glad you put two slugs in him. But shit, why couldn't you have taken a better shot? Aren't you supposed to be some hardcore green beret or something?"

"Retired Special Air Service, and your men seemed content enough to pop off quite a few shots at me. So care to explain why they didn't do the same to Armann?" He narrowed his eyes. "I'm not in favor of friendly fire."

"I'm sure they did all they could. Let the doc fix you up, and we'll discuss this at the precinct." The detective stepped away, calling over his shoulder, "With the rate things are going, maybe I'll get you your own desk, right next to mine."

"Maybe I'd rather put a bullet through my own bloody head," Mercer retorted, and Rowlins chuckled, muttering a few other inappropriate suggestions under his breath.

After far too much poking and prodding, Julian was

free to go. His arm was bandaged and placed in a sling on account of the previous dislocation, and he was instructed to avoid a list of items due to the mild concussion he had sustained during the crash. Other than that, he was given some antibiotics to stave off any infection from the gunshot.

"You still look like shit," Rowlins offered, leading him to a waiting unmarked cruiser. "Are you sure you're capable of protecting Katia Rhoade and Benjamin Styler in your current condition? The captain's been urging them to consent to protective custody, but she's adamantly opposed. Perhaps you could sway her point of view."

"I'm not here to do your bidding. And from what I've seen, there is absolutely no reason why she should trust the authorities."

"And how did you reach that conclusion? Or is that just your paranoia kicking in?"

"Someone with deep pockets hired Armann. Do you have any idea who that might be?"

"Not yet. We're working on it."

"So are we." Mercer maneuvered his arm out of the sling and balled up the blue mesh. "Whoever it is could buy off people in positions of power. You've said so yourself, Detective. And unless you're personally planning to keep watch on Katia and Ben, then I think they'd be safer elsewhere."

Rowlins bit his lip and shifted his gaze to Mercer. "Unfortunately, you might be right."

TWENTY-SEVEN

"Glad to see you're all right," Bastian said, nodding to Julian. "Katia had one hell of a story to tell, but it seems you fared rather well."

"It was nothing I couldn't handle," Mercer replied. Rowlins disappeared into the break room to have an impromptu meeting with his commanding officer and a few other high-ranking officials, and Mercer took advantage of the privacy. "Where are the lovebirds now?"

"A few officers are taking their statements. Carlton showed up, and their personal rendition of World War III played out in the middle of the squad room." Bastian glanced around and leaned closer to Mercer. "Donovan's tracking Armann. He thinks he's found his staging ground, and with any luck, he'll be able to determine where the bastard lives. That is, if the police don't locate him first. Do you think he's gone to ground?"

"No. He won't stop until the contract's been carried out. I put two in his gut, and he kept going. It didn't even slow him down. He must be accustomed to pain. What else have you dug up on his history?"

"You know the basics. He performed unsanctioned assassinations, probably for the government, before becoming his own boss. I'll keep digging, but Donovan can handle it from here. There isn't anything in Armann's background that'll give us a leg up. Plus, the coppers are already digging into every ounce of information they can find, but they don't have him in their sights. Unfortunately, we don't either."

"What about the man who hired him? He needs to be our primary focus since Armann is just a symptom of the underlying disease." Mercer glanced behind him to make sure Rowlins wasn't returning.

"Right, just like a deadly fever is only a symptom of the flu." Bastian rubbed his cheek. "I've analyzed the bank information, Piper Investigations' database records, and the photographs that we uncovered, but you aren't going to like where it leads."

"Which is?"

"Around in a bloody circle. Significant funds have poured out of Carlton Rhoade's business account and filtered into Piper Investigations through the newspaper, which isn't that odd, but the cash withdrawals from Carlton's personal account match the amount that was moved from Welks' hidden account into Piper. It makes Carlton look guilty as sin, especially since Welks said the source of the cryptic e-mail messages from his unidentified employer originated internally from Carlton's newspaper. Carlton has connections to hired guns from his old reporter days and that one questionable newspaper article. He has contacts, means, and motive. And according to Detective Rowlins, that's all we need to make criminal charges stick."

"I thought you didn't believe Carlton was capable."

"I don't." Bastian sighed. "But Rowlins seems pretty sure, and he is a trained investigator."

"Then why didn't the police arrest Rhoade? Or better yet, why hasn't Carlton called off Armann since Katia knows the truth and is refusing to leave Ben's side?" Mercer narrowed his eyes. "Carlton might not be a man to reckon with, but this is nothing more than an elaborate setup by someone intimately aware of Carlton's activities." Mercer smirked. "Apparently, you've swayed me to your side of the argument, Bas."

"It's about time you started listening to me. So now what do we do?"

"We find Armann, make him talk, and put him down." Mercer saw the unsettled look on Bastian's face. "He just killed three cops. Casualties don't seem to be one of his concerns."

"Jules, you tried to stop him."

"If I had really tried, I would have put two in the back of his head when he was still inside the car." Mercer paused. "How did he get out of that car? How did he escape when sirens and lights were looming in the distance?" Spinning on his heel, he stomped toward the break room. "Rowlins," he snarled, "I need a word."

By the end of it, details were hashed out, the city's CCTV feeds were analyzed, and the parts of the police investigation Rowlins was privy to were shared with Mercer and Bastian. It appeared that within less than a minute of Julian's departure from the crashed vehicle, Armann climbed out of the car and took refuge in a nearby alley, eluding the camera feed and disappearing before the investigators could identify the people involved. The rat had crawled back to whatever hole he crawled out of.

"I don't like being accused of things," Rowlins huffed.

"What do you know?" Mercer asked, remembering the comment about Katia and Ben being safer with Mercer's team than the police. "You obviously don't believe your comrades can be trusted."

"Look," Rowlins lowered his voice, "there's been speculation that Carlton Rhoade sourced out the hit. Hell, there's a lot of circumstantial evidence to support that theory. But we can't touch him without a smoking gun since he's close friends with my lieutenant, and he's been known to rub elbows with the police commissioner and the mayor at black tie affairs. That being said, I'd personally like to make sure everything is on the up and up before I jeopardize anyone's life or my career. As you can see, we've already lost three good men, and now, we're out for blood." He swallowed, blinking and looking away. "Goddammit."

"I'm sorry." Bastian squeezed the detective's shoulder. "Were you close?"

"I knew two of them personally. Hell, I trained Stan when he first got out of the academy, and Tom's wife is just about to have their first kid. Now that boy's gonna grow up without a dad. That sick son of a bitch is going to pay."

"Yes, he will," Mercer promised. "But in the meantime, I can't afford for your officers to kill Armann when we don't know who hired him. Do you know anything more than what's already been said or what Bas has disclosed to you?"

"The only thing left is the surveillance footage taken from Styler's apartment building that you asked for. Those two men that were leaving haven't been identified yet, but I'll give you a copy of the photos." He looked at Bastian. "It seems you have your own methods for determining facts."

"Indeed." Bastian nodded, and Rowlins went into

another room to retrieve the data. "What are we doing about Katia and Ben? Armann should be out of commission for the immediate future, but according to what you've said, he won't stop until the job's done."

"You will take them to the safe house we established. Ring Hans and have him meet you there. Two of us will remain on-site to guard them at any given time. I know it will make tracking Armann and the man responsible more difficult, but we don't have much of a choice, especially since we have minimal intel on Armann's two accomplices from the alley." Narrowing his eyes, Mercer thought through the information they currently possessed. "Have you spoken to Welks?"

"Not yet. By the time I had the information, the news had broken concerning the hospital shooting. Hans should be there now."

"Does he know what to do?"

"Yes." Bastian eyed Mercer uneasily. "What are you planning to do?"

"I'm not entirely certain."

"That's never good," Bastian muttered as Rowlins returned with the information.

"We should be finishing up with Katia and Ben, if you'd like a word with them," Rowlins said, hinting at the ulterior motive, and Mercer nodded, letting the detective lead the way to the interrogation room.

"Mr. Mercer, thank you," Katia said, standing and giving him a hug. "This is the second time you've come to the rescue. I don't know what would have happened if you weren't there." She kissed his cheek. Rowlins jerked his chin at the door, and the officer nodded and left the room. "You have to do something to keep us safe. The police want us to stay in custody, but I don't want to be locked up like a criminal." Her cold gaze fixed on Rowlins.

"My team is prepared to move you to an undisclosed location until Armann and the man responsible are stopped." Mercer eyed Styler, wondering what else he might know but failed to mention. "Ms. Rhoade, I was hired to keep you safe, and the farther you are from Mr. Styler, the safer you'll be."

"No. I didn't leave Ben in that alley, and I'm not leaving him now." She looked disgusted. "You sound just like my father."

"Ma'am, do you think he could be involved?" Rowlins asked, but Katia frowned. "Are you sure you don't want to remain under police protection? We will do our best to keep you safe."

"Just like the officers at the hospital kept us safe? I don't think so." Her frown turned to an angry glare.

"Looks like they're your problem now," Rowlins muttered, patting Julian on the back.

"They always were," Mercer replied. As soon as the three of them were alone, Mercer sat in the chair across from Katia and Ben. "We need to have a conversation, and before I take either of you anywhere, we need to get to the bottom of a few things. First, tell me exactly what your father said to you today. If he has any idea who might want to frame him, we need to know, now. Next," he held out the photos, "I want you to tell me precisely who these blokes are."

Styler took the photos, and Katia explained how her father insisted she come home. But Carlton hadn't given any indication that he knew more than what he was letting on. Given Carlton's predilection for destroying those who wronged him, it seemed likely he'd point fingers if he had the slightest inkling of who could be responsible for this mess.

"Who are they?" Mercer asked Ben. "Are those your business associates?"

"I don't recognize them." Styler continued to study the photographs taken inside his apartment building.

"Odd, on account that they are exiting your apartment," Mercer snapped.

"I know I was home that day." Styler's brow furrowed, and he ran his thumb over the date and timestamp. "It was our anniversary. Remember, Kat," he handed her the photos, "you came by for brunch, and we stayed at my place for a few hours. Then we went out to dinner and a show later that night."

"Yeah, I remember." She shifted her gaze from the pictures to Ben. "And like I told Mr. Mercer, I remembered seeing men leaving your apartment that day," her voice grew harsh. "Are you lying to me, Benjamin?"

"I'm not lying. No one else came to my house that day."

"And you were there the entire time?" Bastian asked, joining the three of them.

"Uh-huh."

"So how come you don't remember two men leaving your apartment?" Mercer asked. "What were you doing immediately before Katia arrived?"

"Um..." Ben scrunched his face together, contemplating what happened weeks ago. "I got up, made brunch, popped some muffins in the oven, took a shower, ordered some flowers, checked the market, and did some work."

"Flowers," Mercer's mind flashed to yellow roses, and he inhaled, shaking off the distraction, "did you pick them up?"

"No, they were delivered."

"To your front door?" Bastian was working on a theory but wasn't ready to share it.

"No, they were left in the lobby. I ran down the steps to grab them. I wasn't even gone five minutes."

"I'll get a complete copy of the video footage," Bastian said, leaving the room.

"Fair warning, if you're lying, you will regret it," Mercer warned.

"I'm not," Styler replied, but despite the likelihood of his innocence, he gulped. On his best day, Julian Mercer was intimidating, and on his worst, he was downright scary. And today wasn't one of his better days.

TWENTY-EIGHT

Leaving the precinct that evening was a harrowing experience. Julian had to give his statement, turn over his firearm as evidence in the hospital shooting, and call in a few favors from federal agencies on both sides of the pond in order to avoid being stuck in police custody for forty-eight hours. Thankfully, he still had some friends in government, despite his forced retirement.

Bastian cloned Katia's phone, giving her an untraceable throwaway after placing her cell in Det. Rowlins desk drawer with Styler's. Since the possibility existed that Armann or whoever else might be involved in the hit was tracking Katia and Ben's movements via their phones' GPS systems, this would make it a little more difficult. But the possibilities seemed endless in terms of who might want to kill Benjamin Styler – his business associates, clients, Jack Pierce, any one of Katia's former boyfriends, stalkers, or just a random run-of-the-mill psychopath. And that didn't take into account the slew of individuals who had an axe to grind with newspaper mogul Carlton Rhoade.

Bastian's first order of business once they were settled would be to cross-reference the two lists of suspects and focus on the overlap. Perhaps killing Styler wasn't personal, but it was the best way to place the blame on Carlton. After all, Styler was a blackmailer of sorts, and Carlton had his future son-in-law investigated. So it would make sense that the overprotective and vengeful father would take extreme measures to ensure his daughter's safety. So far, the intel they'd gathered added up to a well-endowed benefactor with access to Carlton's newspaper.

Donovan was tracking Armann. Hans was interrogating the private eye they'd taken captive. Bastian was analyzing the police data and piecing the facts together, and Mercer was barely managing not to be arrested or make any more enemies, which might have been the hardest job of all.

"I'll take them to our safe house," Bastian whispered in Mercer's ear, leaving the commander to finish the paperwork with Det. Rowlins. "Rendezvous when you get the chance. Hans will meet us there."

"Fine, but there are a few things that require my attention first. Then I'll check in with Donovan, and we'll meet you at the prearranged location." He grabbed Bastian's arm, halting his procession. "We have to end this quickly. If whoever hired Armann saw the news report, a secondary team might be set to move."

"Are you serious?" Rowlins asked, interrupting the exchange.

"Wouldn't you have a contingency plan?" Mercer retorted, and Bastian continued on his way, cognizant of his surroundings and the officers watching him. No one could be trusted. And until one of his teammates joined him, he was solely responsible for Katia and Ben's safety.

"I guess, if I was that desperate to kill someone. However, the smart thing would be to pack up and write it off as a loss."

Mercer remained silent, putting the final touches on the forms he was filling out. "Are we done?"

Rowlins scanned the sheet. "Yeah, we're done." He watched Mercer slide uneasily into his jacket. The ex-SAS commander felt naked without his handgun, but they had plenty of excess artillery available back at the safe house. And Donovan always came to the party overly prepared. "When you find Armann, give me a call." Rowlins lowered his timbre, so his voice wouldn't carry. "It makes no difference to me what condition he's in. No questions asked."

Mercer smirked. "I thought you weren't in favor of mercenary work or a body count."

"That was before. This is a no holds barred type of situation."

"Detective." Mercer nodded and left the precinct.

Climbing inside a taxi, Mercer gave the cabbie the address of Carlton Rhoade's newspaper building and settled into the backseat. The authorities were on high alert, and if another crazed motorist wanted to make a run at Mercer, now was the least opportune time to do it. Thankfully, the only kamikaze drivers on the road were the usual rush-hour variety. Paying the man, Mercer exited in front of the building, took a deep breath, and marched inside. He wanted answers.

"Can I help you?" Carlton's assistant, Donna, asked.

"No." Mercer continued through her office to the closed door with the gold nameplate.

"Sir, I really must insist," she began, but Mercer

barged inside. She came up behind him. "Mr. Rhoade, I'm so sorry. Shall I call security?"

"That won't be necessary, Donna," Carlton replied, studying Mercer. "Why don't you take a seat?" Once the office door shut, Carlton stood, clearly angry. "Where is my daughter?"

"She's safe."

"No thanks to you." He glowered. "I was at the police station when they took her statement. Three men were killed. And the person responsible escaped. I hired you to protect her. Obviously, I was mistaken in placing any faith in your abilities."

Waiting for the vilification to end, Mercer studied the dynamics of the room and Rhoade's personal effects. "Are you quite through?" he asked after a time. Carlton made a harrumph noise but didn't speak. "Very good. Whoever wants Styler dead works at the newspaper and knows intimate details about your habits and the investigation you asked John Welks to conduct. A member of my team will be in contact for your employee information, but if you fail to divulge it, we'll get it another way. And I want to make one thing very clear, if you know who did this and can stop it, you better. Whenever the truth comes to light, I will end the person responsible, even if that's you. Do you understand?"

"How dare you?" Rhoade flushed a deep scarlet. "I would never hurt Katia. She's the only thing that's important in this world."

"Says the man who is back at work less than six hours after she was almost killed. Bloody brilliant," Mercer scoffed, standing. He went to the door, opening it with such force that he almost knocked the man on the other side over.

"Excuse me," the man said, and Mercer focused on his face for a split second. The man's expression read smug amusement, and he looked vaguely familiar.

"Daniel, get in here," Rhoade barked, and the man brushed past Julian and shut the door behind him. Heading for the exit, Mercer filed it away for later consideration and dialed Donovan on his way out of the building. They needed answers, and wasting more time with Carlton Rhoade was not going to get them.

Donovan gave Julian his location. Then the two disconnected, and Mercer hailed another cab. His eyes performed a continuous sweep of the area and traffic, but no one followed him or the cab. After paying the driver, Mercer stepped out in front of a pub and went inside to find Donovan seated in the back corner. It was the best and only strategic spot in the entire place. Mercer took a seat across from him, scanning the bar's mirrored back to ensure Armann wasn't hiding inside.

"Here." Donovan passed a gun under the table, and Mercer holstered it automatically. "Isaac Armann frequents this bar and does business out of the back room. I haven't spotted him, but if he's hurt, I'd say the owners would cover for him."

"Have you inquired as to his whereabouts?"

"Not yet." Donovan tilted his chin toward the narrow hallway with three doors. Two were restrooms, and one led to something else. "It's locked, and I wasn't sure how loudly I should knock." He jerked his chin toward the floor, and Mercer noticed the blood smears that were a dark reddish-brown. "I'm guessing he's inside, either hiding out or getting patched up."

"Did you see him?" Mercer asked.

"No. I picked up his trail from what I can only assume is his staging ground and followed him here. Frankly, it's mostly speculation on my part, and it could turn out to be total rubbish."

"There's only one way to find out."

Mercer stood, heading for the door. He stopped in the narrow hallway, waiting for Donovan to join him. The bar was full of regulars. They were grizzled, working class people. But given the neighborhood and the fact that Isaac Armann used this bar to make contacts and run his business, going in loud would only draw unwanted attention which could come with deadly repercussions. Knocking on the door, Mercer waited for a response. When none came, he tried again.

"Yo, Isaac, let me in," Mercer said, once again making a feeble attempt at an American accent. "I got the stuff you wanted."

Donovan cocked an eyebrow, remaining in the adjacent doorway of the men's room. The doorknob turned, and Mercer pressed his back against the wall, waiting for the door to open. As soon as it did, he shouldered his way inside. The woman inside the room screamed in surprise and ran into the bar. From the strewn blood-soaked towels that littered the chair and floor, it was apparent Armann had been here.

"He's gone," Mercer declared after checking the entirety of the room, noting a window large enough for a man to squeeze through.

"Jules, we have another problem," Donovan said, noting the crowd of burly men that were now blocking the exit.

"Shit."

Donovan snorted. "Normally, I'm with Hans when things like this happen."

"Hardy har har." Under different circumstances, Mercer wouldn't have minded a bar fight, but time was of the essence. And despite his invincible attitude, his shoulder ached after the dislocation and stitched up gunshot wound. "Let's make this quick."

"Right-o." Donovan tossed a grin over his shoulder and sauntered into the center of the group. Six or seven men formed a circle in the middle of the room, armed with fat-covered muscles, half-empty beer bottles, and a random pool cue or dart. "Why don't you chaps settle down? We just stepped in for a pint. We'll be on our way."

The woman was behind the bar, and Donovan noted the bartender's stance. He shifted ever so slightly, bringing his handgun closer to reach while continuing his chummy exchange with the men. Two of them decided that taking a seat and downing the rest of their beers was a better use of their time, but the one with the pool cue and two others seemed puffed up by the possibility of knocking in some heads.

"Who the hell do you think you are?" one of them asked. Mercer stepped forward, and the men moved in closer to surround them. "You just think you can barge into our bar with your twink accents and scare the shit out of Laila? It's time you learn some manners."

"Listen, mate," Donovan said, putting a friendly hand against the man's arm, "we don't want any trouble. It's best that we get going."

A bottle smashed nearby, and Julian elbowed the nearest man in the gut, following through with an uppercut to the jaw that had the man teetering backward. He kicked the man in the stomach, knocking him backward into two of the goons standing behind him, sending one of them sprawling across a table.

"I thought you said to do this quietly," Donovan hissed, deflecting a punch that launched at his face and retaliating with a right cross that likely broke the guy's jaw and downed him with one move.

Glass continued to break, and two men grabbed Julian. One wrenched his injured arm backward, and the other pummeled him in the stomach. Donovan ducked down, ramming the attacker with his shoulder and launching him out of the fray. Continuing pursuit, he knocked the guy against the wall a few times until the man stopped throwing haphazard punches and crumpled to the floor.

"Down," Mercer ordered just in time for Donovan to duck and roll before a man could crash a chair over his back.

The man spun, focusing his rage on Julian. He approached, cracking the chair ineffectually against the bar as Mercer sidestepped. The ratcheting of bullets in a double-barreled shotgun brought the fight to a sudden standstill, and the bartender stood with the business end focused on Julian.

"I'd reconsider, mate," Donovan warned, stepping closer with the laser sight of his handgun trained on the bartender's head. "We don't want any trouble. We're leaving. I'd suggest you don't stop us or follow us."

The bartender jerked the shotgun toward the door, and Donovan gave a curt nod, never lowering his weapon as he backed toward the exit. Mercer followed, turning at the door to survey the damage that was done. Three men were out cold. Another two were bruised or bleeding, and a few looked like they might have shit themselves.

"Much obliged, partner," Mercer mused, exiting the bar and heading down the street.

"You and your bloody westerns," Donovan said, once he ensured they were clear and not being followed. "As soon as this job is over, I'm updating your movie collection with nothing but musicals."

TWENTY-NINE

Scouting the area, it was obvious they lost track of Armann. There was no way of knowing when he left the bar. Despite the fact that Donovan had determined where Armann went after leaving the hospital, the former SAS had no way of knowing how long it had been since Armann slipped out the back. With no other leads, Donovan backtracked, taking Mercer to the place Armann used to plan his kills.

The large, self-serve storage unit was housed inside a converted warehouse. Each individual unit had a roll-down steel door and cement walls. When they came to 203, Donovan picked the lock and rolled up the door while Mercer took aim, prepared to decimate anyone inside.

"Bloody hell," Mercer exhaled.

Two of the walls were covered in surveillance photos of Katia and Ben. Their apartments' blueprints were laid out, and a list of restaurants and shops they frequented were enumerated. Their daily routine and estimated arrival and departure times were all listed in black and white. Isaac Armann was definitely a professional who planned for every detail. It was amazing his shot missed. If he had killed Ben in that alley, this would be over, and the contract killer likely would have gotten away clean. Unfortunately, the one factor Armann didn't prepare for was the appearance of Julian Mercer.

"That's not the half of it," Donovan said, stepping inside and pulling a tarp off the wall. On the third wall were photos of Mercer. "At least he got your good side."

"What about the rest of you? Has the entire team been compromised?"

"I don't think so. There's a shot or two of Bas, but that's all I found."

Thinking back, Mercer was positive that Armann didn't know which hospital room was Styler's. If he had, the scene that played out earlier would have resulted in less collateral damage. Mercer scanned the photos, the information, the maps, and the data that plastered the walls. Even miniature, made-to-scale facsimiles of the street, storefronts, and alley where Styler had been shot were inside the storage unit.

"Any idea who is working with him?" Mercer asked, stepping out of the room.

"No."

"How did you find this place?"

"After I determined which pub he used to acquire his clients, Bas pulled the nearby surveillance feed which led here. I broke into the manager's office, skimmed for names, but came up blank. So we kept an eye on the feed, monitoring the people who came and went. Right after the hospital shooting, a man in dark clothes and a hood stopped by. I didn't get a good look at him, but he appeared injured. So I headed straight here."

"Why didn't you intervene when he was in your sights?" Mercer growled, clenching his fists.

"Because by the time I found this," Donovan gestured around the room, frustrated, "he was already on the move." Donovan sifted through another box containing an array of firearms and medical supplies. "This place is closer to the hospital than the bar. He probably had to get the bleeding under control before going there for help."

Mercer blinked but didn't respond. He wanted Armann dead, but first, he wanted answers, names, accomplices, and clients. That was the current focus.

"Let's retrace his steps. Precisely where did he go after he left here? What path did he take? He must have an apartment close by under an alias. In his condition, he can't get far without being spotted since his face is plastered across every news outlet in this city. And he's hurt. He'll need to hole up somewhere secure to mend."

"What about you?" Donovan eyed Mercer's arm. The brawl only exacerbated the situation, and some of the stitches must have ripped, leaving a darkening red spot on Mercer's sleeve.

"I'm functional. And we don't have time for this." Leading the way out of the storage unit, Julian picked up the phone and relayed the information to Bastian. As soon as they captured Armann, Bastian could begin analyzing the information inside the storage unit while the rest of the team protected Ben and Katia and questioned Armann about his accomplices. "Sometimes, I miss having the resources of the Crown."

Donovan chuckled. "That makes one of us."

Night had fallen, and they wandered the streets, checking for signs that Armann had been there. A random red smear on the ground might lead to the bleeding man. But once they mimicked Donovan's earlier path back to the pub, the trail went cold. Checking the side streets, Mercer cocked his head up, analyzing an outdoor staircase used as a fire escape.

"He's smart, but he probably has a place close by, somewhere to duck into if it gets a bit too hot," Mercer mused, scratching his chin. "Someplace with a vantage point to keep tabs on the bar."

Donovan scanned the area, determining which perch provided the best view and cover. When he turned back around, Mercer was making his way to the building across the street. The commander crouched on the fourth floor landing, studying the railing and signaling.

"Blood," Mercer said, pointing to a smear outside the window. "He must have waited here to make sure we left."

"He probably waited for the perfect shot. Unfortunately, we moved westward, and he missed his opportunity."

"Open it." Julian stepped to the side, letting Donovan lift the heavy double-paned glass.

The window wasn't locked, and Donovan held it while Mercer slipped underneath. Once Julian set foot in the apartment, he removed his handgun, holding it down at his side. He silently signaled to Donovan to check the back rooms while he went right, toward the kitchen.

Spread across the dirty linoleum was an unconscious heap. Mercer waited, not moving or even breathing, his focus split between Armann's prone form and the hallway Donovan entered. When the younger man returned, indicating it was clear, Mercer kicked Armann in the side, causing the contract killer to elicit a shriek.

"I thought you said you wouldn't miss next time,"

Mercer taunted, yanking Armann by the collar and dragging him into the middle of the room, away from the cabinets and the few sharp medical instruments which had been used to remove the bullets and suture the gaping holes. "Seems you missed again. You really ought to consider lowering your fee, mate."

"Mercer," Armann gasped, a faint gurgle rattling through his chest, "have you come to finish the job?" He tried to smile, but it looked like a grimace. "You didn't have the stones before. I doubt you grew a pair in such a short amount of time." He chuckled, gripping the side of his abdomen where both of Mercer's bullets had ripped through his flesh. "You had your chance twice. Was this really the best you could do?"

"Who do you work for?" Mercer was starting to see red, and his body tingled with a dark need to finish what he started. Flashes of the slaughtered police officers entered his mind, and he inhaled sharply, looking away. "Who?" he screamed, stomping his heel into the wounds.

Armann's yelp turned into a scream and then utter silence when he blacked out. Mercer stepped back, holstering the gun before he could shoot the guy. They needed answers. Retribution had to wait, but Mercer's entire body trembled with anger and torment. Fighting to control it, he thought he would explode any second.

"Jules?" Donovan asked quietly. He had never seen Mercer so close to the edge before.

"Make sure he's stable. We can't afford for him to die on us before he talks. I'll search the apartment in the meantime."

"Should I call—" Donovan began, but Mercer interrupted.

"I don't bloody well care what you do. Just get him

healthy enough to answer our questions. Dying right now would be far too pleasant an experience for a piece of shit like him."

"Yes, sir."

Donovan set to work while Mercer went to the back room. Sinking onto the bed, Julian put his face in his hands and took a few deep breaths, waiting for the tremors to stop. He never had a reaction like this to any job before. When he was in the military, he followed orders, carried out government-sanctioned hits, recoveries, and interrogations without batting an eye, even the kidnapping cases he'd worked over the last two years never led to anything more than mild irritation and occasionally shooting some greedy, sadistic bastards. But this was different.

Armann was a killer who performed hits for money and sport. There was no personal vendetta to support his gung-ho attitude to destroy Benjamin Styler. He tried and failed twice. And yet, even as he lay a bleeding, destroyed mess, he still had the audacity to gloat. This sick son of a bitch really thought he would get away with killing innocents scot-free.

"Not again. Not another one," Mercer growled, compartmentalizing his anger issues. Finding clues as to who Armann's partners were and who painted the target on Styler's back were far more productive ways for Mercer to spend his time and energy. And at this particular moment, he had a lot of pent-up energy. "You will regret every goddamn thing you've ever done," he muttered, ripping through the closet.

THIRTY

Armann was careful not to keep anything damning inside the apartment. Once Donovan performed some basic first aid to ward off infection and ensure the bleeding had stopped, he and Julian moved the now sedated assassin to the warehouse where they were keeping John Welks. At this rate, Chicago would have a new prison, courtesy of Julian Mercer.

Not willing to risk taking any chances, they shackled Armann to a few metal pipes that ran through the interior, bound his legs and arms together behind his back, gagged and blindfolded him, and activated the jammer to prevent any radio or cell signals from entering or leaving the warehouse. Isaac Armann wasn't going to escape again. Once he was secured and the entire place was locked down, Julian and Donovan returned to Armann's little home away from home.

The apartment didn't lead to anything useful, but the same could not be said for the storage unit. Inside were maps, photos, and enough evidence to put

Armann behind bars for the rest of his natural life or a needle in his arm. Unfortunately, there was no smoking gun pointing to his two accomplices from the alley or any indication of who might have hired him to exterminate Benjamin Styler.

"He must have more of these units," Donovan said. "What do you want me to do?"

"Trade out with Bastian. We'll let him muck around in case we've missed anything." Mercer drummed his fingers against one of the boxes. "It's all we can do."

As soon as Donovan was gone, Mercer took a deep breath and opened another of the file boxes that had been stacked in the corner. Armann kept records, but they were in some indecipherable shorthand. Granted, now that they had Armann locked down, they would eventually get answers out of him, but Mercer wasn't ready for that encounter. Donovan sedated Armann with a tranquilizer strong enough to knock him out for the next twelve hours. It was designed to give them time to search for answers and come up with a stronger basis for their questioning, or so Donovan said. However, it seemed obvious it was to give Armann a slight reprieve because, given the way he looked sprawled across the floor, it was unlikely he'd survive an interrogation at the present. And they needed him to live just long enough to give up a name.

"Bollocks." Mercer replaced the meaningless dossier back inside the box.

"I thought we were meeting at the safe house," Bastian said, startling Mercer who hadn't realized how much time had passed.

"Opportunities presented themselves." He spun around to face his friend.

"Go back to the safe house. You wanted a two-man team guarding Katia and Ben, and you need to sleep. It's been over twenty-four hours, and you've been through the wringer." He jerked his chin toward the door. "Go."

"Cheeky bastard." Mercer was quickly losing the battle against his fatigue. How long had he been awake? So much had happened, he couldn't think straight. "We need to analyze the information. It's imperative I have leverage to use against Armann. He's going to be a tough nut to crack, and..."

"And you'll probably end up cracking open his skull. I'm well aware of this fact, not to mention the promises you've made to Katia and Detective Rowlins." Bastian raised a challenging eyebrow. "I know what's at stake, and I know precisely what to do. Now go." He jerked his chin at the opened door to the storage unit. "Take my car. I'll have Hans pick me up later."

Relenting, Mercer took the car, executing numerous counter-surveillance measures and monitoring the mirrors and traffic patterns for signs of a tail before returning to the safe house. Inside, Hans and Donovan were discussing Isaac Armann's condition and the evidence they'd found. Mercer ducked into the bathroom to shower and assess his condition. His shoulder burned and ached, and the bruises and abrasions on his face and body were darker than they had been. He downed a few of the antibiotics the medical staff had given him, redressed his wounds, and returned to the kitchen.

"Get some sleep," Hans suggested. "Donovan went back to the warehouse to ensure our captives don't try anything. Bastian's hard at work, and I have this situation under control."

Nodding, Mercer sifted through the pile of supplies that were on top of the kitchen table, slipped his arm back into the sling, and went down the hallway to the back bedroom. The sun was coming up, so he drew the drapes before climbing into bed. Propping himself against the headboard, he shut his eyes, letting the dull buzz of his headache combat the errant thoughts that entered his mind. The exhaustion set in, and he slipped deeper into the abyss.

"Mr. Mercer?" A slight knocking sound followed Katia's soft voice. She cracked the door open. "Can I come in?"

He opened his eyes and looked at her. "Fine." His mind felt jumbled, and he wasn't sure how long he'd been asleep or even if he had enough time to fall asleep before her interruption.

She shut the door behind her and sat on the edge of the bed. "I just wanted to say thank you."

"No need."

"Don't be modest." She rubbed her forehead, studying the sling. "Does it hurt?"

He snorted. "It could be worse. What do you want?"

"I just can't stop thinking about the hospital. Every time I close my eyes, I hear the shots in the hallway. I heard your friends talking about it," she admitted, leaning closer to him and resting her hand on his leg. "They said you found the shooter."

"Yes."

"What are you going to do to him?" A fire ignited behind her eyes.

"Whatever is necessary to ensure your safety." Mercer narrowed his eyes at her hand, disliking such intimate contact. "Once he provides answers, I'll do what you asked."

"Thank you." She cocked her head to the side. "Your sling is tangled. That can't be comfortable." She leaned closer. "Let me fix it." She got on her knees, reaching around his shoulders and practically straddling him in order to untangle the strap.

With his mind still sluggish, he reacted instinctively

when her fingers scraped against his bandaged arm by grabbing her wrist and yanking her arm upward and away. She fell forward, catching herself with her other hand and coming to rest inches from him.

"Sorry." He released her hand.

"I didn't mean to hurt you." She sat upright. "I just wanted to help."

"No need. Now if you wouldn't mind getting off of me."

She blushed, suddenly realizing she was sitting on top of him. "I'm such an idiot. I don't know why I do these things. I'm sorry. Please just forget this ever happened."

"Fine."

"Jules," Bastian said, entering the room to find Katia on Mercer's lap. He paused, casting a questioning glance from one to the other. "I didn't realize you were entertaining. When you're finished, I need to have a word with you."

"We're done," Mercer said, and Katia flushed bright red and scurried past Bastian.

Bas watched her duck back into the bedroom she was sharing with Styler, and then he shut the door to Julian's room. "What the bloody hell do you think you're doing with that bird, mate? Her head's not screwed on straight, and she's nuttier than a peanut butter and jelly sandwich. I can't believe you."

Mercer rolled his eyes, too tired and aggravated to address the misguided assumption. "What's so important?"

"I've identified Isaac Armann's two associates."

THIRTY-ONE

Dean Manning and Keith Westin were hired by Isaac Armann to provide a service. However, after extensive research, Bastian decided that the two men were completely useless leads. Armann had taken an ad out in a few of the city's performing arts magazines, posted on various message boards, and hung flyers near a few drama schools for two men to fulfill the roles as extras in a new crime film. It was so stupid that it actually worked. The men that answered the bill had to provide photos and general physical statistics to a post-office box.

Armann was looking to fill a type, and the scary fact was he wanted men that resembled Jack Pierce's co-workers. Along with a strong physical resemblance, Armann found men who had a history of petty crimes in their past. It explained how Katia's wallet and phone were lifted without her noticing. Dean Manning was the lowest level of conman. He ran three-card monte on street corners and had been arrested for panhandling. Westin had multiple run-ins with the authorities. He was a purse snatcher, pick-pocket, and shoplifter. Neither man was particularly grandiose with their criminal records. A few misdemeanors, community service, and parole with no time served were all the penal system was willing to throw at them, which made them perfect candidates for Isaac Armann's new crime movie, except of course it wasn't a movie, and now these two men were accomplices in an attempted homicide.

Bastian found police and court records for both men, but it was unlikely they knew anything about the hit. From what Bastian gathered, they simply showed up to play their parts and returned to their lives. Mercer listened to the news, remaining silent as he contemplated the ramifications. As of yet, it was unclear what the commander planned to do with this new information.

"Where are they now?" Mercer asked, hauling himself off the bed. He was achy and stiff, and he winced as he stretched, removing the sling and straightening his arm.

"What? The bird didn't work out your kinks?" Bastian challenged, and Mercer shot him a look on the way to the closet to change. "After arriving at the unlikelihood that they were criminal geniuses, I passed the intel along to Rowlins."

"Did he ask about the progress we've made?"

"He did, so I gave him the apartment where you found Armann and the storage unit."

"Bloody hell." Mercer grunted, clipping a handgun to his belt at the small of his back. "How are we supposed to get answers with those wankers mucking about?"

"Easy," Bastian smiled, "I already gleaned the necessary information. The paper trail was practically useless. That gibberish Armann uses is a pain in the arse, but I took digital copies. Thank god for handheld scanners. Cheer up, the coppers can work their angles alongside our investigation, but that doesn't mean the streams will have to cross."

"Have you spoken to Armann or followed up with Welks?" It had been a very long day and an even longer night, and the information, photos, and bank accounts they found at the P.I.'s office and home had yet to be fleshed out.

"Just briefly." Bastian let out a sigh and slumped onto the bed, rubbing his face. He was exhausted too. "I don't see why this can't be simple with point A leading to point B which gives us point C." He leaned back against the pillows but thought better of it. "Should I find somewhere else to bunk down for a few hours? I don't want to deal with any residual bodily fluids."

"Nothing happened, Bas. It was a miscommunication."

"Sure, sure." Bastian remained on top of the covers, shutting his eyes. "Whatever you say."

Mercer let out a huff and left the room. The dining room was covered in file boxes, papers, and information tacked up with a web overlay plastering two of the walls. Plenty of progress had been made, but Bastian's words only assured Mercer that they still didn't know who orchestrated the hit. Remembering Rowlins' insistence on discovering means, motive, and opportunity, Mercer made a cup of tea and sipped it while examining every bit of the information they possessed.

Starting at ground zero would be the best way of analyzing the intel. Benjamin Styler was shot by Isaac Armann who was accompanied by Dean Manning and Keith Westin. The two accomplices had no prior connection to Armann, Styler, or any of the other key players, and little involvement aside from tailing and pick-pocketing the couple. However, the simple fact that these were the same two men who were photographed at Styler's apartment building during the time of the alleged flower delivery left a bad taste in Mercer's mouth. How long had this attempted killing been in the works? And if it had been weeks, as the evidence insisted, then why was Armann so desperate to finish it in a single day after confronting Mercer inside the car?

Letting out an uneasy breath, Mercer let his thoughts about Armann and the two actors simmer on the backburner while he shifted his focus to whoever's deep pockets were paying for the hit. First, whoever hired Armann must have provided him with intimate details about Styler. How else would the assassin have known to hire men that resembled Jack Pierce's co-workers? Was the plan to pin the murder on Pierce since he had extensive resources and plenty of motive? Hell, given the facts and Jack's visit to a bar near the scene of the shooting, he might even have opportunity. It made for one bloody wicked frame-up job.

Then, of course, there was the Carlton Rhoade angle to consider. Rhoade had been extorted and implicitly threatened by Styler. Carlton even went so far as to hire John Welks to investigate the source of the extortion. The questionable funds that Piper Investigations and Welks had recently received in their accounts traced back to the newspaper and the media mogul himself. Furthermore, given Welks' responses to the questions Mercer asked, an unknown third party was involved in the mix. Whoever this unsub was, he was paying Welks for tips and information on Carlton's requests. The source of Styler's threat must have a personal vendetta against

Rhoade. Perhaps Styler was simply the weakest exploitable link to hurting Katia and thus Carlton, unless Carlton was being made to look like a patsy for the real killer. And there was also the distinct possibility that Carlton was to blame, and Welks was covering for him, knowingly or not.

Simply put, this unknown accomplice or puppet master worked at Rhoade's paper, had access to Rhoade's professional and private life, and some insight into Styler's past from his days palling around with Jack Pierce. Flashes of the man Mercer encountered outside Rhoade's office crept into his mind, and he reexamined the photographs they found inside Welks' house. Was it the same man that Welks' photographed making a deal with Armann? And since he worked for Rhoade, was he simply doing his boss's bidding when he hired the contract killer to eradicate Styler?

"I don't believe your father is involved. But do you think it's possible he knows who is?" Mercer asked, not bothering to turn around.

"How'd you know I was standing here?" Katia asked from the doorway.

"I smelled your perfume. Now answer the question."

"I don't know. Dad warned me to leave Ben long before we even got engaged. He said Ben was trouble, and he was just using me. But Ben cleaned himself up and got his act together." She snorted and stepped into the room, pulling a chair out to sit. "Well, that was before I found out he took pictures of me and sent them to my father." The anger and disdain were back in her voice. She felt betrayed. "Do you believe my dad knows something he hasn't told us?"

"I'm not an investigator."

"Now who's avoiding the question?" she quipped.

"Whatever's going on has been brewing for a while. I won't discount the possibility Carlton has his own suspicions, but Jack Pierce is connected somehow, just like John Welks." Mercer pulled a few photos off the wall and put them on the table in front of her. "No more lies, princess. Write down everything you know about each of these men and when you remember encountering them, even if it was only a fleeting glance." She started to protest, so he shoved a pen into her hand and left the room.

This job was supposed to be protection and retribution, not some tedious investigation into such a baffling matter. After scouring through the meager foodstuffs that one of his team stocked, Mercer prepared breakfast and tried to clear his mind. The answers were somewhere on that wall. He just needed to figure out how to access them.

Thirty minutes later, Ben came into the kitchen. "Good morning," he greeted, eyeing whatever concoction Mercer was wolfing down. "I heard you had a pretty rough night. When did they let you leave the police station?"

"Why?"

"Just curious. Y'know, trying to make conversation. By the way, I'm sure I've already said it like a hundred times, but thanks for pulling my bacon out of the fire. Two close calls in less than a week," Styler shook his head, cringing, "you'd think I was evil incarnated or worth billions." He shrugged. "I owe you, man. If there's anything I can do, just say the word."

"Good." Mercer continued to eat, but a thought was gnawing its way through his brain. In the distance, he heard ringing and Katia answering her phone. Not allowing for any distractions to derail his train of thought, he swallowed and wiped his mouth. "What are you worth?"

"What?"

"You don't have a significant amount of family money. Your business sense and trading skills leave a lot to be desired. So what would anyone gain by killing you?"

"I don't know." Styler turned, watching Katia enter the room with the cloned copy of her phone pressed to her ear. "What's wrong, babe?"

"My dad wants to talk to you," she said, holding the phone out to Julian.

"Mercer," he answered.

"Return my daughter immediately," Carlton bellowed. "I'm paying you to protect her. I am not paying you to protect her from me. You will bring her home immediately."

"No."

"Do you not understand English? Bring her home. Now."

"No."

"This is kidnapping. I will report you. I'll find you. I'll send someone to stop you from filling her head with seeds of mistrust. They will come to collect her with or without your permission."

"One, this is not a kidnapping. She chooses to be here. If she decides to leave, so be it. Two, who will you send? Since you can't afford to have your security team hospitalized."

Carlton cleared his throat. "Don't try my patience, Mr. Mercer."

"Then don't fuck with me." Disconnecting, he handed the phone back to Katia. "I'd suggest you don't answer the next time he calls."

"But...wh...what are you doing?" she asked, flummoxed.

Wordlessly, he left the kitchen, snatching the list she made off the table before heading to the bedroom to wake Bastian.

THIRTY-TWO

"You do realize how insane that sounds, right?" Bastian asked. He was dressed in a minimal amount of tactical gear, making sure he had at least two handguns loaded just to be on the safe side. "Why would Carlton hire another team to protect Katia when that's precisely what our role is?"

"I don't know." Mercer was replaying the conversation over in his head. "All I'm saying is he wants Katia to come home."

"Well, it's a good thing we're in an undisclosed location, and her cell is still at the precinct. Whatever he tries won't get him very far. If he sends a team of bodyguards to fetch her, they'll come face-to-face with the coppers instead." Bastian smirked. "At least those are slightly better odds than dealing with you."

"Run through the information Katia gave us. Dissect every employee at Rhoade's paper. Track the numbers. Follow the money. Do whatever it is you have to in order to get me the name of the man responsible. In the meantime, I've sent for Donovan.

As soon as he arrives, I will speak to Armann and Welks."

"Are you sure that's a good idea?"

"It's bloody brilliant," Mercer snapped, leaving the room.

"I doubt that." Bastian studied the sheet of paper. He already had some strong leads. It would just take a bit of patience and some luck. Julian had neither of those things, so Bastian returned to their makeshift op center, flipped open a laptop, and set to work, chewing on the end of a pen. "Hey, love, do you have a minute?" he called.

Mercer remained in the kitchen with Ben while Katia went to see what Bastian wanted. Once the two men were alone, Mercer narrowed his eyes at the kid. They had been in the middle of a conversation before the phone call, and Mercer still had questions that needed answering. His silent, unwavering gaze made Styler uneasy, causing the younger man to gulp a few times and rub absently at the bandage on his chest.

"What?" Styler asked when he couldn't take the silence anymore.

"Why would someone want to kill you?"

"I told you I don't know."

"Think," Mercer growled. He was in a horrid mood and likely to lash out.

"Um...I don't have much. My parents don't either. We're comfortable but not millionaires. Everything I have would go to Katia, anyway. I told you that before. But really, you can't think that she wants me dead. She wouldn't be here if she did."

"What about your mate, Jack?"

Ben stifled his chuckle. "I already told you he wouldn't do this. Well, it would be understandable, but he's not the physically violent type. He's nothing like you," Ben blurted, realizing his mistake immediately and slapping a palm over his mouth, reddening. "No offense," he mumbled around his hand.

"That was far from offensive." Mercer leaned back, picking up the cold tea and taking one final sip. "Armann and John Welks had Jack Pierce and his associates under surveillance. Do you and Jack have any common enemies?"

"Not that I can think of."

Mercer squinted, considering the facts and information from Armann's storage unit. "Does Carlton have any connection with Pierce's company?"

"Um...I don't think so, unless he published a story in the business section or included Pierce Industries as part of the exposé series he ran about harmful manufacturing and business practices. I can't remember. There were quite a few scathing stories he published some time ago."

"What was Rhoade exposing?"

"Companies paying off waste management to look the other way when they incorrectly disposed of harmful chemicals. Um...some tycoons making under the table deals with competitors to keep prices artificially inflated." Ben paused, lost in thought. "Some local government guy, the mayor or city council, being paid under the table to vote a certain way or pass a certain law or restriction. I don't really know. It sounded like the same kind of shit that happens every day, and none of that really interests me."

"Shouldn't business deals be your priority?"

"Yeah, I guess, but I don't really worry much with local trends or companies. You remember how great that worked out when I invested Jack's money."

"If you survive this mess, I'd suggest you find a new line of work." With that final comment, the conversation halted.

Mercer stood, stalking the confines of the apartment, impatient to take a crack at Isaac Armann. It was unlikely Armann would remain breathing for too much longer, and given his pallor and the condition they found him in, he might die from infection or blood loss without Mercer squeezing a name out of him. Although, there was still a part of Julian that wanted to draw out the pain and the torment. His mind focused on Katia crying hysterically into his shirt. He knew that type of pain, and since he had yet to find justice for himself, he wanted it for her, despite how childish and melodramatic she could be.

"Jules," Donovan said, entering the safe house to find Mercer's spare Sig shoved in his face, "I come in peace." After Mercer lowered the gun, Donovan explained the lack of progress that had been made with the captives. Welks had slept through the night after answering as many questions as he could. But his answers were still painfully vague. Armann, on the other hand, remained sedated, occasionally slipping in and out of consciousness but never long enough to provide answers. "He won't last long without medical intervention," Donovan concluded.

"Fine."

"Don't you find it the least bit ironic that we're kidnapping resolution specialists, but we've committed two kidnappings in the past week?"

"I don't think of them as kidnappings. We aren't looking for ransom or airing a list of demands," Mercer replied, collecting a set of keys and slipping into a jacket.

"So what are we doing?" Donovan would follow orders, but he was having trouble stomaching the torture they were inflicting. Kill a man and be done with it. That was his philosophy, which explained his preference for long-range military tactics.

"This is a rendition."

"We're not dealing with terrorist cells. This isn't Chechnya or the Middle East."

Mercer snorted, clearly failing to agree, and continued on his way. When he arrived at their makeshift prison, he parked the car, remaining inside and studying the surrounding area. He had learned quite a bit over the last thirty-six hours, and he was determined to put an end to this today. Checking the magazine inside his gun, he chambered a round and emptied the rest of the clip. It would be one bullet or none at all.

Despite the tactical stupidity of such a move, he didn't believe Isaac Armann was in any condition to screw around. One bullet, that was it. It was all he needed and the only thing separating what was left of his fractured soul from the demons he barely kept at bay.

Entering the office space that housed their first captive, Mercer grabbed the back of Welks' chair and dragged him out of the office and into the main room of the warehouse. From this vantage point, Welks could see Armann, but unless either man spoke loudly, the words would not be overheard. Mercer came to stand directly in front of Welks, looking down at him.

"Speak," Mercer commanded.

"What more can you possibly want from me? I've answered your questions. Let's just be done with this," Welks said. He had soiled himself over the last few days on account of his incarceration. He was dirty, exhausted, and probably starving. He had been minimally cared for to ensure his general well-being, but he was a broken man.

"Do you recognize him?" Mercer asked, jerking his chin across the room, and Welks nodded. "Is he the reason you've been too scared to answer my questions?" Welks remained silent, looking away. "Do you want that to happen to you?"

"You're going to do it anyway." Welks was resigned to his fate. He had given up. Perhaps the ex-SAS had broken him beyond where they intended.

"I give you my word. If you answer my questions, I'll let you go. Or I'll arrange for you and your family to be protected. Just tell me what I want to know." Mercer sighed. "That piece of filth is a killer, but so is whoever hired him. It's the same person that hired you."

"I don't know who it is," Welks declared on the brink of tears. He sniffed and shook his head, forcing neutrality to return. He might be broken, but he was fighting to hold on to as much of his dignity as he could. "I've said it before, but I'll tell you again. I received an anonymous e-mail. Payments were transferred into my account. I moved them into Piper Investigations. I don't know who wanted the information on Rhoade and his family."

"How did you report back to this unknown source?" Mercer asked. He believed Welks, finally, but Bastian found no electronic trail for Welks' follow-up communiqués to this mysterious benefactor.

"A dead drop. It was near a coffee cart on the east end." Rambling an address, Welks looked up. "My digging led to discovering Isaac Armann had been hired. His reputation is well-known in the circles I travel. Hazard of being a P.I., I suppose. After that, I tried to walk away, to stop delivering additional intel, but I couldn't. I was afraid. My e-mail contact asked for photographs and documentation of Styler and his contacts, and in my travels, I photographed a meet between him," Welks jerked his head toward Armann, "and someone else. I hoped it could be an insurance policy that would keep my wife and me safe in case someone tried to eliminate me too."

"Did you tell Carlton Rhoade what you had done?" Mercer asked.

"Not in so many words. I began keeping tabs on him and Katia, figuring I could intervene and correct my mistake, but Carlton grew suspicious. He called me into his office at the newspaper to ask what was going on. I said I believed he and Katia might be in danger." Welks swallowed. "He thanked me and said it would be taken care of, but I still kept watch, keeping my ear to the ground for rumblings of an impending hit. That's why Carlton hired his own team to deal with the danger." Welks met Mercer's eyes. "You're going to kill me now, aren't you?"

"No." Dragging the chair and Welks back into the office, Mercer shut the door, knowing that whenever the police arrived, they would search the warehouse and discover the private investigator. Hopefully, they would protect him and his wife, Teresa, in the event Mercer hadn't resolved the issue by then.

Closing the door against Welks' undignified, screeching pleas for freedom or death, Mercer composed himself and strolled across the expanse to Isaac Armann's prone form. He towered over the killer for hire, but the man merely stared up at him, his blue eyes hard and cold. Despite the layer of perspiration that covered his face, a sure sign infection and maybe sepsis were setting in, he didn't flinch.

"Why do you insist on being such a tough nut to crack?" Mercer asked. "Shall I offer you the same consolation you gave me?" Mercer squinted. "Because I don't think you deserve for this to be quick or painless."

"It's just a job."

"Bullshit." Mercer ground his teeth, tilting his head from side to side as he worked out an imaginary kink. "But since you insist it's just a job, who hired you?"

"I'm not sharing my client list." He smirked. "The last thing I need is some other former military hack setting up shop. I asked you to leave nicely. That was your only chance."

"And yet you're the one deteriorating from a gunshot wound. Care to reconsider?" Mercer's voice remained even, and he forced his breathing and pulse to remain steady. This was only a conversation.

"You don't have the stones. You've had far too many chances." Armann let out a wheezing chuckle and spat on Mercer's shoe. "Fuck off."

"You're sloppy. You pretend to be methodical, but you couldn't even make yourself appear professional without hiring two actors to accompany you on the shooting. And despite your failed attempts to eliminate your target, you have a secondary agenda. Elaborate and we'll discuss whether or not you have a future." Mercer wasn't one for words, but years of negotiations did come with a few benefits.

"Follow the fucking breadcrumbs then," Armann retorted, yanking his bound arms and legs so he could roll onto his side. He struggled to get to his knees, the only other position the restraints allowed aside from flat on the floor. "There isn't a goddamn reason why I should tell you anything."

Mercer was smart enough to realize Armann wanted to negotiate. "What will it be? Medical attention, money, drugs, something to make you feel real good?" The ire was seeping into his vocal pattern, and he forced it down. "A bloody commendation for a job well done?"

"Styler's dead?"

"How could he be? You didn't even make it into his hospital room." Julian watched a slight grin erupt. "Who else is in play?" Armann remained kneeling, a sick grin on his face. "You failed. You won't get another chance, so tell me who hired you."

"I want a fair chance to escape." The contract killer was trembling from the exertion of holding himself up, and the wound in his side was seeping blood and, from the smell, pus too.

"Fine, tell me who hired you, I'll remove the restraints, and if you manage to make it out alive, then so be it." Armann looked skeptically up at Mercer. "I give you my word."

"Oh, aren't you the honorable one," Armann scoffed. Mercer remained silent; the only obvious sign of his displeasure was in the clenching of his fists. "Fine. Untie me first."

Mercer assessed him for a long moment. Armann no longer posed a danger. He was damaged, hanging on to consciousness with nothing more than stubbornness. "If you try something, you will regret it." Mercer unhooked the numerous locks that held the restraints around the warehouse piping, taking his time, wary of every shift and sound Armann made. Once the killer was free, Mercer stepped back. "Name."

"Daniel Pierce. Now run along and play. Maybe you can reap some fringe benefits by consoling that piece of ass that's been at Styler's side this whole time. She seems to be pretty good on her knees. And she'll need a shoulder to cry on when Styler's no longer in the picture." He winked. "You're welcome."

Julian didn't hesitate. He pulled his weapon, shooting Armann in the knee. The move was calculated. A blown out kneecap was excruciating and would never heal properly. In the event Armann survived, every day from here on out would be a reminder that he screwed with the wrong man. Furthermore, it was torture, and the thought of this broken man dragging himself through a pool of his own blood to cross the dirty warehouse floor would satisfy the promise Mercer had made to Katia, not to mention the fact it would greatly impede any chance of escape.

Armann howled in pain, and Mercer saw red. Unable to do anything but give in to the bloodlust, Julian braced his palms against the back wall, stomping and kicking the living daylights out of Armann, breaking his ribs and causing vastly more damage to the preexisting wounds. When Julian's vision cleared and his internal rage was back in check, he stepped away, lifting the phone and dialing Detective Rowlins.

"I suggest you send a team to collect the remaining rubbish," Mercer said, providing the address and walking out of the warehouse. "That swine has been dealt with."

THIRTY-THREE

"Mr. Pierce, we need to have another chat," Mercer said. He was waiting in the corner of the darkened office. As soon as Pierce walked inside, Mercer moved behind him, blocking the door. "Where is your brother?"

Jack turned, startled. Flecks of dried blood covered Julian's clothing from the middle of his chest all the way to his shoes. Gulping, Jack took a few steps backward, intent on reaching his desk phone and calling for help. Mercer remained still, watching as Jack listened to the sound of silence in the receiver.

"I disconnected your phone and computer. Your secretary was told to take a long lunch, and building security is preoccupied with an unrelated issue on another floor. I believe there was a slight fire that broke out. It appears to be electrical in nature," Julian continued. "I'm not here to hurt you. Just tell me where your brother is."

"What do you want with Daniel?" Jack asked, his eyes continued to dart around the room.

"Answers."

Jack sucked on his bottom lip, considering his options for escape or the chances of fighting off Mercer. He possessed a valiant streak, but from the looks of the man who was currently holding him hostage with a gun protruding from his open jacket, he wasn't stupid enough to think he'd win in a fight.

"The last I heard, he was still working for a newspaper. This building has plenty of security. I've filed a police report. If anything happens to me, they'll find out who you are and what you did."

Mercer smirked and approached, placing a business card on the desk between him and Jack. "That ought to make it easier for them. However, I'm here to help you. Your brother is seeking revenge. You stole his seat on the Board and the favored position with your father."

"Dad doesn't have favorites."

"No? So it's just an ugly rumor that says he disowned Daniel and crowned you heir apparent?"

Jack sighed. "I had nothing to do with that. I didn't ask for any of this." He gestured around the room. "After my investments started to turn a profit, I pitched a fantastic business plan for the coming year and was promoted. There was no favoritism involved."

"Except until that time, you were shunned because of your childish antics with Styler and your poor investment skills. Your brother stood to gain everything."

Narrowing his eyes, Pierce thought about his previous encounter with Julian. "What does any of this have to do with Ben?"

"Daniel hired a hitman to eliminate Ben and hoped to frame either you or Carlton Rhoade for the murder."

Jack scoffed. "Why would my own brother do

something like that?"

Mercer gave him a look. "Asked and answered."

"We're not Cain and Abel."

"Fine," Mercer stepped toward the door, "but now you are aware of the situation. I would suggest you take measures to protect yourself. This is about revenge. Warn your father and anyone you care about. Your brother is not to be taken lightly." With those ominous final words, Mercer walked out of Jack Pierce's corner office.

Considering Jack's unhelpful comments, there was only one other location Mercer could think to visit. He had yet to phone Bastian to fill him in on these new developments, and frankly, he didn't want to. He was sick of his friend acting as his conscience. It was demeaning and unnecessary. Mercer was a big boy. He could handle matters on his own, even if there would be some disagreement amongst his team concerning the tactics he employed against Isaac Armann. However, no one could argue that the ends didn't justify the means. And honestly, wasn't that the only thing that actually mattered?

Pulling up to the curb, Mercer left his vehicle illegally parked and strode into the newspaper building. Rhoade's paper took up an entire high-rise, and Mercer ignored the row of receptionists, heading for the elevator. Before he made it there, security stopped him. Based upon their dark suits and earpieces, Mercer wagered they were probably members of Carlton's personal team instead of the normal rent-a-cops that provided building security.

"Mr. Mercer," one of them said, "Mr. Rhoade would like a word."

"As would I," Mercer replied. His gaze flicked to one of the cameras in the corner. "But first, I would like to know the whereabouts of Daniel Pierce."

The bodyguard remained silent, but another four men soon joined the ranks, crowding Mercer from all sides and escorting him into the elevator. Mercer's eyes shifted around the tiny metal box. It was close quarters, but there was a fair chance he might be able to subdue these clowns. Then again, this wasn't about Carlton's accusations concerning his treatment of Katia. This was about completing the mission. After all, Carlton hired Mercer and his team to identify the party responsible for the near-fatal shooting and protect Katia, regardless of the cost. And Mercer's team had done both of those things. It wasn't his fault if Carlton got antsy and tried to change the play after the game had already commenced.

The elevator doors opened, and Julian was led down the hallway by the entourage of dark suits. Upon reaching their destination, Rhoade's personal assistant glanced up from her desk. She nodded to the men, offering a small smile to the one on the left, before gesturing toward the open office door.

"Mr. Rhoade will see you now," she said in a professional tone, as if Julian had requested a meeting through more formal business channels. The men in suits remained in the reception area, and Mercer glanced back at them. "Right inside," she said, returning her attention to the computer.

"Close the door," Carlton ordered. His back was to Julian, and he was staring out the large window. As soon as the door clicked closed, he spun, no longer exhibiting the posture or demeanor of a business professional. "Where is my daughter?"

"She's safe."

"You will return her immediately."

"I was hired to protect her."

"Not from me," Carlton bellowed. "We will not have this conversation again. You will either have someone bring her to this office while you wait or I will have you arrested, interrogated, and thrown in jail until you change your mind."

"We don't have time for this. The man responsible for nearly killing Katia's fiancé works here. For you. And if I'm not mistaken, we even brushed up against one another the last time I was here." Mercer took a steadying breath, forcing his anger to remain in check.

"What are you talking about?"

Julian took a seat in the client chair across from Carlton's desk. "You hired John Welks to investigate the source of the extortion. He discovered who sent the photos, and for a while, I believed you hired Isaac Armann to kill Benjamin Styler."

"I would never," Carlton began to protest, but Mercer held up a hand.

"You would. I don't doubt that, but the pieces didn't add up. Frankly, I'm sure you were hoping Styler would die or disappear. But your methods to drive a wedge between him and your daughter have backfired. Having Katia under your roof is what led to their semi-public trysts, and it gave the actual killer the perfect opportunity to act. You're lucky he was only hired to kill Styler, or else it would already be too late."

Carlton slumped into his executive chair. "Who's responsible?"

"According to the assassin, he was hired by Daniel Pierce," Mercer said, watching Carlton's eyes go wide in disbelief. "Where is he?"

"He should be in his office." Carlton took a breath. "After the shooting at the hospital, he offered his condolences and assured me that Katia would be fine. I never imagined Danny would do something like this. Are you sure?"

"Delusional bastard." Standing abruptly, Mercer

went to the door. "Call off the team you hired to procure Katia. I gave you my word that I would protect her, and I've done precisely that. As soon as I get my hands on Daniel Pierce, this will be over." Halfway out the door, he called over his shoulder, "You should call the police now."

Bursting inside Daniel's office, Mercer was confronted with nothing but empty space. The security guards were at his heels, and they monitored his movement as he sifted through the contents on top of the desk and in the drawers. Not finding anything telling, he proceeded into the hallway.

"Shall we detain him?" one of the guards asked as Carlton caught up with the group.

"No." Rhoade met Mercer's eyes. "He's doing what I hired him to do." He studied Julian for a few seconds longer. "I called them." He looked around the room. "Where's Daniel?"

"Find out," Mercer growled.

Carlton snatched a radio from one of the security members and barked a few questions into it, waiting for a response. After a couple of staticky bursts, he handed back the radio, his face ashen. "According to the front desk, he left right after our morning meeting and hasn't been back since, but the police are on the way."

"I won't be here when they arrive, but my team will be in touch. We'll probably need access to Daniel's workspace." Mercer headed to the elevator, pressing the down button. "You should have stopped this," he snarled, speaking mainly to himself.

THIRTY-FOUR

"Bloody hell," Bastian cursed. The team was assembled in the flat. "How long was Daniel planning this?"

"Probably since Carlton hired Welks to investigate the extortion. The private eye got himself in too deep," Hans offered. He had spent the most time with their first captive, but the man hadn't offered much. "The gumshoe was smart enough to know whoever wanted to ice Ben could just as easily turn on his inside man."

"It explains why the funding came from the newspaper and how the e-mails were sent internally," Bastian said.

"What's become of the private eye?" Donovan asked, studying Mercer.

"I assume the police handled the situation. It doesn't matter. Daniel Pierce is responsible. We find him, and we kill him," Mercer said resolutely.

"Or we turn him over to the authorities and let them deal with him," Bastian replied. "Don't you think you've done enough damage today?" His eyes drifted to the blood flecks covering Julian's clothing. "And get changed before we contract hepatitis or worse."

"Donovan, make sure Pierce hasn't hired anyone else to carry out the killing. You've made enough contacts with the local private military contractors, so I don't imagine this task will be too difficult," Julian said.

"Aye."

"Hans, collect as much information as you can from all pertinent locations and players. Bas will tell you what he needs," Mercer said, passing off the command position and excusing himself.

"Bas needs you to stop behaving like a bull in a china shop," Bastian yelled, referencing himself in the third person and hoping Mercer's departing back would take the words to heart.

Once Julian left the room, Katia intercepted his retreat, pulling him into the bedroom. "Don't worry, I'll respect your personal space this time," she teased, attempting to apply levity to the situation. "I heard part of your discussion. You found the shooter?"

"Yes."

She looked up with her big blue eyes. "You made sure he paid for what he did or what he tried to do?" She dabbed at the tears that threatened to fall. They weren't tears of sadness or pain. They were the physical expression of her rage.

"I kept my word."

"Thank you." She looked relieved and let out a sigh. Standing on her tiptoes, she gave him a quick peck on the cheek and returned to the kitchen.

"Birds," Mercer muttered, grabbing a change of clothes and heading for the shower to wash the remnants of Isaac Armann from his body.

When Mercer returned, freshly showered and dressed in something not covered in blood spatter,

Bastian slid a dossier across the desk. Only the four of them remained in the safe house. Hans and Donovan were running errands, and based upon the look Julian was receiving, he knew Bastian wanted a word alone. Mercer took a seat across from him and flipped through the file. All the information he would ever need on Daniel Pierce, the entire Pierce family, their business, associates, and correlation to Benjamin Styler and the Rhoades was spelled out in extreme minutiae.

"Detective Rowlins called," Bastian said, leaning back in the chair and picking up a handful of pretzels. He thoughtfully chewed, and when the silence continued, Mercer looked up from his perusal. "I'm surprised you didn't kill Armann," Bastian squinted, hoping to understand the logical reason for that, "but you let me believe that you did. Why?"

"There was a good chance he was dead." Mercer shrugged. "Really, what was the point of checking? He either was or wasn't. It was no longer my concern."

Muttering curses under his breath, Bastian rubbed a free hand down his face. "Fine, but just know that I don't believe you." The uncomfortable silence lingered a moment more. "Welks is at the hospital. His wife is with him. Rowlins has convinced them to voluntarily enter into protective custody. It seems the private investigator has plenty to say that will corroborate what we've found and solidify the evidence needed for the police to make a strong case against Armann and Pierce."

"Excellent."

"We can stop now, Jules. The CPD issued an all points and will arrest Daniel Pierce as soon as they spot him."

"And you think someone who went to such great pains to avoid detection up until this point will be located that easily?"

"The job is basically over. You determined the identity of the assassin and the man who hired him. The only thing left to do is provide Katia with protection until Daniel is apprehended. Rowlins has assured me that it shouldn't take long. They are maintaining eyes on his brother, Jack, their family's office building, Carlton's newspaper, and Rhoade himself. Daniel will surface. I'm sure of it."

"Maybe." Mercer picked up the dossier and left the room. Bastian was right. Their job was almost done. A couple more hours or days of bodyguard work and this should be resolved, but Julian was having issues separating his personal stake in the matter. After all, the man Pierce hired had attempted to kill Julian twice and taunted him repeatedly. And that wasn't very nice, now was it? "Let me know what Donovan and Hans find," Mercer yelled from the next room.

"Fine." Bastian knew Mercer wouldn't reconsider. The commander wanted to resolve this, so they would.

Settling into the living room, Mercer read through the information on Daniel Pierce. Maybe if they had explored this avenue earlier, those three police officers would still be alive, Ben and Katia wouldn't have been further traumatized, and Mercer wouldn't have been grazed by a bullet or had to deal with the annoyance of a dislocated shoulder. At least they were on track now.

Daniel Pierce was four years older than Jack. After graduating with an MBA from one of the world's most prestigious business schools, Daniel went to work at his father's company. Within a few months, he was made head of advertising, but he wasn't trained for such a position. Marketing wasn't his forte, so in order to gain further insight into that industry, he went on sabbatical at his father's insistence and interned at a few advertising agencies, magazines, and newspapers. His last stint landed him at Carlton Rhoade's newspaper.

Despite the fact that a newspaper didn't offer much insight into a business's marketing strategy, it would earn him plenty of contacts at the big publishers and access to reporters at the major media outlets. This was meant to ensure plenty of positive press for Pierce Industries and the ability to squash any negative stories that might surface; however, Daniel was unlucky enough to be employed by Carlton at the worst time imaginable.

Rhoade was running a series of pieces concerning government and business corruption, and one of the stories at the time focused on Pierce Industries. When Daniel failed to convince Rhoade to drop the story, Daniel's father blamed him. After the internship ended, there was no position left at Pierce Industries for Daniel. The tides had turned, and despite the fact that Daniel had always been the fair-haired child, Jack had recently ended his friendship with Benjamin Styler and his investment portfolio had turned around. Pierce Industries gave Jack a top spot at the company, and Daniel was left out in the cold.

Carlton Rhoade, despite his conniving and ruthless tactics, had a soft spot for Daniel and hired him as one of the business executives. Daniel's fancy education and newly acquired marketing knowledge made him a great asset and quickly earned him a spot as Carlton's right-hand man. But Daniel obviously still held a grudge against his brother and father and decided to do something about it.

After reading the narrative of Daniel's business life and filling in a lot of the blanks with conjecture, Mercer returned to find Bastian scanning the city's surveillance system. Mercer studied the camera feed, noting the special interest Bas was taking in observing the Pierce Industries building and Jack's apartment building.

"Any other targets?" Mercer asked, leaning over his shoulder.

"I'd say his father, but the man is out of the country on business. Styler and Katia are here. And if he wanted to put an end to Carlton Rhoade, he would have done so at the office." He shifted his focus from the screens. "It's pretty fucked up that Carlton just let him walk out that door. This is the man that nearly killed his daughter."

"Maybe Rhoade feels responsible," Mercer suggested.

"Still," Bastian shrugged, "it seems strange. He seemed ready to send a team to eliminate us if we didn't return Katia. Why wouldn't he do the same to Daniel?"

"Are we certain he didn't?"

"I'll have Donovan check, and I'll notify our detective friend." Bastian picked up the phone. "Rhoade strikes me as the impatient type. Worse than you. So if he has any mercenaries on speed dial, I'm sure they're already in play."

THIRTY-FIVE

"Maybe I should call Jack," Ben mused. It was obvious he and Katia were getting stir crazy. "I'm sure he could use some moral support now that we know his brother is a psychopath."

Mercer gave him a hard look, and Ben clamped his mouth shut. The longer they were stuck inside the safe house, the more fervently Mercer wanted to take action, but it was his orders that insisted two members of the team act as guards in the event of a worst case scenario. But as the hours ticked by and day turned to night and then back to day, he wanted to pound the pavement.

Donovan's questioning and search were fruitless. As far as they knew, no one else was hired to replace Isaac Armann. The man was under heavy guard and in a medically induced coma due to the severe infection and injuries sustained. It was unlikely he'd survive the night. Luckily, the two actors Armann hired had been located by the police.

Westin insisted that the cell phone and wallet he

had pick-pocketed from Katia had been handed over to Armann. The two crooks turned actors poured their guts out in the hopes of avoiding criminal charges. After being hired, Manning and Westin were told that they would be playing gangsters in a noir crime film. The men were given suits to wear and told to lurk about. The day they visited Ben Styler's apartment building was the day Armann originally planned the murder scene, but they missed Styler by a matter of minutes. And believing it was a script, they had entered his unlocked apartment, checked for the camera crew and other actors, and left completely confused. Armann told them the scene had been rewritten because the actor hired to play the victim was called away on an unexpected emergency, and the two never called this into question. Even after the shooting in the alley, they still claimed to believe it was just part of the film.

Despite their helpfulness in providing testimony against Isaac Armann, the two actors had never heard the name Daniel Pierce nor could they identify his photo from the pictures the police showed them. Daniel had made sure he insulated himself from the crime in order to paint someone else as the guilty party. And while the bulk of the circumstances pointed the finger at Carlton Rhoade, the question on everyone's mind was why did Armann hire two actors that resembled Jack Pierce's co-workers.

The only man that could answer that question was Daniel Pierce. The CPD was still searching for him. His credit card activity and normal haunts were undergoing heavy scrutiny, but it seemed like the man had simply vanished into a puff of smoke.

"Anything, Hans?" Mercer asked as the younger man returned from his outing, carrying stacks of information and computer disks.

"Tons of feed to be scrubbed," Hans replied, dropping the files and disks onto the desk beside Bastian. "I also asked the detective to pull the police records for Dean Manning and Keith Westin, the entire police file on the current shooting investigation, a copy of his personal notes, and the little things that never became official." He glanced back at Mercer. "Sometimes, the coppers aren't a bad lot."

"Right," Mercer replied sarcastically, picking up the detective's personal set of notes and skimming the chicken scratch that covered several sheets. "The police conducted a follow-up with Daniel's co-workers, but they don't know anything about the hit."

"Daniel still has access to the Pierce Industries building," Bas added, already loading data into one of the computers. "It looks like he accessed the employee database and determined who worked closely with his brother. Then he found the lookalikes to make the frame-up appear even more convincing, as if the falling out Jack and Ben had wouldn't have been convincing enough."

"Cold-blooded bastard," Hans remarked, stifling a yawn. "I'm knackered."

"Take some downtime," Julian instructed. "It'll be a while before we determine what is relevant to identifying Daniel's current location."

"Did the police have a conversation with Jack about his brother?" Bastian asked, wondering if Julian had come across that information yet.

"I don't know. You spoke to Rowlins. What did he say?"

"Not much. He's been too busy keeping our descriptions and involvement out of this mess. Shit, you've been locked up three times. The rest of the police department thinks you're in cahoots with the killer. So be thankful someone is on your side."

"It isn't the first time I've been blamed. Tell Rowlins to do his job and stop covering my arse. I can take care of myself."

The rest of the day was spent analyzing the data. Daniel Pierce had enough access to his father's company and Carlton's newspaper to plant evidence against Jack Pierce and Carlton Rhoade. As far as Bastian could tell, it seemed Daniel was hoping to implicate both men. But why? If Daniel wanted to discredit his brother's character, having him accused of murder seemed like a great way to do that. So why did he also frame Carlton? Sure, Mr. Rhoade had motive and means, but something was still missing.

Around midnight, the computer let out a warning beep, and Bastian swiveled in his chair, focusing on the surveillance feed outside Jack Pierce's apartment building. Daniel entered through the side door usually reserved for building maintenance and deliveries. The police had a few units on-site and the building under surveillance, but Mercer didn't necessarily trust them to make the best decisions. They hadn't so far. And he couldn't be certain they were paying attention now.

"Jules, wait," Bastian called, but Mercer was already out the door. "Bloody hell." Sighing, Bastian dialed Rowlins, relayed the information and Julian's ETA, and then woke Hans and Donovan. "Be on alert here. I'm going after the commander."

As Mercer neared the apartment building, he noted the dozen unmarked police vehicles creating a perimeter around the area. The side streets and main thoroughfare were blocked off, angering the city's occupants who had to reroute. Slamming the car to a stop and blocking half of a dead end alley, Mercer went around to the trunk and strapped on the Kevlar. Briefly, he checked the clip in his gun, stowed an extra magazine in his pocket, and zipped his jacket over his new ensemble. Then he hoofed it the next three blocks to the apartment building.

"Detective Rowlins," Mercer greeted, "what's the situation?"

"We don't know." Rowlins made a face. "A man matching Daniel Pierce's description was seen entering the side door, but no one can verify if it's him. We've made contact with Jack, but he says he got in late and went in the side. There hasn't been so much as a peep from building security or any 911 calls to report a disturbance. We don't want to tip Daniel off if he's not there."

"Goddamn morons." Mercer took a step forward, intent on entering the building and resolving the issue, but Rowlins grabbed him by the collar.

"Not so fast. What do you think you're doing?"

"I'm a professional negotiator. Daniel Pierce is inside. And if he isn't, the dozen unmarked cars rerouting traffic and the plainclothes officers talking into their sleeves have already tipped him off. Either way, you've been made. Now are you going to handle this, or should I?"

Rowlins considered his options. From the grim expression on his face, it was obvious he agreed with Mercer's assessment. "My hands are tied by the white shirts. Good luck."

"Luck has nothing to do with it."

Squaring his shoulders, Mercer took a final deep breath, stretched his sore arm and continued to the side of the building. If Daniel found an alternative method of entry besides the doorman in the lobby, Mercer could do the same. He went around the side to find a metal box requiring a four digit pass code. After giving the door a quick tug, he pulled out his phone and dialed Hans.

"Pass me to Styler," he instructed. And once he

heard Ben's uncertain hello, he asked, "What's the code to get into Jack's apartment building?"

"Two one six three," Ben replied, hearing an unfriendly click echo in his ear.

Mercer entered the code and watched the button turn from red to green. He tugged, and the door opened. He stepped inside. The side door led down a narrow hallway that opened up in three different directions. One path led to the lobby, the other to the basement, and the third to a staircase. Mercer took the stairs up to Jack's floor and exited quietly. Glancing into the hallway, he spotted a man and woman sharing an intimate moment, but the rest of the floor was empty. He passed the lovebirds and continued to Jack's apartment.

Examining the door, Mercer found no signs of forced entry, but it was possible Daniel possessed a key or knew how to get inside Jack's apartment. They were brothers, and oftentimes, family could gain access even when they shouldn't be able. It explained why so many of the kidnappings Mercer had seen revolved around one parent taking a child from the other. Mercer shook the wayward commentary aside, refocusing on the matter at hand. He waited half a minute, debating if he should go in loud. His presence would be immediately known, but he would also have the element of surprise.

"Bollocks." He took a step back and kicked the door just above the knob.

The frame splintered, and the door popped open. Luckily, no one had bothered to lock the deadbolt. He entered the room swiftly, his gun poised in front of him. The apartment wasn't incredibly large, and Mercer didn't have time to perform a proper sweep before two men emerged from a side room. Daniel Pierce was holding Jack at gunpoint, waving him forward with the muzzle of his gun.

"Julian Mercer, it's a pleasure to officially meet you," Daniel said, smirking. "You've definitely made this more difficult than it had to be, but regardless, I salute you, sir. Your reputation doesn't do you justice. And now the final piece has fallen into place."

THIRTY-SIX

"Drop it," Mercer growled, aiming at Daniel's head, but Daniel grabbed Jack and pulled him backward for protection. "Don't be stupid. Let's calm down."

Daniel swayed slightly, keeping a firm grip on Jack. "Your appearance this evening, Julian, is precisely what I was counting on. Y'see, after Isaac failed the first time, I had to reassess the situation. A botched attempt didn't fit into my plans, and he was supposedly the best in the business or at least the best in the area. It's a shame money couldn't buy exactly what I wanted."

"Then you should have done it yourself."

"Probably, but how could I pin it on someone else?" Daniel shook his head. "No. It was supposed to be simple. The day after the shooting, Carlton should have come to work outwardly distraught but utterly relieved that Benjamin Styler was dead. It was one less mooch for him to worry with, and that would mean his daughter stood to inherit everything."

"You wanted to kill Ben so some chick could keep

her inheritance?" Jack asked, stunned.

"No, little brother. You're so naïve. Ben was granted legal privileges to Katia's accounts. It was some arrogant showing of trust and a slap in the face of her father who wanted them to sign a pre-nup. It would have added to Carlton's motive."

"Were you planning to seduce her after you murdered my best friend?" Jack asked, and Mercer realized Jack was asking questions in order to buy time and distract Daniel. With any luck, Daniel would forget to remain in motion and Mercer could take the shot without being forced to inflict collateral damage.

Daniel laughed a low, bitter sound. "Idiot. I can't believe Dad lets you run his company. You have no imagination or ingenuity. If it weren't for me, you would have continued making bad investments. I gave you those stock tips and some insider trading information, but you couldn't even stand up for me when I was thrown out of the company." Daniel edged toward the wall, slamming Jack into it, causing a river of blood to run down from his scalp.

"You wanted the authorities to think Carlton hired Isaac Armann to eliminate Styler because of the blackmail," Mercer said, distracting Daniel before he could clock Jack with the gun.

"Bingo. At least someone else in this room has two functioning brain cells." He made a contented noise. "Then again, if you had thought ahead, you would have figured out my end game and not stepped right into the perfect trap."

"Oh, yeah?" Mercer asked, slowing circling. "Why don't you share it while you can still speak?"

"The evidence points to Carlton. First, the private investigator discovered that Styler blackmailed his future father-in-law, and the communications and money that went to the P.I. filtered through Rhoade's newspaper. There's an easy paper trail for the authorities to follow. Carlton even took a meeting near the dead drop that I established for Welks. It was damn near perfect," Daniel boasted. "And you were just the icing on the cake."

"Explain," Julian said, noticing movement in the periphery.

"You were just another pawn in Carlton's game. And you were led by the nose into believing Jack was responsible. Hell, Jackie's two co-workers were practically accomplices at the time of the shooting. So it looks like Carlton convinced you Jack wanted to kill Ben, and therefore, you should kill Jack." Daniel smiled. "You threatened my little brother. It was caught on the security feed. He even filed a police report against you. But then you threatened him at work, and finally, you came to his house to finish the job. Y'see, everything traces back to you, Mr. Mercer. You discovered that John Welks was the mole. You took him captive, ransacked his apartment, and then you practically beat Isaac Armann to death. Your actions make their testimonies suspect if they were to talk, but frankly, I don't think they will. Welks would be too afraid, and Armann is too proud, assuming he survives. There are enough circumstantial evidence and hints of impropriety circling to discredit anything you might say."

"No one could have predicted I'd stumble upon the botched murder attempt or that Carlton would hire me." Mercer narrowed his eyes. "Even you aren't that brilliant."

"Maybe I am." Daniel's boastful nature surfaced, and the smug look reappeared on his face. "I've always had a contingency in place in the event Isaac failed. Carlton's predictable, and I knew he would hire someone to eliminate the threat. It just happened to be you." He smiled again and held the gun slightly away from Jack's head. "Does this look familiar?"

"My Sig," Mercer said, remembering the police had confiscated it. "I'm impressed. The one thing I don't understand is how you plan to escape. You shoot Jack. I shoot you."

"Not quite. I shoot Jack with your gun, the police bust in, and I say I came to protect my brother. You go down. The evidence is against you. Who would believe a disgraced, former military man who's already been accused of murdering his own wife?" His eyes lit up. "No one. And that's what makes this brilliant."

"Except for the bullet through your brain," Mercer replied calmly.

"You don't kill for sport. You didn't kill Armann, and you won't kill me." Daniel shrugged. "It's that simple."

"Pathetic," Mercer retorted, changing tactics. He lowered his gun and walked around the couch, taking a comfortable seat. "The break-in was reported. The police shall be here momentarily, and you're the only one pointing a gun. It's game over."

"Not if I do it now. I can kill Jack, shoot you, and claim it was in self-defense."

"You're forgetting one basic fact," Mercer replied, his finger twitching slightly at the notion of his next move.

"What's that?"

"I work with a team."

Bastian fired once, having snuck into the room during Daniel's long-winded diatribe, landing a well-placed shot to Daniel's forearm, causing him to release Jack. Immediately, Mercer brought his gun up, firing a single shot to the side of Daniel's head. His skull blew apart, covering Jack in brain matter and skull fragments.

"Dan?" Jack asked, teetering and collapsing to his knees. One look at his brother's lifeless form sent relief and sorrow through him, and he continued to back away, becoming violently ill in the corner of the room. He swallowed uneasily, eventually drawing his eyes upward to find Bastian assessing the displaced handgun. Slowly, he dragged himself toward the couch. "You killed my brother."

"Would you have preferred he kill you?" Mercer asked.

"No. I...no..." Jack swallowed again. And the sounds of heavy footsteps shook the apartment.

"The serial number is the same. There's no doubt it's yours," Bastian said, "which means there's a cop on the take."

"I told you that at the beginning," Mercer declared, holstering his own gun and raising his hands. "Unfortunately, the next few hours won't be particularly pleasant, but the traitor might just reveal himself."

The police swarmed the apartment, separating the three men for questioning before anyone could be removed from the scene. Techs arrived, followed by the coroner and a few higher ranked members of the police force. Mercer narrowed his eyes at them, wondering how many of them were corrupt.

"I'll take it from here," Rowlins said, dismissing the uniformed cop that had been questioning Mercer.

"Detective," Mercer said, pondering Rowlins' potential involvement, "notice anything strange about the handgun Daniel Pierce had in his possession?"

"Like?"

"The fact that you confiscated it from me after the shooting at the hospital."

"Yeah?" Rowlins glanced around the apartment. "Let's head to the car." Mercer stood, and the two went down the steps. "I'm not telling you this, but a few batches of evidence went missing from the precinct yesterday. Some of it was related to Styler, including your gun." He stopped Mercer at the car, opening the passenger's side door. "Your people were snooping around. Did they take it?"

"No."

"Internal Affairs sent someone to investigate. They'll figure out what happened. In the meantime, you admitted to shooting Daniel Pierce in defense of his brother, Jack. From the whispers I'm hearing, Jack's corroborating your version of the events."

"That's because I accurately described what occurred."

"Be that as it may, until it gets sorted out, you'll be held at the precinct. The problem is," he put the car into drive, "if your insistence on police corruption is just as accurate, you really can't afford to be stuck in a place where evidence goes missing or tampering may occur." He tossed a sideways glance at Julian and remained silent for the rest of the drive to the precinct. When he pulled into a space around back, he scanned the parking area. "I can't believe I'm about to do this," Rowlins muttered to himself. He cleared his throat and stared out the windshield. "I forgot I have a quick errand to run. You will wait in the car until I get back, right?" His eyes darted to the door, and Julian understood. "Thanks for helping out on this. If you hadn't gone inside when you did, Jack Pierce would likely be dead. You saved someone tonight, and in my book, that makes this an exception to the rule."

"But there are still unanswered questions."

"Just maintain a low profile while IA works out some of the kinks. I'll be in touch." Rowlins exited the vehicle, walking into the precinct and not glancing back at the car.

Once the detective disappeared from sight, Mercer let himself out and set off in the direction of the safe house. Hailing the first cab he spotted, he got dropped off in the neighborhood, checked for a tail, and returned to update Katia and Ben.

THIRTY-SEVEN

The next few days were an exercise in patience. Katia and Ben bickered constantly. The person primarily responsible for the intended murder was dead, and Mercer was told to stay out of sight. The phone calls were just another annoyance. Carlton called multiple times a day to speak to Katia, apologizing and begging for his daughter to come home. Thus far, she wasn't willing to leave Ben's side until the police investigation was concluded.

Bastian was released from police custody thirty-six hours after the incident in Jack Pierce's apartment. The medical examiner determined Bastian didn't deliver the kill shot, which went along with the statements Mercer provided inside the apartment and Jack's testimony. However, while Bas was stuck at the precinct, he met the Internal Affairs investigator, Detective Smoltz. After Bastian answered more questions than he cared to concerning Mercer's team, Carlton Rhoade, Benjamin Styler, and the Pierce family squabble, Smoltz made some notes and released Bastian on his own recognizance. Detective Rowlins and IAD had his contact information and warned that no one should leave town until the investigation into the evidence tampering and possible police involvement in an attempted homicide was resolved.

Finally, on the fourth morning of bodyguarding hell, Bastian's phone rang and after answering, he passed it to Julian. Mercer glanced at the caller I.D. and took a deep breath. He wasn't in the mood for more police bullshit.

"We need to meet. Do you remember that diner we went to?" Rowlins asked, sounding cryptic.

"Are you planning to arrest me?"

"I'll see you in an hour." Rowlins disconnected, and shaking his head, Julian handed the phone back to Bastian.

"Good news?" Bastian asked.

"Our detective friend wants a meeting. If you don't hear from me in two hours, then I'll probably need a barrister and bail money."

"He won't arrest you," Bastian said, even if his voice sounded somewhat uncertain. "He's been pulling double duty, so he can help out IA and investigate the corruption. Maybe he has news on who's got it out for you."

"I could speculate," Mercer replied, his mind drifting to Rhoade's friendship with the homicide lieutenant. "Two hours. The clock starts now."

When Mercer arrived at the diner, he took a seat at a booth in the back and waited for a squad of police officers to swarm the building, but that didn't happen. Instead, Detective Rowlins walked in, gestured for a cup of coffee, and sat across from Julian. The two remained silent until the waitress placed the steaming mug on the table and walked away.

"What?" Mercer asked, impatient like always.

"I have good news and bad news. Which do you want first?" Mercer continued to stare. "Fine, we'll start with the bad. There isn't enough evidence to support claims of corruption. Yes, evidence went missing and someone tried to run you down after you left the precinct, but no one's talking. IA's focused on the homicide lieutenant, but you didn't hear that from me."

"He's Carlton Rhoade's contact in the police force. Do you think he was also friendly with Daniel Pierce?"

"Yep." Rowlins took a sip of coffee. "At a lot of city and charity functions, Rhoade would invite his staff. They must have crossed paths. It would have been nice to ask Daniel Pierce about that, but dead men don't speak."

"Am I under arrest for his murder?"

"No. It was self-defense. Jack's let us go through some employee info from Pierce Industries, and we've been scouring through Daniel's belongings and communications. It's obvious you did this city a service. First of all, you took care of that contract killer. Second, you dealt with the man pulling the strings. Which leads to my next question."

"I'm waiting."

"What are you going to do about the unidentified officers that covered for Daniel Pierce by attempting to make you look like a killer?"

"It's not my problem," Mercer said, leaning back and studying the detective.

Rowlins snorted as he attempted to stifle his chuckle. "Bullshit, it's not your problem. None of this was your goddamn problem, and yet, you took care of it, even when I told you we didn't need the help."

"Clearly, you were wrong."

"Eh." Rowlins reached into his back pocket for his

wallet and laid a five on the table. "We might want to bring you in for questioning again. Probably tomorrow afternoon. I'd suggest you terminate your employment and hit the road before that happens."

"Was that the good news?" Julian asked, still wondering why the detective was giving him and his team a free pass.

"Yeah."

* * *

Later that evening, Carlton Rhoade returned home from work. In the darkened expanse of his living room, he didn't notice Julian Mercer seated in the armchair, his handgun sitting on the table a few inches away. Rhoade poured himself a drink and turned. Startled by the man waiting for him, he dropped the glass, and it shattered on the floor.

"Tell me why I shouldn't kill you," Mercer said, his tone even.

"Goddammit, you scared me. How did you get in here?" Rhoade made a move toward the security system on the wall, and Julian leaned forward, hovering closer to the weapon. "Where are my bodyguards?"

"I'm sure you'd prefer to have the rest of this conversation in private," Mercer warned. "Take a seat, Mr. Rhoade."

Carlton sat on the couch, his gaze uneasily shifting to the weapon. "Let me guess, you want money."

"No. I want assurances that you will not interfere in your daughter's relationships. Right now, no one is entirely sure what role you played in the assault on Benjamin Styler. You're in the clear. He's alive, and whether the two of them remain together is none of your business. Her happiness should be your primary concern. Do not do anything to make her miserable. Do you understand?" Mercer's tone went from professional to cold hatred.

"Yes."

"Good. Additionally, if you do anything to jeopardize John Welks' well-being, we will have a problem. He made a mistake and deserves a second chance. I trust that you will give him the opportunity to make amends."

"Okay," Rhoade must have thought this was a business arrangement because he relaxed slightly, "would you like your payment now?"

"Payment?" Mercer practically spat. "I don't accept blood money."

"It's not blood money. It's payment for services rendered. All I did was ensure Daniel could never pose a threat to Katia or anyone else again. I wish it could have gone another way."

"Rubbish. You used everyone at your disposal to stack the odds in your favor. How long did you know Daniel was behind this? In your office, you swore you didn't have a clue, but you set a lot of things in motion very quickly."

"That just a newsman's knowhow. We're used to working with close deadlines." He stood and went back to the wet bar, letting the broken glass crunch under the soles of his shoes. He poured another drink and took a sip. "I've been honest with you, Mr. Mercer. Katia is all I have left, and I would do anything to protect her, even if it meant paying you to kill a man." He went to his desk and picked up a document-sized envelope. "But like you and your friend have said numerous times, you're not mercenaries. So I had to take additional measures in order to ensure you would take care of the problem."

"You made sure the evidence that was stolen made

it back into Daniel Pierce's hands, along with my personal firearm, just so I would act accordingly? That was a fucking ridiculous gamble by an entitled, narcissistic egomaniac."

Rhoade smiled, returning to the couch and placing the envelope on the coffee table next to Julian's handgun. "You give me far too much credit, Mr. Mercer. Daniel made contact with a mutual friend that we have within the department, and word traveled back to me. Initially, my contact wanted to set up a sting to lure Daniel out of hiding, but after I presented him with my dilemma, we came up with a more permanent, foolproof solution. Don't forget, I'm nothing more than a businessman with strong ties to only the most upstanding members of this community."

"Bullshit."

"Believe what you like, but justice has been served. Inside, you will find payment for the additional work your team has performed."

"I don't want your money."

"I figured as much, but there must be some agreement we can reach to keep you from sputtering your misguided beliefs concerning my involvement. Perhaps you'll consider some priceless information a fair trade."

"What kind of information?"

"I made a few phone calls on your behalf. I'm not without friends, even in merry old England. In addition to the money, you will find a few newspaper articles detailing similar crimes that occurred over the span of a decade, a reporter's personal notes, photos, and police reports that were removed from the official public case file. It may inevitably provide a lead to your wife's killer." Rhoade stood. "I believe that shall be sufficient consideration for our business to be concluded. I expect Katia to be home by the morning. Good evening, Mr. Mercer. You can see yourself out."

THIRTY-EIGHT

"Are you sure, love?" Bastian asked. "You don't have to go back there."

"He's my father," Katia insisted, "and it's about time we had this out." She shifted her gaze to Mercer. "Don't worry, I won't lose your card. And if anything out of the ordinary happens, you're my first and only phone call."

"Emergencies only," Mercer said.

"No problem." She tossed him a smile. "Thank you. When you came rushing into the alley that dreadful night, I knew you were a hero." She hugged him, much to his annoyance. "Thank you for exacting vengeance on my behalf," she whispered, feeling him nod.

"All right then, Donovan will take you home and ensure your safety before he leaves. Hans will return Mr. Styler to his residence, and that shall be the last time you have to deal with us," Bastian concluded.

When the team dispersed, Bastian and Julian scrubbed the safe house, eliminating any prints or

DNA before repeating the same process with the vehicles. It was an old habit, but it never hurt to be cautious, particularly when the police were only hours away from knocking down the door. After a final check, their remaining belongings were gathered near the front door, awaiting a taxi to the airport.

"Have you opened the envelope yet?" Bastian asked.

"I don't believe him," Mercer replied, but every fiber of his being ached to see what was inside, to find that one clue that he was still missing.

"You're afraid to believe him. Hope can be a crushing thing, but after the shit he put us through, it is the least he could do."

"It's hush money."

"So what? We'll let bygones be bygones for once."

"And what if it's like everything else we've read and uncovered over the last two years? What if there's nothing new? Michelle deserves peace."

"So do you." Bastian lifted the envelope out of the bag. "Shall I give it a look-see?"

"Bas," Mercer paused, unsure how to respond, knowing his friend would dig through this just as doggedly as he would, "whatever you do, never agree to let us take another one of these questionable jobs. We aren't investigators."

"Can you repeat that for the recording?" Bas asked, smirking, and Mercer offered a rare smile. While they waited for the cab to the airport, Bastian opened the folder and began to read.

Don't miss *Betrayal*, the second exciting novel in the Julian Mercer series.

Now available in paperback and as an e-book.

ABOUT THE AUTHOR

G.K. Parks received a Bachelor of Arts in Political Science and History. After spending some time in law school, G.K. changed paths and earned a Master of Arts in Criminology/Criminal Justice. Now all that education is being put to use creating a fictional world based upon years of study and research.

You can find additional information on G.K. Parks and the Alexis Parker series by visiting our website at
www.alexisparkerseries.com

CPSIA information can be obtained
at www.ICGtesting.com
Printed in the USA
BVHW030228241218
536317BV00001B/74/P